Forbidden to

Forbidden to Grow Old

Izaak Mansk

Coach House Press Toronto

Published with the assistance of the Canada Council,
the Ontario Arts Council, and the Ontario Ministry of
Culture and Communications.

Some of these stories originally appeared in *Carolina Quarterly*,
2 PLUS 2, *Rubicon*, *Descant*, and *The Fiction Magazine*.

Cover design: Gordon Robertson.
Text design: Nelson Adams.
Printed in Canada at The Coach House Press, Toronto.

Canadian Cataloguing in Publication Data

Mansk, Izaak
Forbidden to grow old

ISBN   0-88910-347-8

I. Title.

PS8576.A68F67 1988   C813'.54   C89-093070-8
PR9199.3.M366F67 1988

To Shaindy

'Hope! I have quite a genius for hoping. I have done little else but hope during my entire life.'

D'Artagnan from *Vicomte de Bragelonne*

'It is not only certain species of animals that have ceased to exist; certain species of men, too, have ceased to exist.'

Dimi Balien from *Emil Brut*

Contents

Fables and Fairy Tales

Red Hood

This is the story told among wolves.

There was once a wolf who was reckoned a very great gentleman. His land and forest holdings were considerable, with game rights extending to swamps and ponds and fishing rights in streams and rivers and even, some avowed, a handsome house in town, but this he flatly denied. For, he would say among fellows of his own kind, he had a distinct contempt for the ways and manners of men, or most of them at least. But not all his kindred wolves believed him, some muttering between their scaly, yellow teeth or under their bad breath that Gentleman Tom, as he was called, exuded occasionally the smell of Man. But most of this was pure envy, of course, and the idle wagging of malicious, grumbling tongues.

He certainly did have some human attributes, but these were more for the purpose of arousing hilarity than for any other reason. For example, he would get up on his hind legs, lean back against a tree in a lolling man-like attitude, with one forepaw dangling limply downward and the other encircling an empty wine jug, a long straw curling down from between his immaculate teeth, his mouth slightly agape and an expression of dazed, befuddled wonderment in his handsome eyes. It was at the repeated requests of his more simple followers that he would 'do the drunken peasant' to their unceasing, wild amusement.

Tom was also astute when it came to human games of chance and skill, and it was reported that frequently he carried off a bag of winnings in gold coins, obligingly tied to his tail by some of his more gentlemanly human companions. Yet he lost frequently too, but with a good grace it was said, and also sometimes very heavily, because when the mood overpowered his good sense he became obsessive in his play and reckless in the placing of his stakes. At such times, and to amuse his gambling colleagues, he would put on his act of 'the sorrowful wolf', running about the gaming room, leaping over the gaming tables and ever and anon raising his forepaws on a chair to howl piteously, a performance which invariably won him boisterous applause. But Tom insisted, among his gambling cronies as well, that he would never take on the guise of men. When some of his friends, in a gesture of sincere amiability, bought for him a charming, green silk cap, he disdained politely to put it on, averring that despite everything he was a wolf, pure wolf, and was proud and content to remain so.

Tom was very sports-minded too, but more for reasons of prudence than for any sense of fun. When not out hunting, which he took extremely seriously and selected for his followers only the steadiest and most resolute of his band, he organized competitions in running, endurance, leaping, swimming, and dancing. For he was a great believer in the social graces too. But besides that, he used to maintain that a wolf who wasn't fit for the game of life was an abomination, he might just as well be a dog. He was especially considerate of the youngsters whose training he undertook personally, and the womenfolk too, whose rights he often defended when these were abused by their more loutish mates, at which times he would clout the offender severely or, what was more feared, deliver himself of his contemptuous scorn in choice, biting language, while the culprit would slink about with his tail cast down. 'Why,' he would say, 'you're nothing better than a human clod. You don't deserve to be a wolf.'

All in all, between his varied activities, his life was very full and enjoyable, and the days that he spent in the forest and the town gave him a pleasant easy conscience, and a sense of fulfilment.

It was on a day, like other days in autumn, when the sun shone brightly through the cool aisles of the forest, that Tom, in a clearing softly covered with fallen leaves, was demonstrating to a group of cubs various wolf-holds and methods of wolf attack, and speaking betimes of the approaching winter which would present many problems of survival for the pack as a whole. The youngsters were listening attentively at that moment to his authoritative growls when all ears seized suddenly on the clip-clop of an approaching horse. 'Pay attention,' said Tom with an irritable snarl, as several heads turned about curiously at the oncoming sound, 'it's only some human;' and as the heads swung back smartly if reluctantly, he continued his discourse.

As the horse and rider came leisurely on, Tom and his cubs

heard a terrified whinnying as the horse caught the smell of wolf. With a strict command to his charges to stay put, he dashed from the clearing out to the path and saw a young lady on an obviously fear-crazed pony, with its legs splayed rigidly outward. While she tried to urge it on, beating with a small stick upon its head, and crying out angrily, the frightened animal only coughed uncomfortably in its throat.

'I beg your pardon,' said Tom gallantly, stepping out before them. 'I'm afraid I'm the cause of your pony's trouble.'

'Why, you must be Gentleman Tom,' said the surprised but interested young lady.

'If you'll permit me,' said Tom, as the lady watched him curiously though nevertheless coolly, for she apparently knew his reputation, 'I'll just reassure your beast.'

And prancing amiably around the pony in a very wide circuit, he made friendly, chuckling, pony sounds, approaching closer then running off and approaching again with an ingratiating, lop-sided smile. He next did a handstand on his forepaws and even walked along on them for twenty paces, then several brilliantly executed cartwheels, after which he bounded about barking gaily like a dog, then finally approaching very close and looking up into the pony's eyes with an innocence that charmed it, he at last convinced the poor animal of his harmless intentions and the pony relaxed, straightening up nimbly, resuming the lively look in its intelligent black eyes and giving a snort of pleasure.

The lady was amused and elated with the performance, and merrily clapped her hands, and Tom, it must be confessed, blushed under his handsome fur. For it is a fact, but little known, that wolves (and no doubt other animals too) have the faculty of blushing when embarrassed.

As the lady smiled at him with her white, pretty teeth, Tom noticed for the first time that she was in fact a girl, of very fine appearance, perhaps no more than fifteen, with clear blue eyes and a fair white skin, and dazzling flaxen hair which tumbled in curls around her face and from out her hood. That hood set off her face admirably, thought Tom. It was of a deep, sombre red, drawn charmingly round her throat by a large laced ribbon tied in a bow, and descending into a cloak which covered her entirely and almost half her pony. Ever after he thought of her as the lady of the red hood, or simply Red Hood.

As he leapt back with an amiable and contrivedly careless

15

expression, as though calming distraught females was part of his daily affair, she raised her right arm, halting him, and said, 'Won't you at least let me thank you?'

'I have only corrected something which unwittingly I brought about myself,' he replied simply. 'There's no need of thanks.'

But looking down at his eloquent eyes, she imagined she could read his unspoken truer thought, which she interpreted as follows: 'Besides, it is *I* who am grateful for this encounter.'

She paused then before speaking again, attacked by a sudden remorse which she could neither understand nor explain, but charitably it fled as swift as it came, and nodding her head she smiled once more.

'Very well,' she said, 'but I shall remember.' And after a further pause, 'And since you won't accept my thanks, which puts me under the burden of unredeemed gratitude, then know at least my name. I am the Lady Caroline.'

The wolf dropped his head politely in acknowledgement and, without another word, ran back into the forest, while the lady rode on thoughtfully, on her now docile pony.

II.

The winter came and fled. The cold spring sun nurtured the ravaged trees. The plants put out tentative, enquiring leaves and finally blossomed. The forest renewed its greenness.

Yet it had been a hard winter, one of the severest that Tom could remember. The water froze solid in the rivers and ponds. He had not been once into town while it lasted, but had foraged with his band, sometimes desperately, for the infrequent game that came their way. Sometimes the pack had been reduced to gnawing hard, half-frozen roots or desiccated branches. Always he had kept them running in the forest, over his own lands, far away from human habitations, and while this had excited the rage and animosity of several of his wilder followers, who knew for a certainty where fat young sheep could be pilfered from unprotected farms, Tom, true in his divided loyalties to wolf and man, held them in with a savage restraint. The old mutterings came back, snarled with a venomous hate: 'He was more man than brute,' or 'He had enough for his own belly but denied it to others,' which of course wasn't true, or 'It was time he was replaced by a wolf that was wolf right through.' But

when the question arose as to who this wolf might be, no chal-
lengers came forward, and the grumblers relapsed into grumbling
silence, only gazing about with savage grimaces and baleful, flashing eyes, while flexing their powerful jaws and sinews which, they
knew, were no match for Tom's. One thing they could not deny. He
had kept the pack intact. Not one youngster, even the weakest, had
perished. By a severe, equitable rationing, everyone had had their
share, albeit meagre, and those who suffered most had received
more.

For the Lady Caroline the winter had been kinder. Sheltered within
the imposing castle of her father, the Count Berg, she had amused
herself as young ladies do: dancing to the viols and woodwinds of
her father's household band while partnered by simpering or
haughty young noblemen, all of them admiring of her feminine
though sturdy graces; or sewing with her women, or chattering
gaily in French with her governess, or attending Mass where those
mischievous, cool blue eyes of hers brought unreligious feelings to
those whom she coyly ogled; or attending grand balls at the
Margrave's palace where her winning ways won her more admir-
ers; or riding with a few choice friends over the crisp, treacherous
snow, shrieking lustily with pleasure at near spills or other misad-
ventures, her cheeks crimson with high excitement, her blue eyes
shining, her teeth dazzling in a voluptuous smile.

The Lady Caroline was daring and unconventional, delighting
in vigorous exercises and sports which her other lady friends considered to be dangerous. She would listen with rapture to tales of
the hunt, and was herself pre-eminent in the art of duck-spearing.
Idle gossip, mostly of women, condemned her for her many clan-
destine, amorous adventures, and her sometimes outrageous
laughter or her brazen manner. Her powerful wrists and arms,
developed through long hours of sword play, could strike the blade
from many a skilled, male adversary. Thus many men, too,
regarded her with a wary eye, as being a little unnatural, not
entirely female; but most felt a fascination for her curiously
ambivalent charm.

The Count Berg was a widower, a white-haired gentleman
with a stony, furrowed face. His wife, for whom he never ceased to
mourn, had died in a hunting accident, thrown from her horse in a
chase after wild boar and trampled beneath the hooves of her companions' furious horses. From that time on the Count Berg swore,

in his mad revenge, to rid the earth of wild boar, and had succeeded to an extent quite manfully. In his irrational fancy, he had set aside a special room in his castle dedicated to the mounted heads of boar, which numbered then fifty, and which he had sworn he would increase, before his death, to one hundred. Called appropriately The Boar Room, it was here that he assembled his guests whenever his luck and skill had brought him another victim, and the mounting of the head would be accompanied by the frenzied drumming of retainers in Viking dress, followed by a riotous dinner of boar's flesh and pagan toasts to boar. It was on such occasions that the Lady Caroline, at her father's bidding, would serve his guests with her own hands, dressed wantonly in a silken, décolleté gown, the skin of a beast draped loosely over one shoulder, and a small gold crown, like those of ancient days, set on her streaming flaxen hair, so that she appeared like some heroic nordic goddess.

The Count, broken by the loss of his wife, swore never to remarry, although he fully realized that with no male issue his line would cease. The lack of a son to whom he could teach the manly arts only increased his obsessive desire to instil those qualities in his daughter. In this, as we have seen, he had ready material, and the lady's feats, whether on the resined floor of the sword room, or in the field, the ballroom, the hunting lodge, or at the Margrave's palace, filled him with a fierce and overweening pride. It was even said that the reports of her amorous adventures, rather than outraging him, used to cause him a grimaced smile accompanied by a flash of jagged flame across his parchment cheeks, and a lighting of his deeply sunk, sombre eyes.

III.

As the lady sat one late spring afternoon in the great hall of the castle Berg, the sun streaming through the massive stained-glass windows and becoming roseate, violet and gold as it ignited the hidden flame of a knighted figure brandishing an oriflamme in one mailed fist and assailing a fallen foe with an axe in the other, she, sitting dreamily at a long table, basking in the warmth of the welcome rays, and being herself an almost dream-like figure to any who could have seen her then, with the currents of colour of the knighted figure crossing and blazoning her hair, which shone now with a golden aureole and now with a violet, and creating pointed fire in the stones of an emerald and ruby necklace which hung gracefully about her smooth white throat, while casting a flickering sapphirine blue across her face as the leaves without stirred in an awakening breeze, she, sitting there, idly turning over a letter from an unwelcome suitor, bethought herself of that meeting in the forest in the autumn, when her fear-crazed pony succumbed to the ministrations of a wolf, a wolf as handsome, gay and full of grace as any human nobleman, nay, more so, and withal with the secret passion of a beast. What had he said to her, from those eloquent flashing eyes, the message of which she had frequently pondered over ... That he was grateful to her for the encounter ... although his manner was too debonair, too restrained with human or animal dignity, to speak those fateful words aloud. The lady sighed.

Of late she had been feeling irritable, subject to morbid fancies, steadfastly refusing to leave the castle, declining the numerous invitations to balls, galas and fêtes which a lady of her class usually delighted in, and seeing occasionally only one or two select friends who commented with concern on her appearance and urged her to resume her normal ways. One of these, the sister of the Margrave, expressed her surprise that a lady so popular should shut herself away so unaccountably from society. She, the Princess, expressed the Margrave's personal dissatisfaction at not having seen the lady for so many weeks at the hunt, an occasion which he averred was always made more lively by her brilliant presence, and he conveyed through his sister his command that she should present herself at the palace before very long. The lady begged to be excused, but at last wearily consented, and the sister of the Margrave went away, although not entirely reassured.

Her father, the Count, left her severely to herself, understanding full well the potency of unbidden moods of black despair, to which he was only too frequently subject. Her constant companion then was her dog whom, in her wit, she had named Star, a huge though gentle beast who followed her about silently, stretching himself out when she sat and raising mournful eyes which gazed compassionately at her in her dubious distress. For the fact is that the lady's trouble was simply that she found life tedious, the repetitive sameness of her activities leading to an anguished ennui, in which yearnings almost wild, always dolorous, spread their gloomy fantasies in her frivolous head. It was during this time that she dreamed the terrifying dream of the Bergs ... a wall splashed with blood, a metal gauntlet on a severed arm with the metal fingers twitching, and a wolf's head, with phosphorescent eyes, triumphantly grinning ... a dream which traditionally had occurred at least once in every generation to a member of her family and beginning, so it was said, with the first, Alwa, or Alois, the founder of her race: a man reputed half-fabulous, half-human, suckled by a wolf, so legend decreed, and with wolf blood in his veins. Wolves were his invariable companions, he consorted with them in preference to humankind; he hunted with them, slept by their sides in the forest; they devoured the spoils of the chase at a mutual board, they surrounded him as he stalked the land marking out his domain or visited the newly-building castles of neighbouring barons.

It was in those times, so men said, and principally at the initiative of men like Alwa, or Alois, that wolves became a common sight at the courts of princes, some rising to the rank of counsellor, gentleman-in-waiting or chamberlain, while others performed valiant service in times of battle and received from the hands of their grateful lords various signal honours, including patents of nobility and bequests of land to be held in perpetuity by their descendants. Indeed the origin of Gentleman Tom's vast holdings derived from this period, and the truth is that the names of Alwa and Berg were held in special veneration by his ancestors and by Tom himself, with the name of Alwa, or Alois, being given to the eldest in every third generation, a practice followed by the clan of Berg itself. The present Count, the lady's father, was so named, and her own baptismal names were Caroline Aloise Charlotte-Marie.

The lady speculated idly, her thoughts were never deep; of books she had read none, save for the occasional silly tales of marvel; her desires, her instincts, her pleasures, were purely physical. She yawned, very unlady-like, displaying widely tongue, palate, throat and teeth, and groaning pitifully as she did so, while a sympathetic answering whine, followed by a gargantuan yawn and groan from her faithful Star, made her smile, then laugh, then dissolve into merry peals of repeated uncontrollable laughter, at which the dog looked on amazed. The lady twisted a lock of her flaxen tresses. Her cool blue eyes began to sparkle with a wonted light, a cheerful self-assurance, a reasserted determination in her small, well-modelled chin. An idea had occurred to her. She rang a bell imperiously and ordered one of her maids to bring a change of costume, and as the young woman dressed her, in a grey doeskin riding habit elaborately stitched with silver thread and surmounted by a black velvet cap caught to her hair by a pin emblazoning a magnificent solitary diamond, the lady considered deeply on her action. Beyond a well remembered stretch of path within the forest, not more than a league distant, there was a gay little cottage in which there lived, and had lived for as long as she could remember, the lady's godmother. The lady met with her godmother usually only once a year, at Christmastide, when the Count gave his festive parties at the castle. How often had the dear woman implored her to come and visit, and yet she had never found the time. But now there was time aplenty, as the declining of the many pressing invitations to hunts and balls gave her a clear and unfettered way. The lady smiled with confident, anticipated pleasure, as she drew on her long, black doeskin gauntlets and called for her grey pony.

The faithful Star, when he saw her accoutred for riding, leapt about her with exuberant, puppy-like antics, barking ecstatically and beating his tail. The lady rode off at a loping canter, her pony's hooves thundering over the levelled drawbridge, and rousing distant workmen in the fields to raise their heads and doff their caps in mute salute. The dog followed at the pony's hooves, emitting still his sharp, delighted barks, and the lady turned in her high saddle to wave at him, exhorting him on with cheerful cries. All three, lady, pony and dog, felt a surge of high release from the many cloistered days within the castle as the quick, mellow spring air fanned briskly past them, filling their lungs with its intoxicating currents. The lady was pleased as she had not been for years, everything pleased her: her limited horizon seemed to open to a vision fresh, tantalizing in its lustre, redolent of the witchery of illicit promise. Had she but known it, she would have stopped to gaze at herself in the nearest mirror with a self-love and appreciation entirely merited, for she was never again so beautiful, so radiantly alive, as on that day.

She drew in her pony about a half league on, and gave the panting Star a chance to recover his wasted breath, laughing and taunting him playfully so that the dog, in his mad love for her, would cheerfully have met death at that moment in a noble and striking manner and beset preferably by danger on every side, if it would have convinced her of his slave's devotion.

The sun was beginning to angle from the meridian as they entered the forest at a measured pace, with Star now completely recovered and the sturdy pony putting down its dainty hooves with a restrained friskiness, while it shook its heavy mane with an impatience that betokened its eagerness to gallop again. The rich aroma of growing plants and grasses charmed the lady. The path undulated through shafts of brilliant sunlight in which, hovering as in silent ecstasy, thousands of tiny insects with invisible wings took their ephemeral joy. The lady rode through them with unaverted face, though with eyes and mouth sensibly closed, after which she turned her head to watch them form their lazy pattern again.

A yelp from an adolescent wolf ahead caused Star to grumble deep inside his chest. He glanced up at his lady as though to warn her that danger threatened, surged forward past the pony and halted, growling menacingly in intrepid alarm. The lady sought to calm him while the pony, still marching steadily forward, nudged its companion's hind quarters gently with its hooves. The dog's attention was suddenly averted by his lady's spirited voice speaking in high good humour, 'Why, good day, Sir Tom,' at which for the first time he noticed the majestic grey figure who had appeared beside them, with the grace and bearing that signalized him a leader and master of wolves. The dog, recognizing the category of animal that stood before him, and conscious of the familiarity with which his mistress had greeted him, drew back respectfully and dropped his head in obeisance.

'Ah, the lady of the red hood, without the hood,' said the wolf, bowing, then courteously acknowledging the dog's salute.

The lady laughed. 'If it please you, Sir, I shall wear it always when I come this way.'

'I am mindful of your lady's favour,' said he, gazing solemnly at her from his candid eyes. 'I had named you in my thoughts Red Hood.'

The lady flushed and assumed a mock serious air, inclining her head gracefully in recognition of the compliment.

His body, lean throughout the winter, had recovered its accustomed weight, and as he stood before her with the sun burnishing the silvery points of his lustrous fur and igniting sparks of amber fire in his eyes, she thought him more magnificent, more desirable, even than she had imagined.

She explained in her slightly eager voice where she was riding, while her pony tossed its tail impatiently, and he nodded as though it called to him a pleasant recollection.

'Will you guide me to the cottage? I fear it is the first time that I go that way.'

'I know it well,' he said agreeably, 'and to guide you would be my honour.'

Thereafter they conversed less formally, although still in the somewhat stilted way of new acquaintances, neither of them quite sure of the ground of their opening friendship, and withal in the manner prescribed of their rank. The pony, relaxed, amiable, and thoroughly at ease with this unaccustomed walking companion, recalled their past encounter and ever and anon turned its head to look at Tom, when an uninhibited exchange of animal understanding passed between their eyes. The dog, Star, followed on dolorously behind.

To the lady it seemed that the distance was all too short, although their pace, suiting her mood, had been more than leisurely, and the spirited pony felt that its hooves had never dragged so or been commanded to halt so frequently as when the lady wished to admire a particular view – although she had never before expressed such an interest – or, speaking animatedly, wished to make a particular observation. Within moments, it seemed to her, the uninteresting outline of her godmother's cottage descried itself, although in fact almost an hour had elapsed. Tom, springing gallantly to his hind feet, assisted her then from her pony, and the warm collision of wolf fur and doeskin made her draw in her breath hastily, and her heart to beat with a heavy, uncomfortable rhythm. The lady flushed once more and felt her cool blue eyes swimming in an ecstasy that was new and strange, and somewhat terrifying. Her lips, as she enunciated her thanks, drew back from her teeth in a manner not altogether human, but almost at once she recovered herself. Tom, too, was not unmoved by the fleeting contact. The lady's scent was in his nostrils, mingling with the scent of her hair and skin and her riding habit, and the warm, rich, innocent scent of her pony. His voice, always well-modulated and deep, became husky as he bade her an abrupt farewell.

'Not farewell, surely?' she declared with friendly condescension. 'We shall meet again, I hope.'

'I am always here, my lady,' he said, and with that he bounded off.

The lady's godmother knew Tom well, and had responded to his courtly bow with a winning smile on her aged cheeks. She greeted her godchild with unbelief yet nevertheless with undisguised affection, and also, it must be said, with some embarrassment as she had nothing appropriate in her larder at that moment with which to entertain her high-born guest. The lady however soon complained of headache, but promised her godmother that she would make up for her unavoidably short visit by returning next day, at which the godmother expressed her delight and promised that a pleasant luncheon would be awaiting her. The lady then remounted her pony, and the poor animal was astounded at the furious speed with which she drove it back through the forest, yet over a different path, one that she knew quite well from the chase: its thudding hooves meeting only the forest silence and the cries of birds in the trees, while the luckless Star, panting as though his chest would burst, tried painfully to maintain the pace.

The lady's godmother, as we have said, knew Tom well, and had reason often to be grateful to him, for when the season was in swing, he would frequently deposit on her doorstep a brace of handsome grouse, departing rapidly without awaiting her thanks. Pleasantly disturbed by the sound of his arrival and fast disappearing flight, she would survey his retreating form, magnificent in its litheness and furry grace to her admiring eyes, describing somersaults in abandon in the sheer delight of living, and would silently bless him.

She, the godmother, afterward pondered deeply on the reason which had brought her wayward godchild so unexpectedly to the cottage, after so many years of thanklessly pleading for her to come, but could find no ready explanation of the lady's sudden appearance, nor of her desire to come next day again. She brooded upon it as she made a list of the various dainties that she thought would be suitable for her lady's high-born palate, then, shaking her head, sighed painfully, fearing that whether she understood or no, and knowing the character of her god-daughter only too well, the outcome must prove unhappy.

Her son, the Gamewarden of the Margravate, who dwelt with his mother in their grace-and-favour cottage, concurred with her judgement gloomily.

IV.

The lady's radiance and superficial beauty had been remarked by Tom, nor did her amiability and animation fail to stir him. Nevertheless he was not wholly eased with himself. That first encounter in the autumn had given way to moments of wistful musing, a state of feeling not unknown to Tom, but associated previously with thoughts of the forest: its sights and sounds and arcane moods and changes; the full moon riding in tempest over the tops of the trees; the eerie voices of night creatures; the sun half-masked, enchanted, rising miraculously from the depths of water; the unfailing delight of waking at dawn with one's eyes half-blinded in summer dew, and scattering the icy, delicious shower from one's dew-soaked flanks; or the form of a companion, powerful in symmetry, silhouetted at dusk on a rocky elevation, head erect and muzzle upwards, abstractedly scanning a point in the sky; or that of another, less powerful but no less graceful, with deferential humid eyes and pink tongue delicately caught between half-revealed teeth, waiting unweariedly for the sign of his favour; or the impenetrable mystery of eternal silence in the body of a kindred, discovered in seclusion, lying unmarked, unwounded, overwhelmed by the fullness of age.

Tom prized his idle moments, and even his futile speculations. His sorrows were few, deep yet untroubled, and untroubled because their origin lay in the unanswerable, frustrating dilemma which faces all, wolf and man, in the realm between earth and the impersonal heavens. But those sorrows caused him no interior wound or pain, no diminution of his balanced nature.

There were introspective considerations too of his own exalted station. A leader, lonely yet proud, surveying about him his band, his people: those in their full maturity, others in their young manhood or adolescence, some approaching the instability of old age and who required protection, and some, too, equally unstable, who tottered yet on unskilled legs, solicitously attended by their mothers; all of these, or almost all, regarding him with that humility of awe and trust in the majesty and invincibility of his judgement. Tom's flaw was that while both masterful and ambitious, he was too sensible of that accident of birth and heritage, that gift of a peerless body and incisive intellect, which almost inevitably destined him for leadership, yet made him mindful of those others not so bountifully endowed and for whom, even in the rigour of his stern authority, he yet felt a pang of conscience. A too compassionate Prince of Wolves, thus he would style himself to himself. A dangerous lunacy too when there were some within his camp who would rend him from jaw to tail, if they could, at the first sign of weakness. But there was not one, as yet, to challenge him.

Those few moments of idle fancy, reprehensibly repeated in the cool, still days that followed his first meeting with Red Hood, had mercifully been abandoned with the first intimations of winter, and obliterated entirely in the dark, anxious days of snow and storm. This he recollected as he loped with swift, tireless stride through the forest, still conscious of his alarmed senses which had commanded his hasty if polite departure, though her scent lingered yet in his breath and fur. To carry that aroma back with him was unthinkable. At the first stream he plunged in, shivered slightly at the contact of the still icy water, then swam vigorously to the farther shore. There he shook himself furiously, rolled in a bed of pine needles, which sent up a shimmering cloud of the dancing green fibres, and shook himself once more. A few needles remained to mar the perfection of his gleaming fur, but the scent of her, Red Hood, had been replaced by the sharp tang of juniper. Nevertheless he remained uneased with himself. There was no doubt now that she would come again, and perhaps again, and the complexity of his attitude to her bedevilled him. He would not even ask himself the fateful question, whether or no the lady genuinely attracted him, fearing in his perplexity and the novelty of it all that he was unequipped with any objective answer. Yet it was now no abstract matter of chance or destiny, but a real situation, created admittedly by hazard, perhaps developed by intent (although he was not yet ready to concede this to the lady), and one that demanded a direction, a way of behaviour, and truth perhaps as urgent as life.

In his despondency he executed several brilliant cartwheels to loose the tension in his aching head and heart. But beyond providing some unexpected entertainment for several squirrels in the trees above, who applauded him squirrel-fashion, and which the courtly Tom gravely acknowledged, the ache remained. He could, of course, deign to ignore her if she came again, but he was a wolf, not a man, and moreover a gentleman, and such mean uncourteous subterfuges could not be countenanced. Besides, his reasoning could be wrong; the lady was merely in passage to her godmother; it was the first time and he had acted only rightly in showing her the way. The next time, if there were a next time, could well be different, and there was no certitude that they would need to meet again. And yet she, Red Hood, had expressed such a wish with her amiable and enticing smile, and he, ever polite, ever solicitous in his way with men – and with his own kind when the times were mellow – had not demurred, but had spoken with a positive inclination. The wolf smiled to himself grimly, bethinking him of his self-inflicted jibe, the 'too compassionate'.

Yet she came again, and no later than the next day, garbed as she had promised in her red hood, extending in a cloak over her pony's flanks, although the day was warm for such attire. The rapid trot of her now familiar pony's hooves, thudding softly over the leafy path, and the doleful short barks of her dog, Star, aroused him from a reverie. He could no more deny his baffled pleasure that she was there, than dream again. His pace was unhurried though quick as he leapt to the path and saluted her.

'You see,' said she with a flash of her small white teeth, drawing up her pony sharply, 'I have kept my bargain.'

'Indeed,' he said, 'my lady Red Hood.'

She dismounted suddenly, so quickly that before he could move, her dainty doeskin boots were on the ground. 'Walk with me, Sir Tom,' she said. 'I am weary with riding.'

She was smaller than he had realized, now that he strolled beside her. Her long red cloak collected leaves in its train, and she had flung off her hood, freeing her hair, in the warmth of the weather. The pony fell back, its bridle trailing, stepping along idly in front of the dog. The dog with gloomy head dejected, moved his legs as though on weighted tendons.

Her talk was frivolous and he, the wolf, was glad it was so. It was an interlude in his life, he mused, an interlude that had had no real beginning and would, doubtless, have no real ending, when, by accident, or design, she stumbled against a hidden root and fell heavily against him, uttering a little scream followed by a merry burst of laughter as she untangled herself from his legs, but not before gazing into his eyes from beneath him, with the lights in her own sparkling mischievously, her cheeks aflame, her lips parted and wet with her exuberant laughter.

'Nay,' said she good-humouredly at his anxious expression, 'spare your feelings. 'Tis a trifle.' And as Tom extended his shoulder to aid her in rising, 'Your Red Hood's really a robust girl who has had worse spills before.' But as she regained her feet she moaned slightly, managing quickly however to smile again.

'I see,' said he with a wan humour, 'that our forest is no kinder of human feet than four-footed. I beg you to remount your pony.'

'Nay,' said she wilfully, 'I would continue walking awhile, and do you be my knightly arm on which I lean.'

And she placed one of her ungauntleted hands on his massive shoulder and limped engagingly by his side. The lady, we fear, was a consummate actress, limping a pace, walking normally up an incline when more effort was needed, then remembering to limp again. Leaning on him with perhaps more pressure than was needed, she, her hand already warm from warmth and with excitement, burned yet more to his body's heat, while he, the reenraptured, saw nothing before him but the swelling velvet mist within his eyes. Both lady and wolf were perhaps too suggestible to their own temperaments. She would gladly have walked the full distance to her godmother's cottage, had not her sense of prudence forewarned her that her appealing limp and need for aid might not long deceive her presently unquestioning companion. So she whistled for her pony as Tom gazed round with filmy eyes, then quickly alerting himself he helped her to regain her high saddle.

'Leave me now,' she said, 'I shall go the rest of the way alone;' and smiling at him, as though she imagined soulfully, added, 'I thank you for your timely aid.'

'I shall be concerned to know of your lady's well-being,' said he gravely.

'No fear,' she replied delightedly. 'I shall come tomorrow to report myself for your personal inspection;' and pulling sharply at her pony's ear she set off at a lively gallop, with the now recovered Star loping and barking gaily behind her.

The bemused wolf stood without moving on the forest path, turned about slowly and with unaccustomedly tardy steps reentered the wood.

V

The warmth of spring was replaced by the mild sultriness of early summer. Those within the camp of wolves, or some at least, began to mutter of their leader's frequent absences. Within the town, but with more concern than condemnation, his gambling cronies made similar comment. But among these, some, who considered themselves more knowing, merely smiled with worldly comprehension, averring that Tom, no doubt, had more important matters of moment than play or dice, matters of family relative to wolves, at which all the gentlemen laughed heartily. The lady too was missed by her companions, and when the Margrave was asked at one of his fêtes, or at one of his more frequent hunts, what had become of the Lady Caroline, he would reply as though with honest bewilderment, 'The Lady Caroline? Now, who is that?'

Never before had Gentleman Tom been so confounded by his own behaviour. During those days that he and Red Hood traversed new paths through the forest, paths far distant from his own encampment and from that of the godmother's cottage, discovering retreats that neither had known before, and chatting amiably with mutual and growing pleasure, she sometimes riding but more frequently walking beside him, and with the morose Star left sulking at the castle, he felt with a benumbing secret happiness that she, Red Hood, was the epitome of the grace and attraction of humankind. But when, among his kindred or in the somnolence of the night, he would see about him those reproachful but nevertheless respectful faces and the face particularly of her who still unweariedly continued to watch and wait for the sign of his favour, or, alone among the whispering trees, when the reproach of himself by him, the speculative wolf, demanded rational explanations of his actions, he would falter in his esteem of her, the enchantress, Red Hood, and mercilessly berate himself for his wolf's treason. He vowed 'no more', but at the first sound of her pony's approaching hooves at a rendezvous they had designated, he became again victim of his renewing blindness. While she, confident and wilful in her imagined triumph, rode off each day from her father's castle, murmuring to herself in her exultation, 'Soon, soon,' until finally, 'This is the day that it shall be.'

The sun's rays were still slanting when the quarter moon rose in the violet sky, and the dreamy sound of chanting crickets punctuated with a monotonous accompaniment the more continuous high-pitched shrill of myriad tiny flies and swooping insects. The lady's pony contentedly nibbled at choice blades of grass between the trees, as the lady and he, the wolf, watched silently, side by side on a glade still warm from the rays of the departing sun. The shadows deepened and the wolf, with enquiring glance, turned to the lady who with lowered voice said, 'Nay, not now, I would yet stay. Let us sit awhile longer;' and the wolf, serene, yet troubled deeply, sighed unheard in his throat. A star seemed to balance, shimmering, athwart a gigantic old oak when she turned to him and her scent, familiar yet quiescent, now startled him and brought an alertness of wonder to his eyes, as she, peering into them deeply, suddenly and passionately murmured, 'Oh, Tom, what eyes you have.'

And he replied in his courteous, measured voice, 'The better to gaze at you, my lady.'

'And what lovely ears;' and she examined them so intently that he turned his head, replying slowly and almost inaudibly, 'The better to discern your bidding.'

'And what strong, furry forearms, Tom,' and she stroked them playfully as her eyes and teeth glinted in the arousement of her senses.

And Tom was silent. The lady's scent which at first had startled him, then excited and intimidated him simultaneously, began gradually to repel him. He gazed about gloomily, abstractedly, looking for he knew not what, while she awaited his answer. Her own eyes were large and wanton in the moonlight, her mouth agape in a manner which did not charm him, her lips moist and faintly frothy, while a dewiness glistened on her nose and brow. He shook himself then, more like a cat, and a low growl rumbled within his throat. Oh, how he longed at that moment for the clean, kindred smell of wolf. The growl thrilled the tactless lady who mistook its meaning, and raising her chin slightly with nostrils dilating expectantly she coyly asked, 'Well, Sir Tom?' and her smile, to his clouded brain, was hungry, voluptuary, greedy.

At last he answered, 'They are no forearms, lady. You mistake. They are paws.'

'Indeed,' said she, with an amused look at his apparent simplicity, and her voice deepening as she added, 'and cannot paws embrace, nor fondle like arms, those that they desire?'

A sense of pain made him grimace. The lady noticed it not. She placed one hand delicately on one of his ears, drew it out to its length in a stroking, amorous movement, at which he shivered visibly, put her other arm about his neck and leant her face close to his, with her warm breast against his shoulder and her moist breath fanning his eyes.

'Nay,' said he groaning, stirring desperately away, and it was sound like a growl more than a word. A look of puzzled rage sped over her face, when one of cold hauteur displaced it.

'Will you not?' said she quite calmly, her blue eyes cool as crystal but growing wild in their depths, and smiling again in a fixed and unnatural way, 'will you not? Then be it so.' And raising herself from beside him, still calmly, she began re-arranging the sombre red hood about her hair and drawing on her long, black doeskin gauntlets. And then, to his dismay and disgust, she began spitting at him with a tongue of forked lightning. 'Beast! You vile grey beast, will you shame me? Will you shame *me*, you animate hearthrug? Oh, but I shall have quits of you yet.'

And leaping so brutally on her pony that the animal reared and whinnied in its fear, she set its head directly into the forest, pulling at the snaffle till it tore into the pony's mouth, and sent it charging madly through a thicket of brambles. With stoical savagery she carried her head imperiously erect, meeting with disdain the brambles which, in her reckless speed, tore violently at her face and hair, ripped her hood and cloak, bruised her breast and arms and lacerated her body and, when near her godmother's house, she set up such a wailing and screeching that the godmother, followed by her son, the Gamewarden, with halberd in hand, both with staring eyes and startled mouths, flung out of the cottage with a terrified servant who held a wavering light between two trembling hands.

The lady, groaning, was aided off her pony and brought indoors, given a mild restorative and comfortably bedded upon a mountain of pillows, where, with eyes half-mad and spitting, frothing mouth, and between hiatuses of moaning gasps, while her godmother tenderly but vainly sought to calm her and her son, the Gamewarden, moodily looked on, she described how, ambling leisurely along on her pony, she had met the wolf, Gentleman Tom, who had greeted her courteously as he had done for several weeks past, had strolled with him at his earnest insistence to a glade, choice in situation for its view of the setting sun and the rising stars, and there, while rapt in the innocent spectacle of the heavens, he had murmured outrageous and insulting words to her, the Lady Caroline, who in her surprise and contempt had sought immediately to rise and betake herself at once from that place, but had then been pulled down by the now lustfully inflamed wolf who therewith attempted to ravish her, as witness of which she displayed, although there was no need, her pitifully ravaged face, her torn cloak and hood, and to the embarrassment of the Gamewarden even lowered her bodice to show the cuts on her breast. Had it not been for her thankfully masculine training, which had enabled her to repel repeatedly the attacks of the maddened, besotted beast, she feared that she would never have had the strength to make her escape untarnished, or even save herself from a certain and hideous death at his furious claws and teeth. And following this recital the lady succumbed to a suitable bout of hysterics with uncontrollable weeping, while the godmother in her alarm tried incapably to minister to her with words and finally with cordials. The lady then fell into a short but troubled sleep, during the course of which the godmother led her son away into the pantry, where they conversed in low, bewildered tones, expressing their horror at the lady's tale, yet nevertheless managing now and then to convey to each other their incredulity of the wolf's behaviour, having both, particularly the godmother, reason enough to know of his sobriety and perfect manners.

The lady, suddenly waking, called piteously for attention, upon which both godmother and son cut short their rueful colloquy and hastened back to her. The lady was calmer now, but still not too short of frantic, and begged the Gamewarden, despite the lateness of the hour, to beat up his keepers and organize a wolf-kill for the following morning, promising him in her wild passion for vengeance, one hundred gold pieces for Tom's pelt.

'Nay, lady,' said he, 'that I cannot do, it is unlawful and besides he is a great gentleman. It is a matter for His Highness, the Margrave.'

The lady flashed at him a glance of accumulated contempt, and then, urged by her compassionate and weeping godmother, was aided to her room upstairs, refusing with vehemence however the kindly solicitudes of the old woman who begged permission to undress her. At length, after more persistent but futile pleading, the lady finally consented to sit in an armchair by the window, seething still in her uncontrolled fury and sobbing bitterly with hate and shame, and ever and anon striking together her gauntleted hands in attitudes of high tragedy. The lady, as we have noted, was an accomplished actress, who, had she lived nearer our day, would doubtless have enjoyed a certain success on the stages of travelling companies.

A sorrowful procession set off from the cottage next morning: the lady leading astride her grey pony with her tattered red hood flaming in the roseate sunrise, the Gamewarden respectfully a few paces behind on a large chestnut stallion, and various of his greenwoodsmen marching with halberds and staves, both in the van and the rear. This mutely tramping column, at the lady's defiant direction, and against the sober advice of the Gamewarden, took its funereal way along the path leading by Tom's encampment. He, hearing its measured tread approaching, peered sombrely at it from between the trees, but vouchsafing no sound and commanding his pack to be silent, as slowly it passed and disappeared from view.

VI

The old Count, her father, when he heard of it that morning, was, as would be expected, stricken with an overpowering fury, and not solely on account of the reported outrage attempted against his daughter but against her, the lady herself. For now, in his disturbed mind, to his burdensome vendetta against boars – and the wily beasts were learning quickly to evade the thundering harquebuses of his outriders, and the tally of one hundred still lacked forty-four – he had to add the irksome task of extending his revenge to wolves, a wicked vicious lot, as subtle and scheming in their ways as boars, if not more so. And as he summoned up his gouty arms to his old and anguished temples, and mentally considered his age, the thought that the Great Avenger of All would sweep him away before his work was done filled him with a racking cough and a choking despair, and his deep-set sombre eyes glowed with an insane rage.

Glaring wildly at his bewildered offspring, the ancient nobleman shrieked at her in a hardly human, high-pitched frenzy. The lady was aghast at her sire's fulminations, and pretended herself shocked when the maledictions he heaped upon her and himself and the whole accursed line of Berg descended into the coarse vituperation of the cavalry barracks. Proudly she commanded him to recall himself to his rank and breeding, to his office of Master of the Margrave's Horse and colonel in the army, and to recollect too the vile assault which, only hours before, she had been made to suffer. His only reply was a single word, spat out venomously, and of a surprising vulgarity. At which the lady commenced herself to shriek and hastened shrieking from the chamber, interposing between her wild cries quite rational ones for her bodyservant who, arriving at that moment in a distraught fluster, received her collapsing mistress in a purported swoon, and struggling with the assistance of a few other terrified females quickly gathered, carried the lady to her bed upstairs.

Within the hour, the Count, now fully recovered from his rage, which he had forgotten, and reeking pleasantly of old Moselle, knocked at her ladyship's door, was granted admittance by a tearful voice, and seating himself on the bed at her lady's feet, very calmly and deliberately told her, as though nothing untoward had earlier happened, that he had summoned his carriage and was about to pay court to the Margrave, to whom he would not fail to reveal the bitter and degrading events of the night before.

'Rest content, my child,' he said, his sombre eyes winking malevolently. 'You and I shall have our justice and revenge.'

The lady's face, streaked and cut and angry red in its pitiful bruises, made a brave attempt at a smile. The old Count, stooping to kiss the lady gently on an injured cheek, patted her flaxen head and then went off with a soldier's stride, humming under his breath an old hunting air.

The Margrave kept the Count waiting and he, the old noble, fumed, bethinking him in his exasperation – and despite the courteous explanation of a secretary that His Highness was closeted with his council on matters of state – that the ruler was in pique over the wayward and prolonged absence by the daughter from the august presence, and was thus punishing the daughter through the innocent father who, in the august eyes, was doubtless equally culpable. These gloomy, self-incriminatory thoughts were put at rest however when the Margrave, in his glittering dress of Grand Marshal of the army, appeared suddenly by the Count and tapped him amiably on the shoulder, inviting him pleasantly to shake the sleep from his eyes, as the old gentleman was by then nodding, and requested him to join him in his private cabinet. There, after calling for refreshments, he bade the Count to take his ease, and apologized profusely for having kept him waiting, explaining that matters of high importance had necessitated his earnest attention, as he and his advisers both military and civil were then in the midst of meditating war on one of his more unruly neighbours. The Count's eyes lighted up at this disclosure as, with a manly, blustering declaration, he declared himself ready to die in the Margrave's service at the head of his troopers. The Margrave laughed very agreeably and promised the Count that should it come to war, he would not fail to give his old comrade a splendid command.

He then requested the Count to state his pleasure, since his presence and that of his lovely daughter being so rare of late, he assumed that something of moment had brought him there. The Count admitted this with his usual sombre look, but then was silent, and the Margrave noting this judged not incorrectly that the matter was of grave importance.

'Speak out, my friend,' he encouraged him, 'and you will see that whatever your problem, your amiable Prince has the most devoted interest in advising you, and should it be a question of exacting justice for a wrongdoing against you, which God forbid, our righteous arm is diligently waiting.'

The Count cleared the thickened chords of his throat and began in an unwonted delicacy of tone, like a gentle stream, which soon, in the enormity of what he was relating, changed to a bellicose bass that thundered like a raging torrent. The Margrave was faintly shocked, but knowing his old friend well, patiently waited till the dismal recital was done. He then allowed some moments to pass, being aware that the Count's savage animation would soon dissipate itself, and unstoppering a decanter with his own princely hands, poured out two generous measures. Then after both had savoured the first glowing sips of the noble brandy, he bent his head earnestly forward and asked solicitously, 'And what would you have me do? For, after all, he is a gentleman.'

The Count's furious little eyes blazed. 'Gentleman!' he spat. 'Why, my daughter's honour and mine demand quick justice, my Prince, and I as Master of Your Highness' Horse am prepared to execute it.'

'Should I allow it, that is,' said the Margrave thoughtfully. 'No, my friend, that is not the way. We should be like those very beasts whose savagery we abhor. For in our understanding we must act as men, under men's laws and institutions, with the justice of men. Nevertheless, my Lord Count, rest you assured. You shall yet see that our way is best.'

And calling for a secretary, the Margrave dictated a note instructing the chief of his judiciary to render to the Count and his daughter every assistance necessary. And with that he dismissed his now grateful supplicant.

VII.

Those days that followed Tom's last meeting with Red Hood were days admixed of momentary brooding and long periods of exultant happiness. At last he felt liberated of that subtle, penetrating, unnatural poison which had sought to despoil his wolf's paramountcy. He governed his pack with a new leniency of strictness, and with a new ardour, never for a moment leaving them, joining with them as always in the serious matter of hunting, but sharing with them now their games, their frolics and leisure moments, their thoughtful questioning: so that where before they had regarded him as one apart in exalted state, they now with no less deference learned to treat him with a respectful affection; and even the grumblers, though grumbling still, kept their opinions studiously silent.

Yet Tom was apprehensive, and in those moments of brooding subject to a serene sorrow, recognizing perhaps that his new exultancy, keener than ever before, prefigured a knowledge of approaching troubles; and as he surveyed his pack his depth of apprehension about them and about himself, stirred within him the fateful idea of selecting one who, should the need demand, could act as his successor. He did then a most unusual thing in wolf society, where leaders succumb only in the attenuation of their strength or intellect, or in cases of rivalry or dispute are supplanted in single combat: he summoned a conclave of the elders and expressed his wish to name an heir. The elders were astonished, and begged him to give way his idea, or rather fixation, since they saw no necessity of such an extraordinary démarche and expressed their supreme confidence in him and the many years of future leadership to which his vigour and astuteness entitled him. But Tom was persistent and, though conceding that the circumstance might never arise, stressed that it was a matter of simple prudence in the contingencies and hazards of existence, and also that in case of catastrophe, the succession could be handled peaceably without the usual dissension and strife. The worried elders finally though reluctantly agreed, and Tom mentioned as his first choice that fellow who was wont to stand on an eminence surveying the sky, for though given to introspection like Tom, he too possessed resource and qualities of leadership which Tom had observed attentively and secretly approved of. The elders concurred to this also following a short and disheartened discussion. Soon after, a general meeting was called and the announcement made, receiving as one would expect decidedly various reactions, ranging from indignation and sorrow to mutterings from the grumblers, but mostly of praise.

With the weight of that burden exorcised, Tom spent the following days in acute involvement with his appointed successor, Hugh, whose intelligence and bearing well justified his leader's wise and considered choice. Tom imparted to him then various secret matters pertaining to wolf tradition, the knowledge of which is restricted to few, and was delighted with Hugh's ready assimilation of their daunting complexity.

As they strolled one morning beneath the trees, deep in conversation, Tom, moved by a sudden remorse which defeated the warmth and beauty of the day and chilled the deferential look of his companion, turned to him sadly and said, 'I fear my time is fast approaching, I would bid you adieu. Look well to the pack, my brother.'

With that he bounded away swiftly, running purposefully in his long, powerful stride to the path where, in the autumn, he had first met the lady Red Hood. The dismayed Hugh, after first standing for a moment in stunned silence, turned about slowly and trotted back to the camp.

It was as Tom had dreaded yet grimly and confidently expected. At the very moment that he reached the path and paused, his head thrown high, his body extended in the full grace of its matchless symmetry, a column of men-at-arms bearing banners and lances and led by two on black horses, approached steadily from the near distance. As they came up and halted, the two officers saluted and the elder, the captain, politely enquired whether he was Gentleman Tom.

'I am he,' said Tom, nodding courteously. 'What is your pleasure?'

'No pleasure, Sir, I fear,' said the officer. 'I have here a warrant, in the name of His Serene Highness, the Margrave, summoning you to be detained in a dungeon of His Highness' prison for noble offenders, there to await trial on a charge of reprehensible conduct.'

'I am at your disposal,' said Tom gravely.

The officer, surprised, commented: 'Do you not at least wish to know the name of the one who has brought this charge against you, nor the nature of the charge itself?'

'Nay, that is not necessary.'

The officer, astonished, looked with wonder at the wolf of whose repute he had often heard, and was filled with a soldier's admiration.

'Very well, Sir,' he replied with a salute, 'it shall be as you say.' And turning to his lieutenant he added quietly, 'As for that thing,' and pointed contemptuously to a wooden cage surmounting a heavy draught horse which stood in the rear of the column, 'get it out of my sight. Pitch it into the forest. There'll be no need of it.'

The younger officer saluted smartly, and turning his horse's head about galloped quickly to the rear of the column where on his instructions several of the men-at-arms dismantled the cage and unceremoniously sent it crashing into the underbrush.

'We are ready whenever you are, Sir,' said the captain to Tom, and as the wolf indicated his equal readiness to proceed at once, the column wheeled about and returned leisurely to the town, with Tom in their midst, walking silently beside the horse of the captain.

VIII.

The trial of the wolf, Gentleman Tom, ordered on the indictment of the excellent lady Caroline Aloise Charlotte-Marie von Berg, was among the most celebrated of animal trials in history. Its hearings drew the attendance of no less a figure than the Margrave himself, an itinerant Hungarian Prince, four provincial Counts, seventeen landed Barons, twenty-two Barons minus lands, an Italian talmud scholar who afterwards composed a treatise comparing features of the trial with a tractate of that mostly solemn work, and various assorted gentry both animal and human, plus the usual rabble.

The lady's deposition was presented by surrogate, she being still confined at her father's castle in a state of shock approaching a prolonged malaise and, on the orders of the best medical advice, urgently required not to stir from her bed. Defendant's counsel, apprised of the situation before the trial commenced, and after consultation with his client, readily acquiesced in the arrangement. It was then, for the first time, that Tom learned the full name of Red Hood and the indisputed fact that the venerated Berg Alwa, or Alois, of old, was alike the progenitor of the lady and the benefactor of his line.

The charge, read by the presiding judge of the tribunal, a jurist eminent for his rigorous insight into the hearts of malefactors and unbending in his justice, and based on the sworn and witnessed statement of the lady, among the highest-born in the land, of the ancient and honoured House of Berg, generations of whose members had rendered signal service in war and in councils-of-state as devoted and selfless officers and officials, deposed that a wolf, by name Gentleman Tom, arrogating to himself the privileges and ways of a man, and moreover those of a gentleman, and having been accepted as such by various gullible and trusting persons, had, through his animal wiles and man-like lusts, which he had cunningly kept well hidden, beguiled a foolish young woman, a lady, into accepting his wolf-man friendship, until the day that she, in her naive innocence, could conveniently be ravished by him. And were it not for the fortunate and happy chance of her excellent physique and athletic training, the heinous deed would doubtless have been accomplished: nay, even worse might have followed, for the lady's wounds, lacerations and scratches, all of a serious and vicious nature, and indicating the desperate and violent intent of her assailant, and so attested and sworn to by doctors of the highest repute, and here the eminent jurist impatiently waved a vellum document, could have led, had not the lady fought back with her instinctive valiance and courage, that same courage which had so distinguished her illustrious family in time of war, could have led, he repeated, to the monstrous eventuality of a hideous and disfigured death.

A sigh of horror echoed among the less sophisticated members of the audience as the learned judge paused to draw a red silk handkerchief across his sweating brow.

At this juncture various witnesses were called, chief of whom present was the Gamewarden of the Margravate, whose manly bearing and sober countenance impressed all by their quiet, cool objectivity. He deferred to the wisdom of the court in summoning the accused on the very grave charge of the lady whom he had the honour to know slightly as the god-daughter of his mother. He therewith begged leave to apologize for the absence of his mother who was lying then very ill at home, owing to a complaint which because of her advanced age affected her most adversely. The judge at this point ventured to signify the whole court's devout wish that she would soon recover, and urged the Gamewarden to speak out boldly of all that he knew and had witnessed and to return Godspeed to his ailing mother.

The Gamewarden then expressed the view that, to his certain knowledge, he had prior to the event described heard nothing untoward against the accused, Gentleman Tom, but that to the contrary his name and reputation as a lord of the forest had earned him high acclaim and universal praise. He would have adverted at that moment to the viewpoint of his mother respecting Tom, but was informed quite brusquely by the eminent jurist that he must confine his testimony to the facts as he knew them and not to the hearsay of others. The Gamewarden, thus reproved, gazed sombrely and briefly at Tom, who stood below and to one side of the judges' dais, surrounded by four men-at-arms with halberds at rest, and with a heavy iron collar about his neck, from which led two massive chains which in turn were wound around the waists of two further men-at-arms with grounded axes. These two chains had the convenience of fitting to two iron staples in his dungeon, to which he could be attached for the safety of his gaolers when entering there to bring his food, and also of course to inhibit the possibility of escape. The Gamewarden's solemn glance at Tom brought no awakening response from the wolf, who stood proudly with head erect though nevertheless with eyes contracted in their pupils, unblinking, gazing abstractedly, seeing nothing. The Gamewarden then resumed and spoke of the night that the lady, on her pony, had ridden up to his mother's cottage, which he shared, in a state of the highest agitation, and that his mother and he had with difficulty sought to calm her; that she, the lady, had retailed to them an account substantially in essence with the gravamen of the charge, and that undoubtedly she had displayed wounds, cuts and abrasions which admittedly could have derived from an assault, but whether that assault was in fact as had been described, he, the Gamewarden, could not know.

The learned judge, purple with fury, asked the Gamewarden if he had anything further to add, and he replying negatively, the judge commended him to a speedy departure, upon which the Gamewarden turned to salute the regal though unemblazoned curtains which draped concealingly a space in the wall to one side of the judges' dais, and behind which the Margrave together with some friends was following the process of the trial. He then saluted the judge, after which he cast one more swift look at Tom and hurriedly departed the court.

To dispel the perhaps doubtful and unfavourable implication cast upon the veracity of the lady's statement, as suggested in testimony by the Gamewarden, the eminent jurist next ordered a short parade of witnesses, of both high and low station, who spoke with becoming sincerity of the lady's good nature, her rectitude, her absolute devotion to honesty and duty, and of various good works of which several of those present had been the benefactors. As the roll of distinguished, honourable and noble names was called, and those to whom they belonged were in turn each sworn and spoke up in their high-bred accents of the incomparable lady Caroline von Berg and her exemplary actions, the presiding judge beamed good-humouredly and most of those in court nodded sagely. It was then almost anti-climactic and perverse when those of the lower station gave their testimony, and being mostly retainers of the Count and his daughter, the court received their anticipated and poorly declaimed words, all nevertheless in full praise of the virtuous and magnanimous lady, with an air of impatience. An atmosphere of equability having been restored, together with it a heavy smile with all teeth showing in favour of justice, as the eminent jurist saw it, he adjourned the sitting and called for a resumption of the trial next day. The prisoner was returned to his cell, surrounded by his keepers, and the court was cleared amid an air of confident excitement for the following morning.

IX.

The second hearing unfolded more dramatically than the first. The regal curtains concealing the Margrave and his guests fluttered frequently before the Bailiff of the court ground his mace and in the name of His Serene Highness declared the proceedings open. A learned clerk thereupon delivered a resumé of the previous day's process, together with witnesses' statements, which defending counsel approved as correct and fixed his signature thereto, at which the presiding judge cleared his throat and re-enunciated in harsh and compelling accents, for the benefit of those who might not have been there before, the full nature of the charge against the wolf, Gentleman Tom.

A thrill of expectation filled the assembly as Tom was then summoned to approach the space before the centre of the judicial dais, and commanded to know how he answered. He stood as proudly erect as before, despite the weight of that massive collar about his neck and the heavy imprisoning chains suspended from it to his keepers. He paused before speaking and then, in a surprisingly mild tone – surprising that is to many who heard it, who had been expecting the guttural snarl of an insensate beast – he declared, to the consternation of all, 'The lady knows best.'

'Eh?' roared the eminent jurist, and then collecting himself hurriedly: 'Let the accused repeat his statement.'

As mildly as before, Tom said, 'The lady knows best,' and looked about with an air of faint surprise, and then of amusement.

The hubbub which followed this declaration, and which

threatened the solemn nature of the proceedings, brought a stormy thundering of the mace and repeated calls for order. Yet amidst the astounded remarks made by those in attendance were the frequent exclamations of: 'Why, he has condemned himself!' and the almost as frequent rejoinder: 'Nay, nay, one must look deeper into those words.' And meanwhile, from between the regal curtains concealing the Margrave, a lustrous head of jet black curls almost encompassing an exquisitely female and inquisitive face peeped several times through, with a delicate mouth opened in wide amazement. The curtains fell suddenly brusquely shut, silence ensued, and the presiding judge with rueful red face and distended blue veins cleared his throat again.

In an astutely insinuating, gentle voice, which he managed with great difficulty, he recommended to the prisoner that he explain what he meant by those curious words, 'The lady knows best.' Did he, for example, imply that by the lady knowing best, he was admitting the veracity of the terrible charge levelled against him? Or did those very words conceal some evil, wicked intent which he alone, in the twists of his animal mind, was privy to?

Tom, with a neutral and steady gaze as he listened to the judge, spoke once more in his mild, courteous voice, saying: 'I beg the court to understand that, with respect, I have said what is necessary and which is the full and sincere declaration of my mind.'

A milder hubbub ensued but was quickly hushed. 'And will you say no more than that?' came the ominous voice of the judge.

For answer Tom continued to gaze with his candid eyes in the judge's direction, standing immoveably and silently with head erect.

'Ha,' said the Margrave quietly behind the concealing curtains to his friend the Hungarian Prince, 'this is a manly brute. I would get to the bottom of it.' And flinging open the curtains and rising in his full majesty, so that an awed gasp of wonder filled the court as all, together with the three judges, hurriedly rose to their feet, he pronounced in his clear and ringing voice: 'Sir, will you answer *me* with an explanation?'

Tom bowed deeply his head, a fairly simply matter with all that weight attached to it, then raised it with difficulty and said, softly yet distinctly: 'I thank Your Highness for his noble favour. Yet I have said what I could and have nothing to add.'

The Margrave, frowning deeply, reseated himself while a lackey hurriedly drew the curtains closed.

An air of bemused wonderment settled over the court, as the presiding judge consulted animatedly with his colleagues. This discussion excited and apparently divided the gentlemen into opposing viewpoints, but after a few minutes he, the eminent jurist, seemed to win his way. Looking about him with his marble-like, frosty blue eyes, set in their deep purple pouches and surmounted by bristling, wildly unkempt white eyebrows, he first glanced at the Margrave's box, to which he inclined his head humbly, then turned to face the court, gazing beyond the prisoner as he enunciated the words: 'The statement made by the accused is incomplete testimony, implying on the one hand culpability for the crime alleged, and on the other a subtle mystery, known only perhaps in its meaning in the accused's mind. The court on pressing for an explanation of his statement has met with blank refusal, and even the august and generous intervention of our noble Prince,' and here he bowed again in the direction of the concealing curtains, 'has elicited no further information from his recalcitrant and stubborn tongue. The court therefore is left with no other alternative in proceeding for the moment.' And here he ordered Tom to the torture in an effort to loosen his wayward and wicked tongue. The hearing was then adjourned till further notice.

X.

These events, together with the details of Tom's imprisonment and the dire accusation of the lady Red Hood, were soon known by a principal few in the encampment, and one need not guess too hard at the origin of the intelligence, but for those left in wonderment it will only be necessary to mention the Gamewarden. It was then decided by Hugh, in consultation with the elders, since he felt still somewhat inexperienced, to post a reliable scout within the court, one with the most agile legs, who could report back the news as it developed. The plan was adopted without dissent and Hugh was congratulated on his perspicacity. The appointment was duly made and the fellow chosen, proud though dignified in the consciousness of his responsibility, set off for the town. Unbeknownst to Hugh and the elders, however, word of the assignment and of Tom's predicament spread to a few others, including those grumblers who had still not forgotten nor forgiven Tom for having prevented them from attacking defenceless farmsteads during the late, bitter winter, and who for other numerous and twisted reasons bore him deep malice in their hearts. Two of these, after an agreement among themselves, also set off for the town.

Late that evening, after many hours of introspection, Hugh called the principal elders away with him from the sleeping encampment and deep into the forest, where he proposed to them, under the hidden silence of the stars and the tenebrous trees, various plans of action whereby in the uncertain vagaries of the trial's outcome, the pack should act. The most dramatic of these concerned the possibility of Tom's condemnation to death which, with heavy heart, Hugh conceded existed. Were this to come about, and he needed not mention how his own deep feelings and those about him militated against the horror of it, it would be essential to move the whole pack from the area with the utmost speed. Two of those there immediately agreed with the wisdom of this course of action, adding that even in the dire eventuality of Tom's condemnation with its inevitable ending, it would only be necessary after a suitable period to return a reliable scout to ascertain whether the pack was still to be tolerated in their chosen encampment. 'You have completed my thought,' said Hugh with gratitude, but before a consensus could be reached, the two other elders advanced the opposing view that even in the event of Tom's death, it would still be premature to leave such choice grounds which from time immemorial had provided the pack with a friendly environment and with comparatively good hunting. At this point Hugh expressed the opinion that since time would probably not be available to them when the ruling of the court became known, an immediate decision on method of action had to be agreed then. After further discussion which went on for several hours more, it was mutually covenanted that should the judgement of the court go against Tom in the manner dreaded, three in addition to Hugh would give orders to their section leaders to decamp at once. The fourth, despite the viewpoint of the other three elders and Hugh, declared with confidence that he was content for his people and himself to remain. All five then pledged themselves to a discreet and binding silence on their plans, and returned to the camp.

In the town, where the events were known at once and created much furious speculation, and particularly in the gaming club, the views were mixed. Some averred that the gallant wolf, with his handsome and eloquent eyes and his lithe grace and becoming ways, had finally overreached himself and his rank, and that his protracted and unusual absence during the spring and early summer certainly pointed to his being up to something. After all, one couldn't blame him entirely either, what with a sultry moon and a dark velvety sky, and a docile and friendly companion well known for her attractions. Others though declared with passion that they were convinced of his absolute innocence and honour, and were willing to wager heavily that the outcome of the trial would not only vindicate their opinion but enrich their purses. Some of these, particularly the younger and more idealistic, asserted too that they would attend the proceedings and would be honoured to speak in defence of Tom's blameless character, despite the power and intimidation of those arrayed against him. They were admonished expectedly by their elder, more experienced companions as being rash and in danger of courting unknown trouble and possibly damaging their futures. Nonetheless, it must be said, they swore not to be deterred from their good resolves.

XI

The court was not assembled again until a further week had elapsed, and a solemn hush filled the chamber as Tom was aided to his accustomed place beside the dais of the tribunal. A confused buzzing ensued amid which the three judges entered and were acknowledged by the assembly rising to its feet and thereafter sitting, following the usual proclamation in the name of His Highness and that the court was now ready for its business of dispensing justice.

All eyes were fixed in fascination and horror on the wolf who stood, still with the heavy iron collar and depending chains yet with head painfully erect, on two legs, balancing delicately on a third. The fourth was raised clear of the floor. He had been blinded in one eye, maimed permanently in one leg, which now acted as a kind of crutch, while the one which was raised had a paw brutally crushed. The presiding judge, after a hurried look at Tom, requested the Bailiff to enquire from him whether he preferred to recline during the proceedings, but was answered with a mild negative shake of the wolf's head.

The eminent jurist himself, for the benefit of the court, then summarized the events of the second hearing, and the dire and necessitous action imposed on the court through the accused's own contumacious conduct in refusing to clarify the meaning of his statement in answer to the grave charge levelled against him, which statement consisted of the obscure and misleading words, 'The lady knows best.'

The presiding judge then whispered briefly to one of his colleagues on the bench, after which he gazed sombrely at the court for a moment without speaking, and cleared his throat gently.

All men, he said, were possessed of certain reserves of strength and fortitude, which aided them in the midst of battle or in the trying pursuit of fulfilling their duty as servants of the state or in the humbler occupations of life. There was a time too when all men, before the Maker of their lives, unfolded their hearts in absolute truth and with sincere devotion. These were men, however, possessed of men's minds, men's sensibilities and finer emotions. But what of the beasts? What were their standards, their morals, their comprehension of right and wrong? Moreover, what could a beast feel in comparison with a man? What could he endure without, like a man, giving way finally to the compelling need to tell the truth? There were black hearts amongst men, it was true, none denied this, otherwise there would not be courts of law to interrogate and punish the guilty, as justice demanded. But who could compare the black heart of a man with the black heart of a beast, a beast withal who could withstand, apparently without feeling, without speaking – other than those selfsame words as before – the subjection of the boot to crush his limbs and the poker from the fiery brazier to thrust out his eye?

The eminent jurist paused in consideration of the magnitude of Tom's wickedness, hiding for a moment his piercing eyes behind the sheltering shield of his two enormous, veined hands. He was recalled from his abstraction by one of his colleagues who whispered urgently into his ear, at which he looked up with such surprise that his purplish lips dropped open. 'What's that?' he asked vehemently, so that the whole court could hear him; and when it was confirmed to him that what he thought he had heard was the case, he nodded vigorously, and a malevolent smile invigorated his senile lips into two sinuous serpents.

'We have a surprising and new development,' he said, caressing each word as he pronounced it: 'two who would speak of the accused, Gentleman Tom, not as men but as kindred wolves, and as members of his own company. We have heard the testimony of men, but who can know the heart of a beast so well as a fellow beast?

Therefore let them be brought in, but nevertheless well attended,' at which remark the learned judge attempted a sombre smile, with which his colleagues and a few among the assembly joined in, and all eyes were directed towards the prisoners' gate.

The two grumblers were now led in by a small troop of men-at-arms fortified with lances, and furious at the subterfuge which had been played on them. For after first being greeted courteously by the officer in charge of the court's security, and thence accompanied to the judges' chambers where several anxious-looking clerks nervously took down their statement and transmitted it to the bench, they were then unceremoniously manacled together on the orders of the officer, who had meantime remained discreetly in the background. Laughing good-naturedly, the officer assured the grumblers that it was only a formality and begged them to excuse him for his seemingly high-handed action, but since there were ladies in court, and, between men, so the officer demeaned himself, there was bound to be the possibility of some feminine hysterics. The grumblers however would not be soothed by these sweet words, and grumbling as usual were led in by their watchful escort.

Looking about with surprise at the vast number of human eyes watching them intently, and the novelty of the three aged heads on the bench staring down at them with old men's looks, the grumblers felt a certain elation mixed with apprehension and awe, at the grandeur and wonderment of their situation. It was then that they noticed Tom for the first time who watched them too with a cool, contemptuous expression. That look was enough to set beating again the old malicious hate in their unnatural hearts.

When a degree of composure had settled over the court, the presiding judge instructed the clerk to swear the new witnesses in due form, after which he read the following statement:

The two who stood before the court [they shall be nameless], as voluntary witnesses desirous through their own sense of duty of adding to the court's information with particular reference to the character of the accused, Gentleman Tom, were members of his own company who had grown up alongside him, had accepted his authority as leader although many times with serious doubt and misgivings, and had noted his developing interest in the lady, who was styled by them Red Hood, on account of a certain costume which she was wont to wear on her visits to the forest, which visits had occasioned many absences from the encampment of wolves by the said Gentleman Tom. These absences had raised in their minds the serious question, a question which had troubled them previ-ously, whether in fact their leader was not more man than wolf and with instincts similarly directed.

A loud intake of breath throughout the court interrupted this last statement.

Not content enough with this damaging insinuation, those two went on to relate how, in the late winter, with the threat of starva-tion facing the pack, they had urged Tom to be permitted to plunder a neighbourhood farm with good fat sheep, but that Tom had severely rebuked them and angrily refused, which in their estima-tion was another sign of his man's nature unnaturally closeted within a wolf's body.

The judge then enquired of the two whether his reading of their statement was in essence correct, and the two nodded balefully, with pleased treasonable hearts. They were then required to affix their marks to the document and were led out again, gazing about the court with a self-consciousness of importance and pride, although studiously avoiding Tom's glance.

But at a gesture from the presiding judge, which brought his clerk rushing to his side, an instruction was conveyed to the officer who, with the most sincere expression of sympathy, informed the two that unfortunately their manacles could not be immediately unshackled, at which the grumblers in unison shouted, 'Betrayal!' and struggled savagely in their bonds, at which the officer reproached them for their bad-mannered impatience, and advised them severely to be of better behaviour, and that meanwhile they would be lodged with great comfort and convenience, until released quite shortly, in a very fine room where good food would be plentiful. The two accepted this with a better grace, and marched off docilely between their captors.

Tom's gaming friends would, at that moment, have stood to beg permission of the court to give their evidence of his blameless conduct and excellent character, had not the eminent jurist at this point declared the court in recess, to be reassembled after consulta-tion with his learned colleagues in several hours. The assembly then rose reluctantly to its feet and withdrew, while the prisoner was aided back to his dungeon.

Following a long peroration by the presiding judge, in the midst of which he cited again the charge which had brought the court into session and the accused before the bench, and repeated the essential points of the witnesses' statements, including that of the latest, the two grumblers, which had only verified and confirmed the contention that a wolf, with the arrogance of a man, had through his animal wiles and man-like instincts and lusts prevailed upon the innocence of a trusting and foolish young lady, yet one of the highest rank and honour, to grant him her friendship so that eventually he could beguile her to a cloistered spot in the forest, there to attempt his foul ravishment which, thank God, she in the excellence of her strength and boldness of manner had valiantly resisted, but at the expense of terrible wounds, bruises, lacerations, et cetera, after which he continued:

Moreover it was a fact that the accused himself did not deny the charge, nor offer any other explanation of the lady's bitter testimony or of her grievous condition than that of his words, freely offered in court and unchanged under the stresses of torture, 'The lady knows best,' which in context could be interpreted as confirming that what the lady had said was the truth. Bearing in mind all this, and after much learned discussion, the court could move now in only one direction. At this point the jurist turned to an awaiting assistant and was handed a hideous, crimson, silken cowl, which with the assistant's aid was transferred to his parchment-white skull. Following this grotesque procedure, a thrill of awe and horror went through the assembly, and as the judge resumed speaking, Tom, with mournful humour, mused to himself, 'Ah, it is my fate to be twice doomed by Red Hood.'

Tom was condemned to be hanged, and his properties confiscated, although, added the judge sombrely, amid the hush and gloom of the assembly, it had been the court's first intention to inflict a severer form of punishment for the heinous crime involved, but that in deference to the value of the pelt, the court had consented to see him hanged rather than destroyed by the wheel.

At the conclusion of this statement Tom was asked if he had anything to say but declined with a shake of the head, and was led slowly from the silent chamber.

Those nearest him then said afterward that he seemed to murmur to himself in passing, and even discerned the indistinct syllables 'Alwa' or 'Alois'. What he said in fact, as he thought solely to himself, was this: 'The Alwa of old gave to mine ... surely it is right that through the Alwa of now I render back ...'

The eminent jurist in a now brighter vein, which set some of the assembly laughing, made reference to the last two witnesses who, by their culpable candour, had revealed such dangers to society as their existence threatened that merited the same punishment as their former leader. The two grumblers were accordingly also sentenced to hang.

They who had laughed, and those many who had not, alike left the court with a disquieting feeling of unease, sensing despite the evidence of the trial and its inexorable direction, that that solitary, maimed figure, who held his head so invincibly in the face of his detractors and the biased declamations of his judges and who, by those curious words 'The lady knows best', had intimated a potency of honour and grandeur rare even among the annals of men, was indeed as he had been called, Gentleman Tom, a gentleman in name and in deed though in the body of a wolf.

XII.

He, the valiant, the agile of leg, the trusty scout, betook himself swiftly from the courtroom to a more secluded part of the town where he lingered until dark with a heavy, brooding heart, and then, under a moonless, starry sky, by unfrequented byways, and passing occasionally the feebly lit hut whence issued the strident, drunken voices of men, came swiftly back to the central square with its numerous dark and shuttered shops, and, not far distant, the open quadrangle paved with massive blocks of red granite, the Margrave's champ-de-mars, where his soldiery on state occasions paraded, and behind which in turn loomed the ghostly white pile of the palace, with proud pennons flying from its battlements, with tall, noble windows brilliantly lit and the sound of gay music of horns and viols which, carried to him as he paused, gazing about watchfully, struck him with pain by its alien tones.

Without the deep grounds of the palace, surrounded by a forbidding wall of stone and iron, marched the sentinels of the Margrave's guard, some with shouldered halberds, others on horseback carrying lanterns and moving at a walking pace, still others on foot beside harquebuses, standing silent and immoveably alert.

On a further side of the square stood the ponderous court of law, shuttered now, and dark and heavy to the wolf in its portentous evil; and between the palace and the court the high-gabled, turreted fortress with moat and drawbridge, with lanterns flashing at its entrance where stood a small group of officers chatting gaily among themselves; and ever and anon the disciplined cries of watch and greeting from the fortress guards. It was there that his leader rested, awaiting the awful dawn of his extinction.

The wolf stirred restlessly, leaning for obscurity's sake into the embrasure of a nearby wall, his shadowed eyes flickering in their own brilliance, his body poised with the tension of a powerful bird ready to launch into immediate flight: he, the runner of the pack, the bold messenger, the faithful spy, trusted for his intelligence and the incomparable speed of his agile legs. His mandate for action had been clearly defined to him: to report on the trial as it progressed each day; to return to the town for further observation; to report back finally when the trial was over and the outcome known. Yet he lingered, though he knew that his news was fateful and should be carried as quickly as possible to the elders and that powerful young subordinate leader, the wise Hugh. A compelling urgency and a devotion to him who would forever be supreme in his wolf's soul, the magnificent and peerless Tom, kept him waiting, dangerously, with the precious moments slipping by as the night advanced, for he would speak, convey a farewell to him whose kind would nevermore walk the face of earth with such nobility and majesty.

The wolf crept out of the enveloping embrasure with a swift, crawling gait: in all matters of movement he was the most versatile, the most imaginative, the most daring. Like an elongated spring, closing slightly on itself then reopening, he hurried silently over the stones of the square, shuddering as he sped more slowly by the grim and frightful law court, with the fortress and its guards not far ahead. Then he paused, then started up again on shortened legs so that his body resembled a flattened parcel of fur moving incongruously over the ground. Then at the crucial moment outside the drawbridge on its outer side he waited, sheltered rashly behind a wall which came no higher than his shoulder, standing immobilized, rigid, like a sculptured wolf of stone, till with incomparable judgement and timing of the distance across the drawbridge and his own reckoned speed for covering it, he perceived the officers separate and look opposite ways, at which like a ball from a musket he discharged himself across the intervening space and within moments reached the protecting shadows of the fortress walls. The officers turned to each other again and resumed their interrupted conversation with no knowledge of what had happened, and began laughing gaily at some shared pleasantry.

The scout paused and shook himself carefully, breathed in with a deep reviving breath, and commenced moving with a circum-spect, quick gait about the fortress enclosure. Where he came to bolted windows, whether at ground level or above, he halted, and with a discreet wolf signalling signified his presence. He had made almost an entire circuit of the fortress walls as, with sinking heart, he approached in the distance the drawbridge again, with its yet chatting officers, when an answering sound, attenuated in its thin-ness, made him stop short, with the fine hair in his inner ears tin-gling at full alert. The wolf repeated his signal, with the added dis-tinctive warble of Tom's pack, and heard the same warble return-ing to him. A soft voice in the wolf tongue whispered to him then from a scarcely visible slot in the wall some few yards above his head: 'Is it thou, Gari?' The wolf answered with a deep humility and affirmative joy, and conveyed to Tom his mission, omitting however to mention that the mission did not include instructions for paying farewell to him, the soon-to-be departed leader. 'Then all is not lost, for I see Hugh's purpose. It is well, very well, I am more than content. They will yet survive.' And as a silence fol-lowed, the anxious voice of Tom came louder, 'Gari, art thou still without?' And when a discreet warble answered: 'Then go, my friend, my brother. Go swiftly and vigilantly. Go as the wind in storm, as thou alone can on thy agile legs. Back to the forest with thy message, and fare you well, noble friend, till we meet once more. Fly, Gari, fly.'

The wolf, with a low shuddering moan, turned on tensile though trembling legs, and ran headlong with reckless speed until catching himself with instinctive alertness he drew up, tested the strength of his matchless legs, loosened with a shake the taut muscles in his shoulders, and watchful, with large, glittering, star-ing eyes following the movements of the hateful men, he discerned again an opening, that momentary unheedfulness which he could always count on, and gathering up once more the coiled speed and power in his massive tendons, he launched himself across the drawbridge like a vanishing grey phantom.

XIII.

The wolf, Gentleman Tom, had that fateful night another unexpected visitor, and one of the highest degree, who came masked, accompanied by two great dignitaries, one of whom was commander of the army and the other his chief-of-staff, both with helmets and burnished cuirasses yet unarmed save for small sheathed daggers. The deeply humble Governor of the fortress, himself unlocked the grating door of the dungeon and admitted the trio, leaving them with a large smoking lantern before withdrawing silently. The wolf, with the heavy iron collar about his neck, lay for convenience on the stone floor, but on the entrance of the masked figure and his companions, sought painfully to raise himself, at which the man who was leader, he of the mask, spoke with a gentle solicitous voice: 'Nay, stir not. There is no need,' while his companions gazed with horror at the black, unsightly hole that marked the wolf's missing eye, and the grotesquely maimed leg on which he tried with the aid of his others to rise, then fell back again. 'It were as though you had risen,' said the gracious Prince, for it was the Margrave, 'and I make full acknowledgement that the form has been observed. Now listen, I would speak with you, for my heart troubles me about this trial and its sentence,' and here he removed his mask, revealing to Tom the sincere and anxious lines of his face.

'I ask you, Sir Wolf, to treat the sanctity of these walls as reposing your confidence in me, your Prince, and these my comrades-in-arms, whose lips will remain as silent as mine, to speak with a full and open heart of all that concerns you in your great trouble, and, if what you say will alter in some manner the grievous evidence against you, I will, and this I swear, even at this late hour, remit the pending execution and call immediately for a new hearing. Therefore speak, Sir Wolf. I command you.'

The wolf was silent. The accents of the Prince's voice, though sweeter than those of his gaolers and the malignant cackle of his judge, were yet human, and the human voice to Tom had become an abomination which he, the wolf, would use no more. Nor had he shaken himself from that fatal and irreversible resolution when he learned that the lady, Red Hood, was of that same line of Alwa and Berg to which he and all his forefathers were long-standing debtors. To men, in addition, he owed the disfigurement and abasement of his once matchless body. Death, for him, was then a release, a welcoming end to a life finished badly. And the wolf gazed at the Margrave sadly with all these thoughts in his mind, while the Margrave, his temper rising at the wolf's disrespectful silence, tugged suddenly at his beard.

'He has lost his tongue!' cried he angrily, with his eyes flashing. 'Ah, he is but brute after all,' and the Prince spat in his fury. And donning his mask again, he departed with his astounded companions.

His gaolers reported of him that he was mostly silent that night, only occasionally did they hear a muttered growl, as though the beast were communicating with himself. But before daybreak, as the hangman's and his assistants' footsteps sounded hollowly in the corridor, all shrank in terror as a warbling, majestic and overpowering wolf howl went throbbingly throughout the fortress and even over the moat so that those living near the square were shaken from their slumber. It was answered by two others, less powerful in their separateness but no less feeble in their savage unison, which echoed up from the underground cells.

The execution party was immediately enlarged and strengthened on orders of the Governor who, in his alarm, was astonished at the mild complaisance with which Tom allowed himself to be lifted onto a pallet and carried outdoors.

The two renegades, grumbling to the last in their discomfited fury, joined Tom on the gallows. At the end of a week the bodies were cut down and expertly skinned. Tom's pelt was presented to the Mayor as a rug for his council chamber. It is still to be seen, somewhat the worse for time and wear, in a pleasant town in Germany.

The lady's father, the noble old Count, was granted permission to conduct a wolf-kill on the very day of Tom's execution. His bag however was disappointingly small, for even that elder of wolves who had expressed his intention to stay, had, with the swift evacuation of the main pack following the urgent news of the agile Gari, begun instructing his section leaders to decamp with the others. It was he, faithful to his charge of rearguard responsibility, together with a few stragglers, who fell to the guns of the Count's outriders. From these unstartling beginnings, commenced man's remorseless and unremitting war on wolves.

The lady herself, a few years later, married a nobleman not exceedingly younger than her father. She died some eighteen months after giving birth to a sickly child, of the plague it is said, and her husband quickly followed. The child, whose life was despaired of, nevertheless grew up to be a lean and ferocious killer of wolves, and a huntsman renowned for his prowess. He died in a boar shoot at the age of sixteen, pierced through the temple by the lance of one of his companions, and deeply regretted by his maternal grandfather, the old Count Berg, who lived yet at the time of this happening, and with a tally of boars' heads still far short of a hundred.

Although these events took place many years ago, among numbers of wolves in Europe Tom's name is still execrated. Among the more tolerant, thinking minority he is regarded as a brave and resourceful leader who notwithstanding was contaminated and finally destroyed by his too close contact with man. Most do not think of him at all, being more concerned with the vagaries and threats of their daily existence. But for those very few who take a scholarly interest in their history and origins, those in fact who provided this chronicler with his information, the name of Red Hood is synonymous with the human word Satan.

NOTE.

Trials of animals were common during the close of the medieval period since, like men, animals were adjudged responsible for their actions and thus answerable to the laws of the land.

The practice tended to abate in later ages, mostly due to the influence of the Church who, in her wisdom, opined that animals had no souls and so no concept of morality or sense of right and wrong; although cases of animal trials continued to be reported, and some have even taken place as late as our own day (in Central and South America).

See recently re-issued *The Criminal Prosecution and Capital Punishment of Animals* by E.P. Evans, *Faber*, June 1987 (first published 1906).

Legend of the Narcissus Warbler

The Narcissus Warbler lived long ago.

The ancients tell of it in folklore and story as undoubtedly the most attractive yet enigmatic of all the smaller denizens that inhabited the Mediterranean world.

Various descriptions of it have come down to us, each remarkable for their striking divergence from the others.

Some would have had it that this fascinating mammal, or bird, was coloured an emerald green, with a square brachycephalic head, cobalt eyes and a mass of waving golden whiskers, withal decorated in a columnar pattern of dense silky fur, or feathers, majestic and flickering in movement: which inspired its original names, the 'animate peristyle', the 'dragon's auxiliary'.

Yet others pictured it reversely, with its fur, or feathers, a deep lapis-lazuli blue, its *eyes* emerald green, and its nodding whiskers black as ebony.

Some assigned to it additionally a pair of languid flamboyant wings, mottled in irridescent purple and silver, and almost inert when in flight.

Still others concurred with all the known descriptions, averring in explication that the creature was capable of achieving transformations and subtleties of form and colour beyond the sweep of man's imagination.

No wonder then that it was semi-deified and regarded, when luckily observed, as a forerunner of good things to come.

Although men's opinions differed wildly, all agreed that its beauty was transcendent and moreover that its song, which few nevertheless could claim to have heard, was of a quality which rendered even the nightingale's coarse and vapid by comparison.

However, it was only the young who had heard this song, and for this reason: that it was only they, with their as yet undefiled sense of hearing, who were capable of apprehending such micro-auditory music, the effects of which, it was said, were such as to astonish the onlooker, as the child or youth succumbed to its ineffable tones.

Those lucky enough to have heard it were ever after reported to have lived lives of unexampled happiness and good health, attended by an unfailing succession of strikingly fortunate events.

Thus it was that parents, as soon as their offspring were at the age of understanding, would take them strolling among the woods and flowers where the creature most frequently dwelt, and always at the time of the summer solstice when, it was claimed, the Narcissus gave voice to its supra-earthly mating call.

Now whether or no it is right to call it a 'mating call' has always been in question among the ancients.

Alas, there is no consensus; on the contrary much bitterness that the Narcissus occupied such a brief span in men's reckoning, and this at a time, like our own, when everyone was desperately in search of good fortune.

Was it, sage men wondered, that the Gods in their undisputed wisdom had retracted their generous gift when they learned of its threat to their own authority? Or worse – erred in overlooking its benign potency, and thoughtlessly expunged it as another misdirected experiment in creation? Or worse still – erred in a more capricious way, more shameful to mention: that of beguiling the progenitive instincts of this unique being towards self-indulgence?

Thus it was noted that the Narcissus, when seen, was almost always perched on the underside of a branch projecting over a silent pool of water, whose unimpaired reflection gave back to it the form of its peerless, picturesque beauty: at which time its so-called 'mating song' was said to be heard.

Men, attuned to Nature's wonders by their own ways and those observed of conventional wildlife and domestic animals, had assumed this to be the Narcissus' mating music, when, more critically, it should have been understood as a serenade of *itself*.

For among all the sightings of the Narcissus, none mentions any but a *single*, full-grown member of the species.

And so, when it was but a memory in men's anxious and eternally questing minds, the descriptive terms of 'peristyle' and 'dragon' were replaced by the more mundane 'warbler', the name which the ancients with infallible hindsight and sorrow decreed for it.

The Exorcist

I said to him, 'You've been considering it such a long time that surely you've come to some conclusion,' and he smiled. Then he raised his head and what I had taken for his pubicly-fuzzy beard turned out to be a spray of asparagus fern garlanded round his collar.

'No, I've not – and that surprises you?'

I smiled too and pressed the flat of my hand against my side where it was beginning to throb again.

'Are you in very great pain?' he asked solicitously, raising the garland and sniffing at it delicately.

'I've other things to think of,' I said perversely, and 'when do you think –'

' "When do you think" I'll decide about it?'

I nodded. His eyes began to cloud over, iris merging with cornea, till the whole seemed infused with a uniformly azure colour, like those eyes of Modigliani's.

'I'm afraid,' he said, and I leant upon his words, feeling them, like flies, articulating on the surface of my tongue, 'I'm afraid [again] it will be a little while,' then the water of compassion must have melted him for he added, 'but surely before morning.'

'Can I wait that long?' I asked him, as a fly reached the roof of my mouth and looked over, down the slippery slope.

'May God illumine my task and ease your impatience,' he mumbled with silky unction. 'Let me begin then.'

And he began by paring off the nails of his left hand, setting them in a concave sieve on top of a small metal tripod, and burning them to ashes.

'Familiarity with the smell of death will help us,' he said. 'Stand with your face to the window and tell me what you see, everything you see.'

'But this is quite stupid,' I argued. 'I need a physician, not a sorcerer.'

'Do as I say and tell me what you see!'

'The street,' I relented, 'only the street, and the houses. The alleyways, the street lamps ... the road, refuse bins. A blue neon light advertising funerals, a red neon light advertising hot beef sandwiches – all night service.'

'What else?'

I smiled. 'A large black dog – micturating.'

'In the act or finished? Go on, tell me.'

'Very well, in the act but finishing, snuffling now and scraping its heels. It's crossing the street, coming over here.'

'Open the window and look out.'

'It's in front of the street door, scratching at it.'

'Go down and let it in, then bring it up here.'

'I detest dogs.'

'Do as I say.'

'Part of my cure?' I mocked, dangling my tongue at him, like a dog, and releasing the tiresome flies.

The dog had that urinatory smell characteristic of dogs and tangled itself between my legs in its eagerness to get in. It rushed up the stairs in front of me and went straight to the room, nuzzled the door open and walked in, then it stopped, perhaps underdogged by its rashness or sudden fear, and began whining softly. I patted its head and it subsided into growls.

'Splendid,' he said.

'"Splendid?"'

'We shall call him Canaan.'

The dog grinned.

'Call it whatever you like,' I said indifferently; 'only remember you promised before morning. Anyway, hadn't you better examine this beauty in case you want to call it Sheba?'

Both of them looked at me disapprovingly.

'Really,' he said, 'you are most uncooperative.'

'Have you forgotten my pain?'

'Are you accusing me of frivolity?'

'Go on,' I said sourly. 'Carry on.'

He took a small bottle from his pocket, placed it on the table, unstoppered it and released a stench from it, then he relaxed into a stupor which, if it weren't for the wide open azure eyes, made him appear to be sleeping. The dog began rubbing its head against his legs, then it too relaxed and lay down, with its jaw across his feet.

I put a bent cigarette in my mouth and struck a match, but the flame began to flare with such magnesium-like intensity that I blew it out, and only with some difficulty. It was two in the morning.

At two-fifteen the dog began moaning, doubtless from the effects of a doggish nightmare: its front legs caressing the wooden floor with a scratching sound from its unkempt nails. Then with a grotesque bark it suddenly stiffened, relaxed again and turned completely over onto its back, with its four paws dangling limply downward. The air was clearing slightly. I lit another match and this time it flared normally, but there was an unpleasant reproving hiss and the words, with a curse to their edge, 'Put it out!' and I complied meekly.

It was two-forty-five. I began experiencing an urgent need but managed to control it. At five minutes to three the dog stiffened again, rolled over and stood on its feet with its eyes glaring horribly, like the saucer-eyed dog in the fairy tale, then it collapsed sideways as though invisibly struck, and lay as though flattened by an omnibus.

The sky was beginning vaguely to brighten. My need was becoming part of the general discomfort of my tired body, but the pain in my side was miraculously lighter. I touched it tentatively, I pressed – both the lump and the pain were gone.

His eyes were deep pools of lapis lazuli flecked with volitant clouds as he smiled at me.

'Feeling better?' he asked dreamily.

I shook my head.

'You're lying,' he said, easing his shoes off by means of his feet, and placing his feet on the recumbent dog; 'aren't you?

'Is it morning yet?' he asked.

I looked out. 'No, not quite.'

'You see?'

'I don't know if I *am* cured,' I grumbled, feeling a renewed oppression in my side.

'That's only because of your distended bladder. Go and empty it.'

I had almost forgotten until he recalled it. 'But don't you –?'

'No,' he smiled sweetly. 'I hardly ever feel the need.'

When I got back his shoes were on and he was still slouched in the same position, but the small metal tripod with the concave sieve, the vile-smelling bottle – and the dog – were all gone.

'Where's the dog?' I asked.

' "The dog?" ' He looked puzzled. 'Was there a dog?'

'You're playing with me.'

'I assure you.'

'Look here–'

'Sh-h, I wouldn't speak of it. Most of my patients admit to seeing symbols of one kind or another during treatment, but this is quite exceptional. A *dog*, did you say? I've been told of nursing mothers, two-headed calves, achondroplastic dwarfs, embryos and foetuses, even' – he began lifting his shoulders with amusement – 'even scapegoats and scapechickens – but a *dog*! This is really quite unique.'

'That's what I thought it was,' I said morosely, 'a scapedog.'

'Never mind,' he said consolingly, removing the garlanded fern from round his collar and handing it to me. 'Keep it as a memento of the treatment.'

He rose, brushed his jacket with small white hands, placed a black velour hat on his head and walked by me, smiling, to the door. Then he turned and nodded at me several times, very benevolently, and went out.

There were streaks of purple and red in the morning sky and the peaks of the houses were beginning to glisten. I saw him emerge from the front door and walk up the street. The colour from the neon signs was bleaching, but they were still aglow. Under the red one, by the arcade of the shop dispensing hot beef sandwiches, a large black dog was pensively micturating. By the time he reached it, it was just finishing. I leant out the window and could see him signal to it, then both disappeared inside through a gust of beefy steam.

The pain in my side erupted again with a sharp intensity.

In the Beginning

And Marwa, as was to happen again and again, was beguiled by Arduk, while Fire which had not been yet officially named became the plaything of Horla.

Horla, his thousand arms radiating out from his shoulders, backbone and sternum, like the struts of a primeval ferris-wheel, ranged upon the crust of middle earth, frolicly leaping over torrents, chasms, exploding seas, erupting volcanos, until, singeing the frowsy fur which hung in ropey strands from his myriad ears, he ignited in playful exuberance one of his flammable arms and, in amused idiocy, watched as it burned, slowly at first then furiously.

As the deliciously novel fragrance penetrated his cascade of nostrils, they streamed in flood with sensory mucous as passionate greed overwhelmed him. A tentative nibble at one of the finger joints elicited a shriek of pure gourmet delight, followed by grunts of orgiastic gluttony as he crunched off the hand with one bite, tore with his teeth up the succulent forearm, and ripped off chunks of roasted flesh up to the shoulder which, still ungrilled, repelled him. Sensitive beast!

Almost mad with his lust, he ignited arm after arm until the frightful scrunching and belching reached Marwa on High who, gazing out, descried the wretch in the act of consuming his nine hundred and ninety-eighth member, at which with a burst of divine inspiration, He endowed him with a nervous system. (After that, men had two arms only.)

The scream that penetrated to the thirty-third Hell, split three of the three thousand pillars of Heaven as Horla, howling and disgorging piecemeal, rolled flailing in his vomit.

And Marwa began again, while insidious Arduk, he of the hood-lidded eyes, purred with contentment. Arduk it was who devised the Cat, delineating a face like unto his own.

And Marwa found it good.

Then Marwa announced a change of style to Arwa, thence to Ramah, thence to Gama, thence to Yama, thence to Yahwa; while Arduk paralleled Him with Garduk, Yarduk, Rukman, Lukman, Lucefur.

And Chaos reigned...

The Royal Physician

Rinaldo XXIII, King of the Cats, was growing very old but had not yet named a successor.

'Your Majesty cannot live forever,' said his principal adviser, Count Corfu, 'much as I should like Your Majesty to do so, and while I do not have to remind Your Majesty that it is already eighteen months beyond the usual time assigned for the naming of an heir – in the manner prescribed by tradition and fastidiously fulfilled (with perhaps one regrettable exception) by all your illustrious ancestors – may God be resting them contentfully! – I must courteously, but firmly, bring to your attention the latest protocol drawn up by the Council of Notables which decrees – I beg your pardon – which declares, or rather affirms –'

'Oh, shut up, Corfu,' interrupted the King irritably.

'Your Majesty?' said the miserable Corfu, dropping the protocol then stooping painfully to pick it up.

'My dear old friend,' said Rinaldo more kindly, 'I didn't mean to snap at you like that, but really, I'm quite tired of all your moralizing, and I'm fed up with that senile assembly of balding tails. I want you to tell them that I've never felt better in all my life. Tell 'em, in fact, that I'm as fit as a tiger on the make.' The King leered at his own witticism and Corfu smiled back, albeit rather feebly. 'Is that quack, de Salis, here yet?'

'He is awaiting attendance on you now, Sire.'

'Then send him in, and tell that scamp Prince Kuralu that I want him too.'

'His Highness is in the royal stables examining a new racing animal.'

'I don't give a whisker where he is – just get him here. And Corfu –'

'Sire?' replied his adviser, pirouetting precariously on one paw.

'Remember that tune which went down so well last Halloween

– the one all the youngsters took to so madly? You know – tum, tum, tum,' sang the King in his grating off-key voice. 'The *name* of it, Corfu – what was the *name* of it?'

'I believe Your Majesty means, um, *A Little Less Solemnity, A Little More Gaiety.*'

'That's the one! Splendid song and I wish you'd take it to heart. Corfu, that's an order.'

'I obey with trembling, Sire.'

'Oh, bother the trembling, just obey. Now scat!'

'I could not forbear hearing that Your Majesty was at home,' said a distinguished, nasal, gallic-sounding voice.

A rather small black cat with tinges of grey on the tips of his ears, one of which was ornamented with a discreetly tiny gold ear-ring, and with hunched scholarly shoulder bones and a fine semitic nose, now walked into the royal chamber.

'Binyamin,' cried the King pleasantly, 'my dear Binyamin – forgive me, Bertrand – come here and lick my paw.'

After the newcomer had performed this obeisance, with an almost unnoticed sneer, the King asked him to recline on the pillow beside him and regale him with the latest Paris jokes. This was a task which Binyamin de Salis (or rather Bertrand de Salis, as he preferred to be known), member of the Geneva medical directorate, author of the famed handbook on the pathology of the feline aorta, and honoured by the Linz Academy for his exquisite violin-playing, heartily loathed. And he loathed it simply because the King, in his forgivably boisterous way, always managed to burst out laughing precisely *before* the punch-line was told.

'Kh-kh-kh-kh,' wheezed Rinaldo helplessly, holding his royal diaphragm, as the dénouement of a particularly risqué story was left incomplete on the doctor's facile tongue which, curling intra-orally, articulated, '*Idiot.*'

'Royal grandfather,' exclaimed an exuberant high-pitched voice, and de Salis turned with a morose smile as the personable, if frenetic, Prince Kuralu dashed into the chamber.

'Kh-kh-kh,' continued the King. 'Why are your jokes always so funny – kh-kh. And why is it – kh-kh-kh – when I want to tell them to someone –'

'You can never remember the punch-line,' filled in the indiscreet doctor.

'Binyamin – how did you know?' Then becoming mockly

severe the King added: 'But, my dear, that's *lèse majesté*. In the old days –'

'We'd chop off his head,' interrupted Kuralu savagely.

'Kh-kh-kh,' spluttered Rinaldo. 'Not very nice, but true. Quite true.'

'I humbly apologize,' said de Salis silkily. 'If my head gives you offence, Sire, I pray you to have it removed.'

'Ah, you high-spirited Jews, I mean, Gypsies, always so quick to take umbrage. No, no, my dear Bertrand, you stick to your lancets and stylets – and jokes – and let me take care of affairs of state, at least for the present. And Prince –' said the King warningly, as he noticed the lad preparing for another outburst.

'Royal grandfather?'

'Hold your tongue, boy.'

As Kuralu flushed hotly under his golden fur and clenched a paw round his small jewelled sword, de Salis sighed inwardly and mused, '*Another enemy.*' It was only too true.

'My dear doctor,' announced Rinaldo in his most regal manner, 'can you guess why we have summoned you here today?'

De Salis assumed his well-known medical attitude. 'Your Majesty, I trust, is well?'

'Come, come, Binyamin, I'm sure you know the reason.'

'I confess, Sire, that on this occasion at least I must disappoint you.'

The King beamed. 'Really?'

De Salis bowed.

'Prince,' said Rinaldo to his grandson, 'hand me that box.'

'This one, Sire?'

'Yes, my dear. Now,' said he, opening the clasp and exposing the interior so that the trapezoid jewel it contained sparkled like a miniature sun, and the gilded collar to which it was attached reflected the brilliance in its heavy lustre, 'do you know what this is?'

'The Claw of Manio,' said de Salis in a suitably awed whisper. 'The ancient emblem of kingship.'

'I don't as a rule wear it,' admitted Rinaldo. 'I detest collars.'

'Sire?'

'For you, my dear Binyamin.'

'But Sire!' exclaimed de Salis, genuinely startled, while Kuralu's volatile eyes opened to double their size.

'You mean you refuse?'

'I cannot accept.'

'Hm-hm-hm,' murmured the King thoughtfully, scratching his chin with a point of the resplendent jewel while Count Corfu, who had just re-entered the chamber, winced incredulously. 'Hm, must I mar the last year of my reign with an execution?'

De Salis who meanwhile had been scrupulously, if nonchalantly, passing his penetrating diagnostic eyes over the King, remarked with a trace of sadness, 'Your Majesty is not well.'

'Are you asking me that?' cried the King testily.

'No, Sire, I am informing you.'

'My dear de Salis, will you stop being so Gypsyish, pardon me, so Jewish. I've never felt better in my life.'

'Sire,' persisted the doctor, 'you have ruled long and wisely. It is time you relinquished the heavy cares of state and turned yourself to simpler amusements.'

The King beamed, while his eyes glowed with what has since been called 'the Rinaldo light'. He clapped his paws softly together and murmured, 'Splendid. Truly splendid. My dear de Salis, your intuition is positively Roentgenesque. Then you *do* know why I have summoned you!'

'Your Majesty?' interposed de Salis gently, with an eloquent raising of his brows and a self-depreciating smile.

'Come, my dear, sit closer to me,' said Rinaldo. 'I want to show you something.' And as de Salis languidly obeyed, the King stuffed the jewel case with the royal insignia under a cushion beside him, and withdrew from the same place a small book bound in yellow silk.

At this manoeuvre, Prince Kuralu and Count Corfu, who were on reluctant speaking terms with each other, exchanged glances. Corfu, disturbed by the breach in royal etiquette in vouchsafing such familiarity to a commoner, wore a reproachfully troubled look on his kindly senescent face. Kuralu, on the other hand, could not repress an ill-concealed hiss of hatred.

'See, my friend,' said the King, pointing to a passage in the middle of the book, much scored over by claw marks, 'in this, the *Chronicle of the Cats of China*, a very interesting event occurs. I should like to read it to you.'

The King's paws trembled as he reached for his spectacles and de Salis scrutinized him intently and anxiously. He knew now with certitude that the King was exercising a considerable will to retain his composure, but that his almost imminent end was foreshadowed in the visible evidence of his eyes and the sound of his breathing which, at the negligible distance now separating them, de Salis was able to analyze critically.

'Your Majesty,' he said, his voice quietly urgent, 'I beg Your Majesty to stop talking instantly and to take a draught of this potion.'

A look of sudden fear flashed through the King's eyes as the breath seemed to suck from his lungs and an agony of the most intense pressure threatened to collapse his chest and ribs. Hurriedly but deftly de Salis inserted a phial of green liquid between the King's lips, in a manner which allowed the liquid to pass safely down the royal throat and avoid the windpipe.

'What are you doing to the King?' shrieked Kuralu, dashing forward with his sword upthrust, then holding the point menacingly to de Salis' throat. 'Answer, you dog!' (The worst insult among cats.)

'I am trying to revive him,' replied de Salis coldly. 'But I fear it's too late.'

'Your Highness, I beg of you,' said Corfu, in a voice tremblingly betraying his age. 'I implore you.'

'Whom are you imploring?' demanded a familiar voice as Rinaldo, apparently recovered from the effects of his attack, sat up and licked his lips. 'Fine stuff,' he commented, 'damned fine stuff. Ouh! my chest.' And then, noticing Prince Kuralu, he growled: 'Boy! Why is your sword unsheathed?'

As Kuralu put away the weapon and muttered unpleasantly between his attractive teeth, the King turned to de Salis and whispered, 'Bad, isn't it?' De Salis nodded sombrely. 'The fourth time,' murmured the King so that de Salis alone heard him. 'The fifth will be the last.'

'Why did you not summon me sooner?' asked de Salis reprovingly.

'Summon you?' said the King, and his eyes flashed with the well-known 'Rinaldo light'. 'Summon you! You, at least, de Salis, should know better. We cats, we royal cats especially, recognize when our hours are numbered. Our "existential clock" you once called it – have you forgotten?'

De Salis bowed his head gravely.

'Come, my friends, my friends all,' said the King more loudly to his grandson and Count Corfu, so that both approached close to the throne. 'What I have to say is for you too — you, Prince!' he added crossly to Kuralu who with rapt expression was watching the nuzzling antics of a pair of royal pigeons on the window ledge, commencing the opening stages of their love play. Frowning, Kuralu turned away and glared at de Salis.

'The *Chronicle of the Cats of China*,' said Rinaldo, 'tells us that in the legendary days of the first Emperors there was one, Yao, famed for his wide-embracing wisdom, and under whose reign the nobility and commoners alike were supremely contented and at peace. I shall now read from the text itself.

' "Yao, feeling the effects of his advancing years, looked about him. While he had worthy sons and kinsmen he did not however see in any of these those qualities necessary to fit them for the weighty office of Emperor. Reports had come to him of a certain Shun, a cat of middle years who, notwithstanding that he shared his dwelling with six sets of relatives in addition to his own wives and numerous children, managed to maintain there an atmosphere of such perfect peace and familial harmony that all who lived about were confounded with wonder. Thereupon Yao asked that Shun be brought to him, and after questioning him in various subtle and searching ways, determined to his own satisfaction that the reports were well founded. With great tranquility of mind therefore he relinquished his seals of office to the noble Shun, in accordance with the mandate of Heaven, and harmony and happiness, as in his own reign, continued to prevail throughout the Empire." '

For a moment following the King's reading there was silence. The import of his words, clearly intelligible to each of his listeners, produced a dramatic effect. Prince Kuralu's mouth relapsed into a savage grimace, which revealed in all their enviable perfection his immaculate white teeth; while Corfu's mouth, by dropping open in wide amazement, displayed the ravaged and lamentable condition of his. De Salis, oppressed by the King's unmistakable reference to himself, passed an elegant paw uneasily over his dark forehead.

Kuralu was the first to react. Stamping a paw, from which all the claws had sprung ferociously loose, he screamed, 'Sire, you *cannot!*'

'Cannot?' roared the outraged Rinaldo, rising to his feet with a severe effort. 'You dare to say I can – ah-h? Ah!'

The violence of his protest was such that the word was never completed. He groaned once, his jaw fell and his eyes glazed over. As he sank back, the yellow book, still open at the page he had been reading, toppled over on his face.

De Salis bent quickly over him and shook his head. 'He's dead,' he muttered helplessly. 'The King is dead.'

'And you killed him,' shrieked Kuralu. 'You, you dog, you foul Jew and Gypsy. *You* killed him. Guards! Guards!' he continued to shriek, and when three of those heroes appeared running: 'There! There he is. Seize him! Seize him before I slay him myself. He has murdered the King, right before our eyes. Has he not, Corfu?'

The honest though shaken counsellor, thus addressed, could only stammer, 'Your Highness, but Your Highness –' whereupon he collapsed.

The Prince, tearing his regalia as he went, ran weeping to the King's body, fell upon it and began uttering loud lamentations just as the Colonel of the Guard and several notables presented themselves.

'Ah, Your Majesty,' wept Kuralu feelingly, 'dear Majesty, must I bid you farewell in this dark way, murdered before your time by the evil of this wizard doctor, this Gypsy whom you so long, so unwisely, trusted? For your sake, for the sake of the justice you taught me, I have spared him that he may be brought to trial before his condemnation and sentence. All my royal blood clamours to tear his foul ungrateful heart from his breast – with my claws, such is my grief, rather than my sword.' And here he fell into the most pitiful wailing, to which the Colonel and notables also lent their voices.

'A worthy successor,' whispered one to another, between heartfelt sighs, at which the other nodded. 'A worthy successor, indeed. We could not ask for a better. Look there,' he added, pointing to de Salis and shuddering: 'have you ever seen such satanic malevolence?' 'Malevolence, indeed,' concurred the first.

The Colonel of the Guard, with tears streaming from his dark impressive eyes, unsheathed his sword and raised it high. 'The King is dead,' he proclaimed. 'Long live the *new* King!'

'Long live the *new* King!' came the answering response, as from palace room after palace room – excepting those where the royal wives of Rinaldo were sobbing bitterly – the royal retinue of nobles, counsellors, servants and hangers-on echoed their approval. How, you wonder, did all those hear of the catastrophe so quickly? Cats, you must know, do not have to be informed in so many words of such matters.

The newly elevated monarch, afterwards known as Kuralu xix (or more commonly as 'The Cruel'), now stripped of his regalia as custom demanded, broke his sword adroitly and laid the pieces at his feet, then placed an enquiring paw beneath his late grandfather's body and manipulated the jewel case from under it. With moisture-laden eyes he fixed the heavy collar of The Claw of Manio about his slender throat as the notables nodded approvingly, descended the throne steps without once looking at de Salis who contemptuously watched the proceedings, and walked with bowed head past the Colonel who with clipped martial tones exclaimed: 'A thousand years to His Majesty!' And as the King, followed by his notables, left the throne room, the Colonel turned menacingly to de Salis and growled, 'As for you, you blackguard, come with me. Guards! Escort the prisoner.'

Late that afternoon, Kuralu, in a rare demonstration of kingly tolerance, went to visit Count Corfu in his apartments but was told by the sorrowing Countess that her master had never recovered consciousness. 'Too bad,' sympathized the King. 'I'm sorry to hear that.' But as he walked down a corridor, smiling secretly to himself – they say that grief sometimes dispossesses reason – he flung a small packet through one of the open palace windows and heard it splash into a pond. Next morning, curiously enough, all the carp in one of the royal fish ponds floated to the surface belly-side up and were pronounced, by the royal toxicologist, as having perished through some potent poison.

True to the King's justice, de Salis was ordered to trial and shortly after condemned to be beheaded. His Majesty himself offered to perform the office, so agonizingly, he said, did he feel the enormity of the crime. At length it was agreed that he would stand on the scaffold to witness at first hand the execrable de Salis' execution.

'Prisoner and condemned,' said the judge of the court, a cat of learned mien whose wife had been saved from a supposedly fatal female complaint by the skill of de Salis' surgery: 'dear friend, I mean, dear prisoner,' and Kuralu glowered, 'have you anything to say before I pronounce you dead, excuse me, before I sentence you to life? Pardon me, Your Majesty, but we haven't had an execution in nineteen years and I am somewhat unused to the forms –'

'Carry on, you idiot,' roared the King. 'And we may regard the punishment meted out today as a precedent for others. Do you understand?'

Amid the hushed silence of the court the judge glanced up at his wife in the gallery who glared back at him as he replied humbly,

'As Your Majesty wills.' She, at least, had warned him the night before that if he condemned de Salis to death she would not guarantee that any of his future children would be of his exclusive progeny, and other wives of her circle had made similar threats.

Thereupon, fastening his brows together as well as he could, which was difficult since the judge was essentially a kindly savant more versed in the norms of international cat law than in the rigours of the criminal code, besides which he had often played chess with de Salis: thereupon he murmured low in pure Aramaic, for the benefit of de Salis who stood on a small dais facing him, the words: '*Shahray li ma'ri*,' (which mean, of course, 'May God forgive me'), and followed this more loudly with the awful sentence of beheading, over which he stuttered so painfully that almost none could apprehend him, and then in clear tones declaimed: 'Prisoner, have you anything to say?'

De Salis nodded abstractedly, then passed his eloquent eyes round the assembly. 'Friends,' he said, 'or rather former friends, since I now must so regard you, but enemies never –' at which one of the ladies in the gallery began sobbing hysterically and had to be removed by an usher, while all eyes, including those of de Salis, followed her, and the King shook his head with a furious grimace: 'Former friends, and you, Your Majesty, by whose royal word alone evidence has been so adduced as to make me guilty of the highest treason, I plead nothing in mitigation since, with deference to Your Majesty's opinion, I –'

'Briefly, my friend, briefly,' interposed the judge under the storm of the King's glare.

'Very well, I shall be brief. We, cats, of differing racial origins and beliefs, owe a special allegiance to our species and above all to our chief, the King, may God grant him numberless years.' An uneven chorus of 'numberless years' was repeated round the court while the King strained his eyes to discern where the voices had been feeblest. 'Therefore I, of alien blood to most of you, deem it a privilege that I have been received among you and allowed to practice my skill as an equal among equals. If the King's heart will relent to me in future, when he is somewhat older, I shall consider that justice today has been done.

'For the present, I have but two things to ask of the court. That, in the interest of our people everywhere, my clinic, subsidized by the late royal favour and maintained for the purpose of exploring the morbid increase in mental debility, be continued.'

The King nodded and the judge murmured, 'Granted.'

'That my extensive library of ancient and contemporary medical and other texts be acquired by the clinic, and that a modest part of the proceeds be used as a pension in support of an aged maiden aunt of mine, Miss Anatolia de Salis of the city of Lyon, and the balance as endowment for a refuge of other aged or homeless cats.'

The King nodded again and the judge repeated, 'Granted,' then added: 'Nothing more?'

'No,' replied de Salis with a quiet smile, 'except to say that I, as all of you in time, go now to submit myself to the most baffling experience of life.'

The prisoner descended the small platform on which he had been standing, with two palace guards flanking him on either side, and preceded and followed by others of the Guard he was escorted through a small portico into the royal courtyard where the scaffold had been erected. The King followed after a suitable interval, accompanied by his Council of Notables and various of his highborn friends and relations. The ladies were sent home.

'Pleasant day,' said de Salis to his executioner, a large grey Caucasian who was mute. 'See here,' he continued amiably, 'I have made a mark on the back of my neck where you should strike. Do you see it?' The Caucasian nodded. 'If you strike exactly there, my head will come off neatly with one blow – everyone will be impressed. Do you understand?' The Caucasian nodded again, very happily. It was his first execution, and he was pleased with the advice and anxious to make an impression.

The King mounted the scaffold with his Colonel of the Guard. At a signal from the Colonel a troop of youthful drummers set up a low, sustained but uncertain rolling, interrupted at intervals by uneven staccato beats. They had been practicing assiduously the evening before. The prisoner placed his forepaws into two receptacles just below the surface of the block, dug his claws in securely and knelt his chin on top. The Caucasian raised his sword, aimed it directly over the mark that de Salis had made for him, and struck with assurance.

The world for de Salis condensed into the microcosm of a speck of dust before it exploded into a wide windy universe. All at once he felt himself being rushed away in a huge black cumulus which, as it mounted towards the pole star, revealed itself as a gigantic cat outlined against the darkening heavens by ragged streams of phosphorescent lightning, punctuated by a monotonous polyphonic thundering coming from below. The tail was a causeway of shimmering basaltic infinity, stretching backward and dividing the horizon into two enormous arcs. De Salis' eardrums vibrated painfully to the screaming intensity of the speed. Without clinging to anything, he seemed yet immoveably attached, and his perspective confirmed to him that he was secured somewhere on the face of the colossus, possibly near one of the ears. He attempted to speak but the wind sucked his breath away.

'Louder,' said a voice, high-pitched and quavering, although not unfriendly. 'Speak louder.'

'Who are you?' cried de Salis.

'Can't you guess?'

'No, seriously!' protested de Salis, his fur rising for the first time he could remember.

'Mocker,' returned the voice, 'sweet mocker. That is the way I want you always to be. Give me your paw.'

De Salis laughed. 'But where shall I find yours? All I can see is this immensity of parched black fur filling the sky and shrinking the stars. Is there a paw in this gigantitude to which I can fit mine?'

'No,' came the answer, 'there is not, but I shall fashion one for you, a paw as sensitive as your own, perhaps more so, and a body joined to it such as you may have dreamed of when your shoulders were still straight, your fur gleaming, and your eyes not probing into the exposed viscera of your diseased patients. See! The miracle of generation without seed is still within me.'

De Salis shuddered as a shadowy blur alongside him took shape in the tactile form of the most exquisite feline body that he had ever seen, a body which to his exacting professional and aesthetic criteria was perfection realized, and with a curvatured tail that expressed in itself the whiplash of impatient love. Yet where its head should have been, there remained only the parched spectral fur, and de Salis groaned quietly to himself.

'After all, if He had to exist, He had to be senile, since He began decaying aeons ago.... Old gods should not seek to perform old miracles in the expectation of their working anew.... Yet if this is the best He can do, why shouldn't I make the most of it?'

And he put out a tentative sensitive paw and a tentative sensitive paw met his, and he rested his head close to where the other's should have been: but those haunches were no chimera's, nor was that searing brilliant heat which made him almost shriek before he thrust past its barrier and felt himself tugged into a space almost too small to contain him, yet so yielding and firmly tensile that every spasm of his pain was followed immediately by a spasm of intolerable pleasure, until the very force of his rising flood thrust him out gasping, whereupon two subtly insistent forepaws manoeuvred him in again.

'Oh, God!'

'What is it now?' came the querulous high-pitched whisper.

'What a crescendo!' moaned de Salis, the musician, feelingly.

'You see?' said the soughing voice sententiously: 'it is always the same. God the model-maker, God's creatures the artisans and imitators. Don't interrupt, please ... I tell you this, de Salis, cats of your kind are becoming altogether too scarce for my liking. A God watches, but sometimes He must also move. I have moved, de Salis, that is why you are here with me now: procreating.'

'A people probably without heads – without brains?'

'They will be less vulnerable for that in the future.'

There is no hope for him, thought de Salis, *if ever there was. His mind is as parched as his ravaged fur.*

'Good,' interrupted the voice. 'Your unspoken reproach is far dearer to me than your unforthcoming praise. A God condemned is at least a God acknowledged.'

'But I never thought of you before,' protested de Salis.

'Silence!' quavered the voice irritably: and 'Look there ...'

De Salis' scope of vision suddenly thrust so far forward that his eyeballs seemed to hurtle through space. All at once the muddled patchwork of the earth below erupted into vistas of sharply defined fields and hedgerows, trees, terraces, rivers and ponds, and even bullocks with forelegs half-submerged standing in the shallows, dreaming yet awake. And there too was the forecourt of the Royal House of the Cats, burgeoning with a glittering assembly of nobles in court dress about a raised dais covered in black sacking on which stood a familiar, slender, kingly figure with a jewelled claw round his throat, holding aloft in two exquisitely-gloved paws a curiously aged feline head with a fine semitic nose: while on the block beside him, almost ignored, with tail upright and back arched above the hunched shoulders, and foreclaws dug deep into the wood as though still tense in expectation of the blow, stood the headless form of Binyamin de Salis, late doctor extraordinary to the King of the Cats.

———————

A German Fable

Arno Lutz was telling his fiancée, Sophie, of a dream he had had of her. She in immobilized terror was standing at the top of a burning building while he, with arms outspread below, was pleading with her to jump. As the flames rose about her, a small crowd assembled on the pavement. They too implored her to jump. At last, closing her eyes and enfolding her arms about her breast, she leapt forward. Arno spoke as though the event had actually occurred. The vein which like a fork of lightning dominated his tall white forehead, spasmed violently.

'I wanted to catch you as you fell. But at that moment someone distracted me by asking what time it was, and when I looked into the clock face – because somehow it was a clock that was fastened to my wrist – I saw *your* face, with the clock-hands, at 1105 hours, piercing your lower eyelids.

'Then I heard a frightful sound of masonry or bones breaking and suddenly I was all alone, on my hands and knees, crawling along the pavement, searching for you everywhere, and discovering nothing but evil metal splinters which lodged in my fingertips. And then, without surprise, I saw myself on my back and you sitting on my chest, with the hands of the clock dangling from your lower eyelids.'

'But, how horrible!' said Sophie.

'Yes. And I had the feeling too that where the arrows of the clock-hands had penetrated, there were tiny blisters of blood, already furry and black, where the blood had matted with your mascara.'

'Arno, please! It is quite revolting. I wish you would stop. Now it is getting dark and I want to listen to the Kuhlau flute trio. Won't you put it on?'

'Just let me tell you a little more, please. You were more beautiful than ever I remember, and the disfigurement of the clock-hands was in its way compellingly attractive. In no other manner were you wounded, *mein liebchen*. Yet it was with the weight of death that you straddled my chest.

'Do you recall uncle Dieter telling us that his greatest nightmare on the Eastern Front was that one night, while he lay bivouacked, one of our tanks would come grinding over his chest? Well, it was this nightmare which suddenly invaded my dream, and I wanted to banish its traitorous memory because it was *you*, in the purest form of German womanhood, who were killing me.

'It was like the weight of our whole Fatherland, our united Germany, which sat upon me, and I was happy to die so. Believe me, Sophie, it was glorious!

'From you there came an aroma unknown to modern senses, an aroma rich with the fields and woods and flowers of our pristine land. Finally with a movement I could not discern, you lay down upon me – knee to knee, stomach to stomach, breast to breast, lips to lips. And now the weight of you became unendurable as your body seemed to sink into mine – *through* mine, in fact – in a coalescence of all our atoms.'

Sophie's eyes were shining now, with something of pride and anticipation. 'That part I *do* like,' she said. And as Arno, still trance-like from the recital of his dream, went to put the Kuhlau record on the turntable, Sophie unfastened her brassiere-bands and arranged her blouse more décolleté.

———————

The Contumacy of Wolves

Of all the animals created, the wolves proved the most intractable and ungracious.

Their delegates, after several lengthy meetings, submitted a petition which declared they could see no salutary benefit for their species in the role designated to them; and that while they found the novelty of their lately effected existence not unpleasant, they, the wolves, preferred to be omitted entirely from the experiment.

When the Heavenly Counsel drily pointed out to them that this was contumacy of the basest, implying moreover a stricture on the wisdom of the Highest Authority, and, if acceded to, extinction of their kind, they replied with simple dignity it was extinction that they sought.

At this a thrill of pleasurable horror suffused a number of the other animal representatives. The hyenas coughed to cover their embarrassment. The younger of the two lions emitted an anguishedly amused growl, for which tactlessness he received a cuff from his elder. While the condor and eagle delegates nervously rattled their fearsome feathers.

Whether strange or no, those like the ram, bullock and boar were totally unresponsive, for which 'saintly restraint' they were commended by the Heavenly Counsel, who augured for them and their people a happy future, and then in patiently reproving tones redirected his brief to the wolves.

No – despite their egregious request – they would be denied, for kindness' and equity's sake. They would learn that to defy Authority was not to diminish it, and to accept their role in the scheme of things. And, if it turned out as badly as they wrongheadedly feared, they would have but themselves to blame. Decisions once taken were irrevocable.

Saying which the Heavenly Counsel, with a benignly weary smile, stroked one of his golden vestigial wings to signify that the conclave was closed.

The True Story
of Hansel and Gretel

A Not-So Grimm Fairy Tale

There was once a poor woodcutter who lived near the edge of a large forest. Formerly he had dwelt in the local village a few miles away, but as this had involved him in tedious trekking backward and forward, and as he had no horse to carry his burden – since horses in those days would consent to work for only the rich or the noble – he decided to relocate himself. Alas, he soon discovered that this merely put the problem in reverse. For where once he had gone from the village to the forest and thence to the village, he went now from the forest to the village and back again.

His first wife having died, of boredom some say, he took a second, a gorgonish woman called Gerda. Gerda's triumph proved to be Jerome's, our woodcutter's, undoing however. From morning to night her raucous voice filled the cottage and frightened the neighbouring wildlife away. But the marriage had one salutary effect: whereas Jerome had previously been content to lie abed till noon, he was now getting out of it at the crack of dawn – by Gerda's expedient of tipping him out.

Three children came of the union, although to imagine the circumstances in which they were conceived is far too horrible to consider. These were Hansel, the first-born, Gretel, and Peter who followed seven months after. There was also a blind cat, Puss in Boots, who was under the firm conviction that it was dead and was now inhabiting Hell, and a deaf dog, Guerdon, who was friendly and loyal.

At the time our story opens there was famine in the land, and some chroniclers say that the cat and dog had already been eaten. Others, less polite, suggest it was Peter who had temporarily assuaged the family's hunger. Be that as it may, the dog, the cat, and Peter, have only a tenuous connection with the events that follow.

Jerome, as usual, was complaining. 'Wife,' said he (he could never bring himself to call her Gerda), 'wut'll become on us? 'Ow kin we feed the kiddies when we ain't no more t'cat arsellufs?'

Gerda's reply is mutilated at this point. One ludicrous reconstruction begins: 'Dear little children...'

A more plausible reading from the Croat edition runs as follows:

'Poor children, poor little Peter. I never had a good day from him. First he gave me morning sickness, now this awful heartburn.'

The authentic text continues:

'Puss ware better, waren't she?' muttered Jerome, massaging his gums in recollection (he had lost all his teeth some years before). 'Well, no use frettin', be there, lass?' And then he whispered, 'There's still vem uvver two.'

Gerda was silent. Was she thinking perhaps of those carefree days when Hansel had suckled at her mountainous breast and brought her the first joys of motherhood? Or of Gretel, tender Gretel, who wept so bitterly when she discovered that Peter was the 'chicken'?

'I'm gnawed frough wif 'unger,' Jerome went on suggestively, spitting on his axe and rubbing his shapeless thumb along the edge of the metal. 'Ain't you?' And as if to make the point stronger, his gut rumbled ominously.

'Quiet, you beast, I'm thinkin',' replied Gerda. A suggestion of remorse cast a faint pallor over her thickish lips, which resembled slabs of red sirloin.

'Thinkin'?' mumbled Jerome sombrely, while his microscopic eyes glared venomously. 'Thinkin', be it? Aye, thinkin'.'

A long spiral of saliva flared out of his sunken mouth as he sprang up suddenly with a howl, and loosed his bottled-up feelings by letting fly with his axe at a wooden cupboard which, bursting asunder, discharged in a seemingly endless cacophonic rout: crockery whole and smashed, splintered sucked-out bones, clanging cutlery, meat tenderizers, whips, mops, dusters, tallow candles, a family of furry spiders which promptly scuttled away in terror, and an emaciated, startled, though pathetically grinning dog.

'Guerdon!' roared Jerome. 'So thet's ware you bin.'

'Quiet!' shrieked Gerda. 'Oh, me nerfs, me poor nerfs. Jus' lookit the mess you've made, you beast.'

'Beast, be it?' grumbled Jerome querulously. 'T'ware Jerry once't, aye, Jerry.'

His almost invisible eyes seemed to glow for a moment, then relapsed into their customary vacuity.

''Ere, doggie.'Ere, Guerdon,' he beckoned. 'Nice doggie.'

Guerdon, no longer grinning, looked uncertainly towards Gerda, then to Jerome. His tail drooped mournfully as he uttered a little howl.

At that moment there was a knock at the door. Gerda, rousing herself from her reverie, muttered, 'Oo kin thet be?'

'Tax collector,' blubbered Jerome cravenly, and with an agility surprising in one of his bulk he dived adroitly under the nuptial bed, at which a cloud of feathers burgeoned up like a miniature snow storm, while that same family of furry spiders which had sought refuge under the bed as well, scuttled away again in terror.

Gerda, grumbling with contempt, went to the door and opened it, and there she saw a little old lady in a flowered straw hat, with iron-rimmed spectacles on a sharp little nose, and wearing a rather dear, old-fashioned grey frock.

'Good morning,' said the old dame pleasantly.

'G'mornin',' replied Gerda sourly. 'An' wut may you be wantin'?'

'I'm Miss Grumberger,' said the crone, and smiled with little iron-grey teeth. 'Dear me, this famine is dreadful, isn't it?'

'Well, we ain't got nuffin' t'offer you, ef thet's wut you're after. Ain't got nuff t'feed arsellufs nor the kiddies.'

'Why, that's exactly what I've come about. You see, my dear, I've managed to put by something for my old age, and I've just been to the village – quite dreadful, you know – and I thought to myself: "Alice" – that's my given name, you know, Alice, Alice Grumberger – "Alice, you simply must do something to relieve this suffering."

'And do you know what I decided? Well, I thought how nice it would be if I asked some of those poor, dear children to my lovely house in the forest – just while the famine lasts, you know – and feed them up. Poor dears, some of them really need it. Why, just at this moment, round the trees, I saw two sweet children, a boy and a girl, and they looked so dreadfully thin, and I said to myself: "Alice, why don't you make a beginning right here?"

'Well, my dear, I asked them where they lived and they said in this nice little cottage, and so I thought I would call on you.'

Gerda eyed the crone suspiciously, and then enquired somewhat unworthily, 'An' wut might you be gettin' outta this?'

'Oh dear,' said the old lady, 'I assure you I never – well, I never –

I hope you don't think –' and pausing pitifully she raised a dainty handkerchief to her lips.

We interrupt the narrative at this point to note that while this colloquy was in progress, the dog Guerdon sidled unnoticed through the doorway, past the women and out into the forest. We wish this estimable creature a happier fate than that likely to overtake him had he remained.

Meanwhile Jerome, snorting heavily under the nuptial bed, and noticing that the voices at the door were merely those of his wife and another female, took heart and, creeping out, moved stealthily close to them, shielding himself behind the colossal bulk of his wife's back.

If only he could have seen himself at that moment! His normally uncouth face was streaked with dust, cobwebs hung from the thick lobes of his flapping ears, and a coronet of loose feathers and down festooned his stubbly straw-like hair. He listened with a cunning expression in his deadened specks of eyes.

Gerda was saying: 'I do 'ope I ain't offended you, dearie.'

'Oh dear, no,' said Miss Grumberger. 'I do understand. But doing good has its own rewards, you know. I only wanted to help as I so love children. However, I certainly wouldn't want to burden a mother's heart, separating her from her little ones, even if it's only for their own good, of course.'

Strange to say the mother's heart in Gerda's ample breast felt no burden whatever. 'I ain't said I ain't agreeable. I allus wanted the best fer the l'il dears, poor l'il tykes.' And here she too took a handkerchief from her bodice and pressed it to her eyes.

'Sly,' murmured Jerome to himself, 'sly lass,' and busily applied himself to an obstruction in his nose.

'Of course,' went on Miss Grumberger, 'I think it only right that the children's minds should be set at rest too. It won't do for them fretting for their dear Mum and Dad while they're getting fatted up, I mean, regaining their poor lost weight. And, oh dear, I don't know how to say this, it's so embarrassing, but would you take these?' and she extended three gold pieces. 'Because you know,' she added confidingly, 'it's not that there isn't enough food in the village, but you've got to have something to buy it with.'

'Well, I dunno,' said Gerda uncertainly. 'P'raps thet'll be awright.' But at a warning thump in her back she added, 'Still, food's expensive –'

'Don't I know!' said Miss Grumberger beaming.

And at length it was agreed at five gold pieces, with a sack of corn and a side of beef to be handed over, against Miss Grumberger's signed order, by her provisions merchant.

II.

As Hansel and Gretel accompanied their benefactress into the forest, they listened with innocent pleasure as she told them of all the delightful things they were soon going to eat, even as they munched greedily at some confections she had given them.

It must be said for these children that after enduring the trauma of their dreadful home life, it was a positive thrill to be going away, even with this odd little woman, and goodness knows where to. Although she said it was to a charming house set in the wood, surrounded by flowers and berries and all sorts of fruits; with its ovens constantly churning out cakes and rich creamy pastry; with lots of milk to drink from a dear little cow and butter aplenty; and no fixed mealtimes either, just eating, eating, eating whenever. It sounded like Heaven.

Let us be candid, too, in admitting that with a genetic background such as theirs, these children were not over-refined in taste or physical appearance. Although Hansel's eyes, like Jerome's, were not large, they were nevertheless discernible, and of a friendly blue colour. His hair likewise was of a coarse Saxonic tow, and his nose rather wider than most children's noses. Yet emaciated as he was he was still a manly little chap, albeit of a simple, trusting disposition.

Gretel was swarthy with dark straight hair and her smile, which came easily, would have been charming had she not the misfortune to display more gum than teeth, and these were somewhat carelessly ordered. When not smiling, her face very often took on a quizzical look, especially in the company of older people, as though she mistrusted the sense of what they were saying. It was a look, of course, which had infuriated her parents.

Although their walk through the forest was unremarkable, save that it led along paths with which neither child was familiar, they did have one encounter which made them, or Gretel rather, aware that Miss Grumberger was not all that she seemed. It happened this way.

That famine, which had caused so much deprivation among

the people, had inflicted similar effects on the wildlife, so that animals large and small had succumbed to hunger or hunters, or roamed about disconsolately.

It was at a turning overshadowed by gigantic elms that Hansel, Gretel and Miss Grumberger were arrested by the fierce challenging growl of an enormous bear standing on its hind legs, with its cavernous mouth wide open and loose salacious saliva dripping from its numerous teeth and unsightly jowls. It was apparent from its tiny hunger-crazed eyes and beckoning paws – beckoning to them – that its dinner had been long delayed and it was impatient to repair the omission.

It was at this point that Miss Grumberger, smiling with her little iron-grey teeth, raised her tiny parasol and murmured some outlandish word. The bear, with a totally un-bear-like little howl, dropped to all fours, lay its head on the ground as though in a contrite bow, and, at a further outlandish word from Miss Grumberger, shambled off slowly into the trees, ever and anon turning and bowing with a foolish ingratiating smile.

'He's really quite a dear creature,' said Miss Grumberger sweetly. 'Come along, children.'

'Blimey,' said Hansel, 'thet was a big 'un,' and hastily stuffed another handful of sweets in his mouth.

The sagacious Gretel, however, after first being too startled to think or move, gazed curiously at Miss Grumberger, while a frown of concentration marred for a moment her not altogether pretty face.

'Oh dear,' she said suddenly, 'I've lost all me sweets. They was settin' in me pinafore pocket, an' me pocket's gotta nole in it.'

Indeed, if the truth must be told, the child's clothes were almost entirely in tatters and holes.

'Don't fret, girl,' said Miss Grumberger, 'there's lots more.' And she handed her, and Hansel too who was watching enviously, another fistful of the delicious confections, each of which sparkled with a delightful rainbow-like hue. 'And we must get you a new frock too. Would you like that, dearie?'

Gretel nodded gratefully, her eyes radiant, her mouth being too full to articulate her thanks.

These sweets lost by Gretel – whether by accident or design – have caused much confusion among the various chroniclers of this tale, being described as pebbles, bread crumbs or nuts, and invariably proceeding from the pocket of Hansel.

We should like to lay the matter at rest, once and for all, by stressing that Hansel was too stupid to have thought of any ploy, devious or simple, and altogether too greedy to let anything in the shape of food escape him. Nevertheless, where all chroniclers (and the present one) agree is that these objects *did* serve to lay the trail of Hansel's and Gretel's progress through the forest.

But if a trail, a trail for whom? Certainly not, it would seem, for the children themselves, who were in no mind then of returning to their revolting home, unless the far-sighted Gretel had reason to assess in its truer guise the suspect kindliness of their curious guide.

Meanwhile Jerome, grinning imbecilely at the five gold pieces he held lasciviously in his oversized palms and which ever and anon he jingled, turned his toothless gums to Gerda and gurgled, 'Lass, lass, this be a nappy day.'

Gerda, sombre in her mountainous bulk, merely grunted. Then, 'Better 'and 'em over t'me,' she said. 'Stop playin' wif 'em.' And after a pause, 'Ain't it time you went t'village an' collected are eats?' And she extended the slip of paper with Miss Grumberger's instructions to her provisions merchant.

'Aye,' said Jerome agreeably. 'Almos' fergot I ware famishin'. 'Ere, lass,' and he handed her the coins. 'You blow up a fire an' I'll be back presently.'

His empty head filled with the clank of coinage, Jerome paused as he saw something glinting on the ground. He stooped to pick it up and almost as a first thought put it in his mouth. It was one of the rainbow-coloured sweets, and its delightful flavour so excited his palate that he peered about for more.

Soon he saw another, then another, and drooling greedily he began following the well-marked trail through the forest, hunched forward like some ungainly animal, grunting with pleasure as he sought and found the enticing sweets and macerated them between his gums.

It was at a familiar turning, overshadowed by gigantic elms, that Jerome, snuffling along in his happy search, was brought up suddenly by a ferocious ear-splitting growl.

"Ere,' he shouted, "Ere you, clear off!' to the gigantic brown bear which stood before him on its hind legs, with its cavernous mouth slavering and its forepaws eloquently beckoning.

As the bear advanced, Jerome retreated, uttering frenzied out-landish words. Alas, these did not include the outlandish words which Miss Grumberger had used and which, as we saw, had such an extraordinary effect on the bear's behaviour. To spare our more tender-hearted readers, we shall merely relate that the bear dined well that evening, heartlessly ignoring Jerome's horrendous last squeal for mercy which echoed appallingly throughout the forest.

Hearing it far off, Hansel, his mouth stuffed with the same confection that had proved so fatal to his Dad, mumbled, 'Wutsat?' and Gretel too looked startled.

III.

Presently, the dark aisles through which they were walking thinned out, and, in a sunny clearing before them, they spied the smartest little red and white house they had ever seen.

The garden at the back was filled with a profusion of flowers and fruit trees, while in front and round the sides there was a terrace in crazy paving of multi-coloured stones, each set cunningly against its neighbour to form the outlines of boars roasting on spits, steaming pots of goulash and, everywhere, fat little children with apple-round cheeks and plump little bottoms cavorting about in highest glee.

From the smoking chimney there came an oily wisp, heavy with the fragrance of baking meat, which, carried to their eager nostrils, made their mouths water shamelessly. And what was their surprise when, on approaching closer, they noticed that the red gables were not, as they had thought at first, made of the usual tiles of the district, but rather of strings of small plump sausages maturing in the sun.

The white walls, which looked like icing sugar, turned out to be good solid stucco, for, as Miss Grumberger explained, it wouldn't do to have her house melt away in the rain. To make up for it, however, she pointed out the festoons of sweetmeats, nuts, gingerbreads, rich little pastries and curlicues of gristled fat which, like a bead curtain, hung round from the gutters.

Smiling amiably, Miss Grumberger led the children round the house, inviting them to sample from each festoon of goodies, when, almost bursting from the pressure of their amply-filled bellies, she remarked, quite charmingly, 'Oh, dear, I shouldn't have let you eat all that before supper.' Then she led them to the front door, on which was painted a fearsomely huge and glowering black cat, with its pink mouth open and its tongue arched in the act of spitting. It was as they entered, through that forbidding door, that Gretel noticed the small white board above the lintel which proclaimed, in chocolate-coloured letters, that the house was called *Good Enough To Eat*.

Inside, everything was as neat as clover, with gaily-flowered sofas and easy chairs, and pretty little doilies with pots of plants set daintily on them. Bustling about too with duster in hand was a large shapeless individual in a grey woollen gown, which, it must be said, her backside filled entirely, while on her head was a small, ridiculous-looking maid's cap. As she turned about, startled, and curtsied to Miss Grumberger with a look almost of terror in her eyes, Miss Grumberger said, 'It's alright, dearie. I've brought some children. Children, this is Miss Braun, my housekeeper. These are Hansel and Gretel.'

As the woman stared at them stupidly from her enormous, popping eyes, and with mouth wide open – so much like a frog's – Gretel thought: 'Why, ef her skin waren't grey – ef it ware green instead, she'd be a frog, a whoppin', great, ugly frog! Ugh!'

As they sat about the table, with the little cow mooing contentedly in the garden, Miss Braun silently ministered to them bowls of soup with thickly-buttered bread, jugs of foaming creamy milk, platters stacked with greasy meat and potatoes swimming in gravy. Hansel's eyes enlarged with sheer wonder and pure gluttony. 'Cor,' he murmured happily, tucking in with no restraint whatever, while Miss Grumberger beamed, herself eating fastidiously from a heaped platter of the small plump sausages which sizzled deliciously. Gretel, who had had enough from the dainties outside, left her soup untouched and only nibbled at a piece of bread and butter.

'Don't you like your soup, dearie?' asked Miss Grumberger, as her little iron-grey teeth clicked together merrily. Her mouth was lightly smeared with sausage grease.

'It's too fat fer me, mum.'

Miss Grumberger's red little eyes peered anxiously from behind her spectacles as she said, 'You're a naughty girl. It's only because you've shrunk your stomach from fasting. You *must* eat. I insist upon it. Why, you don't want to go on looking like a *stick*, do you? It's so unhealthy.'

'C'mon, Gret, it's good,' said Hansel grinning, plunging a whole potato in his mouth, from which a rivulet of greasy gravy trickled down his chin. Thus urged, Gretel made a severe attempt to bolt some of the unsightly food but could manage only a mouthful, while Miss Grumberger glared. But when the sweet arrived, a mountainous custard with a corona of whipped cream girdling its centre and sides, she managed two helpings followed by a mug of milk, and Miss Grumberger smiled. Dear woman, she seemed so keen to make those children plump and healthy.

Although Gretel wanted to go outside again and see the pretty cow, Miss Grumberger insisted that both children go to their room and rest before sleeping. For, she cautioned them, in their delicate state of undernourishment, it was essential that they moved as little as possible, so that the good things they had inside them could be properly digested. She gave Hansel a large bowl of nuts, just in case he felt any 'gnawings' during the night. Gretel refused any further provender, promising to help herself from Hansel's hoard if necessary, and Miss Grumberger looked rather piqued, thinking probably to herself, 'That's the thanks one gets for being so considerate.'

As Hansel went and lay upon his bed, nibbling at his nuts, Gretel exasperatedly hissed at him: 'Oh, 'Ansel, must you be such a pig?' And Hansel, very hurt, muttered back: 'Wut's eatin' you?'

Shortly after his eyelids settled drowsily and Gretel tucked him in, then she went to her own bed, sat upon the edge with chin in her hand, and considered very deeply.... How bewildering to encounter such seeming good fortune. The hard knocks she had known made her wary of gratuitous kindness. Besides, it was all so odd: the house, the curious Miss Grumberger, and that awful-looking Miss Braun...

Next morning, both children were astonished to learn that each had had the selfsame nightmare.

It began with two glowing eyes peering in at the window with a hideous phosphorescent glare, startling them so badly that both had dived their heads under the coverlets in terror. The owl, for owl it was in fact, murmured into its snowy beard as it flew off into the forest, 'Alice has guests again. Hm-m, more pickings.'

There followed then the sound of weeping and whimpering, amid which piteous moans they heard the voice of Miss Grumberger, against a background of the frenzied croaking of toads, gloating, 'Ah, you'll do, my lad, you're nice and fat. You'll do lovely. Into the oven with you, quick!' Then some dreadful shrieks, a more ominous din from the toads, the clanging of a metal door being slammed shut, and silence. Several hours later the nightmare resumed to the dissonance of whirring, clanking and grinding, a further silence, and the voice of Miss Grumberger calling: 'Come along, Emma. It's ready.'

As they awoke, it was Hansel, his hair standing upright in tow-coloured spikes, who spoke first. 'I'ad a 'orrible nightmare,' and he shuddered.

Gretel lay too worn out to move.

''Dja 'ear me, Gret? I said –'

'Yes, I 'eard you. I 'ad one too,' she replied in an exhausted whisper.

'Br-rrrr,' said Hansel: 'them eyes ... them toads ... them cries!'

'You too?'

''At's funny,' said Hansel, his guileless face imbecile with perplexity: 'you an' me 'avin' it the same. Wunner wut Miz Gumberger'll say ef I tell 'er.'

'Don't you dare!' said Gretel severely.

'Awright. On'y, I wuz thinkin' –'

'Yes, brother.'

'Wut time's breakfust?'

As Gretel turned to survey him with undisguised contempt, a lilting voice came up the staircase. 'Yoo hoo, children. Breakfast's ready.'

''Ear thet?' said Hansel grinning. 'C'mon, Gret.'

They splashed their hands and faces in a basin of clear cool water and dried themselves. But when Hansel tried to put on his *lederhosen* he found them too tight. They seemed to have shrunk during the night.

'Me breeches's got smaller,' he declared with amusement. 'Fancy. Wunner ef Miz Gumberger's got me a bigger pair.'

'Oh, I'm sure,' said Gretel disdainfully. Her tattered frock and pinafore still fitted her perfectly.

Miss Grumberger greeted them cheerily as they came down the stairs. She had just come from the garden where she'd been snipping wart-lilies, and the children were amazed that she'd made a bouquet of these sinister flowers.

'Don't stand there gawking,' she said amusedly. 'Go to the scullery and ask Emma, I mean, Miss Braun, to give you your breakfast.'

''Zer name Emma?' asked Hansel, with a slow but not very

clear awakening. "S' funny, you know, cuz –' but at this point Gretel pinched him warningly.

'Because what?' said Miss Grumberger quietly, as her little red eyes glowed behind her spectacles.

'Oh, I dunno – me breeches's smaller. Look,' and he grinned, 'the buttons won't button. They've gone an' shrunk.'

'Oh,' said Miss Grumberger with a surprising little giggle. 'Ask Miss Braun to fetch you another pair.'

Miss Braun was a sight. Her frog-like face with its puffy frog-like cheeks was even puffier this morning, and it appeared she'd been crying, for great luminous tears still dripped slowly from her enormous eyes, and she sniffed unhappily. She dried her large surprising-looking hands on her apron, put aside the small casings on strings which she had been stuffing with minced meat from a tub, covered the tub against a swarm of flies which were dancing eagerly round its edges, and blew her nose long and sorrowfully.

Gretel watched her thoughtfully as she laid a thick slab of butter and a half-loaf of bread on each of their plates, added a jug of warm cream, pots of jam, sugary buns, a large ham studded with cloves and with a rich glazing of syrup, and a gargantuan platter of eggs swimming in butter.

As Hansel began glutting himself as happily as before, he found that his appetite and capacity had increased enormously.

'Please, Miz,' he said to Miss Braun, half-way through: 'me breeches's smaller. Miz Gumberger said you wuz t'gimme anovver pair.'

Miss Braun raised her almost invisible eyebrows, and without a word went into the pantry and returned, holding up a pair of *lederhosen* remarkable in their width.

"Scuse me,' said Hansel politely as he took the proferred trousers, went out to the garden and returned shortly after. 'Ah, 'at's better,' he remarked luxuriantly, reseating himself and tucking in once more.

As Gretel nibbled at a bun, her sharp brain ached painfully. 'Ah, me,' she thought. 'Wut's t'become on us? Sure as sure thet Miss Grumberger's a queer ol' hen – mebbe a witch. An' those screams in the night! Lordy, lordy, thet t'were no nightmare. Thet ware *real*. An' thet stupid 'Ansel, jus' like 'is Dad. Daren't let 'im outta me sight while thet crone be about. 'E'd be sure t'blab. O lordy, wut kin I do?'

While the wretched girl tormented herself, the curious Miss Braun, who appeared to have taken a fancy to her, very secretively laid a small gold ring beside her plate, and when Gretel opened her eyes in wide surprise, the anxious-looking housekeeper with a silent gesture bade her put it on. Gretel did so, with some misgiving but also with a kind of fearful pleasure. A ring, a *real gold ring* – she had never known such riches before.

Straightway, unbeknown to herself, her swarthy skin took on a refined, creamy-textured hue. Her hair, oily and lank with accumulated lack of care, began shining with a lustrous if oily-silken sheen. Her eyes grew larger and more brilliant, her lips fuller and rounder, so that even her gums and teeth reversed their previous characteristics when she smiled, as she smiled now at that ring on her finger: the gums being hidden discreetly by the fuller, shapelier mouth; and even the ill-arranged teeth seemed noticeably less so, even charming. In short, if she could have had a good wash and brush she could have passed for beautiful.

Miss Braun noted the transformation with unconcealed pleasure, and went back into the scullery with a tearful sigh. Alas, poor lady, if the truth must be told, she was none other than an enchanted Princess, metamorphosed through the malevolence of the witch Alice Grumberger – indeed, she *was* a witch! – into the semblance of a frog, and not entirely successfully, as we have seen. And a frog, moreover, without a tongue, which accounted for her muteness. Crafty Alice Grumberger! And that ring, useless to her now but which, as a young Princess, she had had from a Good Fairy, with its guarantee of ensuring striking beauty, she had nobly sacrificed to Gretel. For, thought she hopelessly, she would ever remain in thrall to this ghastly horrid witch, with her cruel lust for children in the shape of sausage meat, which she, the once proud Princess, prepared for her.

And thinking this, she burst into bitter tears. Alas, alas, what would become of her? Escape she could not, for even if that were possible, how could she appear at the palace of her father, the King, in her misshapen frog-like presence, and declare, in her ugly frog-like croak (or rather by writing, since she was tongueless), 'I am your daughter, Emmeline.'

Poor King. He too knew the remorse of a broken heart as he sent couriers throughout the land, futilely searching for his long lost child.

IV.

And Hansel grew fatter and fatter, while Miss Grumberger, gig-gling gaily, took to measuring him daily with a tape-line and com-plimenting him on his expanding girth, upon which the doltish boy would reply with his imbecile smile, 'I've 'ad to loose me belt anovver notch, Miz.'

Whereupon Miss Grumberger would throw up her skinny arms and giggle more engagingly, so that if you were a stranger, come upon the scene, you would have found it difficult not to think, 'My, what a jolly little lady.' But if you had lingered a moment longer you would have been astounded to see her turn, with a surprising change of mood, on Gretel, and, as her little red eyes smouldered behind her spectacles, spit with fury:

'Faugh! You ugly bag of bones, you skinny wretched baggage. Just look at how nice and plump your brother's become. Why, he's good, he's –'

'Good enough to eat?' put in Gretel thoughtlessly.

'What?' shrieked Miss Grumberger, so violently that her spec-tacles leapt off her sharp little nose, bounced once upon the ground and then, quite astonishingly, turned into a small grey mouse which, after gazing about mischievously, dashed off into the forest.

'Me specs,' wailed Miss Grumberger, dropping her better-class accent, 'where're me specs?'

And if you had been lingering there still, you would have nod-ded sagely to yourself and said, 'Aha, I see it all now. The woman's nothing but a witch. Scandalous!'

For of course one of the sure signs of identifying witches is their little red eyes, and the fact that they are almost blind without their spectacles. The sagacious Gretel perceived and understood this quite clearly, and a wise determined look replaced the momentary expressions of wonder, terror and amusement, occasioned by both the mouse and Miss Grumberger.

As Miss Grumberger continued to wail – it would be a mistake to say 'heart-rendingly', after what we know, although the sound could be so construed had she had a heart, but quite ear-splittingly in any case, so that Miss Braun within, with a feather duster in one of her ungainly hands, turned noticeably greyer, and Hansel, stu-pid Hansel, was so dumbfounded that his mouth dropped open –

she, Miss Grumberger, suddenly recovered herself and her accent, and laying one of her hands on Hansel's arm, she said, 'Take me inside, my dear. I've just remembered I've got a second pair.

'As for you, my pretty,' she added menacingly, pointing a scrawny arm at a nearby tree, although Gretel well understood it was meant for herself, 'get you off to the forest and collect a bundle of brushwood, as big as you can carry. And when you've returned with it, mind you go off and collect another, *and* another. Do you hear, you hideous bag of bones? I'm baking tonight.'

Alas for Gretel. Her short-lived pleasure at seeing Miss Grumberger flailing about blindly and vulgarly screeching for her spectacles was now turned to despair, as she ran off into the forest with tears coursing down her lovely cheeks.

What could she do, and where could she turn? And as she went about collecting twigs, she heard from a branch high above her head a bird speaking in rhyme:

> The witch's baking
> Is Hansel's unmaking
> Tu whit, tu whit.
>
> The witch's baking
> Is Hansel's unmaking
> Tu whit, tu whit.

As the bird continued its monotonous refrain, Gretel with a small shriek placed her hands over her ears and ran deeper into the forest. Unknown to her, the mouse on escaping had taken the opportunity to gossip to all its cronies, of which the rhyming bird was one, about the sinister doings at Alice Grumberger's.

'Must collect my wits,' thought Gretel desperately. 'It simply won't do if I give way like this.'

Surprisingly, with the more becoming change in her physical appearance, the magic ring seemed also to have conferred a distinct improvement in her manner of speech.

As the poor girl put the finishing touches to a bundle of twigs and raised it to her back, she speculated with horror on the fate awaiting Hansel, realizing how helpless she was. There was no use, she knew, in appealing to Hansel to flee. Even if she could convince him of his danger, that stupid boy's disgusting bulk made it impossible for him to move quickly, if at all. And then there was the mute Miss Braun: well-disposed, certainly, but so ineffectual, and completely subservient to Miss Grumberger's will. And that witch herself ... it was obvious, with her power over the bear, that she was a formidable enchantress. If only she hadn't bethought herself of that second pair of spectacles and had remained half-blind!

'Oh dear, oh dear,' murmured the distraught girl, as she came to the cottage and was directed by a silently weeping Miss Braun to deposit her load of twigs inside the scullery beside an enormous oven.

It was on her last trip, with darkness already falling, that Gretel, quite exhausted, staggered into the scullery and was shocked to see Hansel in what appeared to be a monstrously large, child's nursery chair, and with the odd addition of castors, happily gorging from a mountain of food on a tray before him. His eyes, imbedded in creases of fat, were almost invisible but were twinkling merrily, while he made uncouth grunting noises as he slopped and half-chewed before swallowing in an unseemly ravenous haste.

'O Hansel!' cried Gretel with despair in her voice: 'if only you could see how horrid you look.'

And the miserable girl thought that the best thing she could do was run deep into the forest and allow herself to be torn in pieces by the first savage beast that she met.

'Wut's wrong wif you?' whined Hansel disagreeably. 'Don't look ef you don't like, see? 'Sides, Miz Gumberger ast me t'cum down 'ere cuz she's spectin' guests t'morrer, so you'll 'ave t'clear off anyways. Sez she gotta speshul treat fer me t'night. See? Th'oven's bin lit. Ef I wuz you, I'd clear. She 'ates you somethin' fearful.'

And that dolt began tucking in again as nonchalantly as though his sister had suddenly evaporated.

Without a word the unhappy girl turned and walked out of the scullery, past the silently weeping Miss Braun, and out towards the forest.

At the first line of trees she stopped, leaned sorrowfully with one arm against a massive trunk, and almost at once sank to the ground overwhelmed by slumber.

Straggling ants on late night rounds crawled over her, depositing some of their painfully accumulated gatherings on her clothes and face in their reckless haste to get home for supper. Later, a powerful young rabbit cleansed the bottoms of his hind feet, sending up a shower of earth behind him, most of which fell into Gretel's hair.

94

Then a lusty breeze sprang up, shaking the trees so that they shivered and dropped leaves and small branches on the sleeping girl below. And still Gretel slept. Finally a light cold rain began falling, and her eyelids fluttered open.

'Oh dear,' she said, becoming suddenly awake. 'Oh dear, oh dear.' And drawing a sleeve across her face to dry her eyes, she rose and peered through the trees at the cottage in the distance.

Pretty or no, Gretel was a fright. Her lovely hair stood up in matted spikes, her face across which she had drawn her arm was smeared with a blackish unwholesome scum which emphasised the wild brilliance of her eyes. Fortunately, she had no mirror to discover this, although one wonders if it was not too dark to use a mirror and, besides, too awesome a moment to be thinking of personal appearance.

All the lights in the cottage, save one, were out, and this was in the scullery. Taking up a large, stout stick at her feet, Gretel crept forward silently, her heart beating uncomfortably. As she approached the cottage, it was as quiet as could be. Then all at once she heard the loathsome sound of toads croaking in high excitement, and when she peered through the window this is what she saw:

Hansel, fast asleep in his oversize nursery chair, with six giant toads propelling it smartly along on its castors towards the open door of the enormous oven, and the witch, Alice Grumberger, with a hideous grin on her open mouth, leading the procession.

Thrusting the window violently open, and with a cry as of some demented tigress, Gretel leapt through the aperture, accidentally knocking over Miss Grumberger, who promptly lost her spectacles again but regained her feet more quickly than one would have imagined, and was just about to set up her vulgar howling when the toads, at the sight of that apparition with its mud-stained face and frightful hair, hopped away in terror, releasing the nursery chair which immediately spun out of control and careered into the witch who, like a cannon ball, shot straight into the open oven, and with such force that the door clanged shut behind her.

This dreadful scene was enacted almost entirely in a moment, so that before Gretel could draw breath or regain her wits, the last expiring shriek of Miss Grumberger had sounded, the toads had disappeared in bursting puffs of dust with her death and vanished enchantment, and Hansel, finally awake in that unholy din, had opened his little eyes to bleat, 'Wut's 'appenin'?'

Early next morning, while the children slept an exhausted slumber, a gay sound of horns trilled through the forest, and presently a troop of splendidly-attired cavaliers, each more dazzling than the other in plumage and costume, rode up noisily in front of the cottage, and with swords and spurs jingling merrily, dismounted.

'Would you believe it?' said one, apparently the leader, a rather silly-looking young man with a long pink chin, pointing with undisguised hilarity at the lintel over the door: 'It's called "Good Enough To Eat",' and all the gentlemen exploded with laughter.

At that very moment the door opened, and very timidly an enchanting young lady appeared, garbed in a coarse, voluminous, grey woollen gown which hung about her in massive folds, and with a startled look on her delicately beautiful face.

'I say,' said one of the cavaliers in honest admiration, 'well-named indeed, "Good Enough To Eat",' and the others applauded noisily, bowing gracefully to the beautiful lady.

'Why, it's the Princess!' exclaimed the leader. 'Her Highness in drab. By Christ, we've found her at last!'

At which the Princess, still unaware of the transformation which had delivered her, with the death of the witch, from the unsightly frog-like form of Miss Braun into the fresh youthful beauty of her former self, recoiled in embarrassment, blushing furiously.

And when the gallant young men clustered respectfully about her with joyful smiles, talking excitedly among themselves, Gretel, with face washed very nicely and hair smoothed down, and in a pretty frock she had somewhere discovered, peeped out the door.

'Well, I declare!' said one of the gentlemen after a moment of admiring silence, 'we seem to have discovered another,' and there were further shouts of high-spirited laughter.

As Gretel and the erstwhile Miss Braun stared at one another in wonderment and pleasure, and each asked simultaneously of the other, 'Gretel?', 'Miss Braun?', and both, with true feminine instinct, dashed back into the cottage to examine themselves in the nearest mirror, the gentlemen roared again with perplexed laughter.

'You dear, dear child,' said the now overjoyed and grateful

Princess, after having gazed at herself lovingly and lingeringly in the mirror, and after listening with tears streaming from her lovely eyes to Gretel's adventure and how the execrable Miss Grumberger had met her deserved fate, 'I owe you my life. There is nothing in my father's palace that I would not give to you.' Dear Princess! And then she begged Gretel to consider coming as her principal lady-in-waiting, at which Gretel demurred, saying that for the present she must look after her brother Hansel, but that if the Princess were agreeable, she would come in a year.

And so it was decided, and the Princess, after embracing Gretel, rode off surrounded by her gay retinue, with the horns trilling merrily. And we may conjecture at the delight with which her aged father, the King, greeted her at long last.

That ass Hansel was inconsolable for his 'Miz Gumberger'. Despite Gretel's exasperated pleas that the woman was a witch who had feasted on children, and that he himself, by the merest chance, had been saved from her terrible oven, the doltish boy continued to sulk and repine.

Meanwhile Gretel searched out what Miss Grumberger had 'put by' for her old age, and this turned out to be an enormous hoard of gold coins, rings, jewels and, curiously enough, spectacle frames of every description. With firm insistence she at last managed to get Hansel to busy himself with something useful, and at length a garden of vegetables grew up under his haphazard efforts. But his gargantuan appetite persisted, and Gretel despaired of ever seeing him back to his normal size. In time, his eyes did manage to re-emerge through their folds of fat, but he remained, as so many do, a lad with a weight problem, not that he considered it a problem at all.

At the end of the year, a courier from the Princess came to ask Gretel if she would now consent to accompany him back to the palace where the Princess was keenly awaiting her arrival. Brother and sister bade each other a temporary farewell, and Gretel rode off to what we learn in time was a dazzling career in the council-of-state.

Hansel remained at the cottage. A ponderous figure who moved slowly about, and open in hospitality to all passing strangers, to whom invariably he told his story and extolled the kindness of his late, lamented benefactress, 'thet dear Miz Gumberger,' he continued to live there for many a year. He may be living there yet.

Metamorphosis

Joseph Paul Marian Gordeony, a middle-aged importer of glassware and novelties from Bohemia, was very disturbed because he had woken that morning to discover that his hands were not his own, that is, not the ones he had grown up with: those which in childhood were small, irresolute, and with difficulty had formed into fists; which in adolescence had developed with fine lines and sensitivity, becoming more prehensile for the objects they desired and skilled in expressive eloquence, while doing certain things in secret of which they were ashamed; and which in manhood had achieved a noble white regularity and persuasive purpose, besides performing for the world the usual actions that hands are made for: scratching oneself, taking money, manipulating artefacts, caressing a desirable anatomy, pulling dogs' tails, shaking other hands, et cetera.

He stared at the hands beneath his wrists with disbelief. They were earthy brown, monstrously large and coarse with calloused thumbs and discernibly purplish cartilages, thick prominent knuckles, swollen veins and filthily unkempt blackish nails. One had even an obscene illustration tattooed on it. Gordeony did the obvious: he rolled up the sleeves of his pyjamas and was relieved to note that his forearms at least remained as he knew them: round, white, soft, with fine blond hair and the plump modelling of his good Gordeony heritage. 'I am going mad,' he thought, placing the hands on the telephone table beside him and again examining their outlandish appearance, 'quite mad.' He let them fall to his sides where they dangled like the iron pineapple weights on old-fashioned grandfather clocks, so ponderously did they drag down his shoulders and disorientate the natural fluidity of his body.

How would he wash, he wondered, comb his hair and moustache, stroke his face, shave, show those masses of horny flesh to the world? He was filled with revulsion; even horror. The telephone rang suddenly. Rather than use those hands he kicked off the receiver, knelt down to it and awkwardly placed the instrument against his mouth and ear. He heard a voice, far off, saying, 'Mr. Gordeony? Is that Mr. Gordeony?' 'Who is it?' he whispered back sharply in disguised sibilants, although he recognized quite well the nasal accents of his American secretary; and then, 'Not home, not home.'

The connection broke and Gordeony left the receiver off its cradle. 'I must be calm,' he said, beginning to sweat. 'No panic ... Merolenko. Let me see Merolenko.'

He knew it was a mistake as soon as Merolenko's wife ushered him into the waiting room. The doctor's flat and office were several floors beneath Gordeony, and the two played chess together frequently. A few moments later Merolenko was beckoning him into his surgery with something of a guilty smile.

'My dear Joseph, an unexpected pleasure. Sit down, please.' Gordeony stared at his friend with such a fixed, sorrowful expression that the doctor, genuinely moved, asked, 'Why, what's the matter?'

'Look,' said Gordeony, raising the unsightly hands.

The doctor rose from his armchair and came round to him, examined the upraised hands with perplexity then smiled. 'I was not aware that you were tattooed.'

'They're not mine,' burst out Gordeony passionately.

'I beg your pardon?'

'These hands – they're not mine!'

Merolenko paused with incredulity, went round his desk and reseated himself. He shook his head sadly. 'You are overwrought, my friend. Ill. You are not sleeping enough. I shall give you a sedative.'

'No!'

'No? I tell you Joseph, you are overstrung. Have you business worries?'

'No.'

'Any worries at all? Private, financial?'

'I tell you, no! These hands –'

'They are quite normal. Indeed, most remarkable.'

'But they're not *mine*!'

'Joseph!' Merolenko said this with deep reproach. 'It is an hallucination, you must take control of yourself.'

'You fool,' exploded Gordeony, 'don't I know my own hands

when I see them? These hideous shovels – do they look as though they belonged to *me*? Look at them!'

Merolenko paled at the insult. With ill-concealed fury he spat out, *'You* are the fool who refuses sound medical opinion. You need the services of a psychiatrist, not a physician. I try to help you but you rebuff me. Please, leave my surgery at once.'

Merolenko's wife, Vera, hearing her husband's apoplectic tones, and having in fact heard the whole of the dialogue from her position outside the surgery door, retreated quickly to the external door of the apartment, so that when Gordeony, his face no less pale and furious than the doctor's, reached it too, she beckoned to him and followed him into the corridor, closing the door softly behind her. He gazed at her irritably, and in a grating whisper said, 'Not now, Vera, I can't speak now. Something dreadful has happened.'

Vera, innocently, put her face close to his. 'Listen, Joseph, we aren't exactly strangers. Whatever it is, I must know too,' and very coyly and obliquely she glanced at the suspended hands, dangling unnaturally low beneath their dressing gown sleeves, but just as quickly sensing the exposure of his deformities he slipped them behind his back.

'Not now,' he hissed. 'Later, we shall talk later. Besides, Nick – anyway, there must be a patient coming, I just heard the lift.'

Vera, soothingly, kissed him lightly on the cheek, gave him a voluptuously reassuring smile, made her lips into a farewell rose-bud and whispered, 'Alright, later. Shall I phone you at the office?'

'No,' he groaned. 'I'm not going to the office today.'

The sound of the lift door clanging open on the landing impelled Vera hastily back into the apartment, and the distraught Joseph to glare atrociously at the innocent cause of the interruption, an elderly and richly-clad beauty in a large black straw nodding with funereal feathers, whom he almost jostled in his choking rage as she squeezed past him, muttering between her expensive teeth, 'Beast.'

Gordeony went back into his flat and slammed and locked the door. Unthinkingly, his first act was to replace the telephone receiver on its cradle, performing this service to the dictates of technical conformity and the neatness inherent in his orderly nature, yet at the same time grimacing with nausea as he directed the hands in their task while trying to look the other way. But no sooner had the instrument received its predetermined outline again than it burst into savage ringing, as though in frustration of having to remain silent for so long. With a wild cry and an enraged kick Gordeony displaced the receiver again, and hearing the frantic, high-pitched nasal quacking of his American secretary, he moaned, 'Lieber Gott,' restraining himself at the very last moment from placing those grotesque hams of hands against his beating temples, and rushed into the bathroom where the compelling twang of his secretary, whom he had once ironically dubbed 'Doris Duck', although in fact she was Ms. Alison Thomson of a good Bostonian family, so she had told him, was mercifully obliterated by the torrent of water which he released into the basin. Kicking the bathroom door violently shut, the near-deranged importer of glass novelties from Bohemia squirted into the seething water a well-known brand of bath jelly which exploded into an emerald foam, and plunged the 'Moravian shovels', as he now began to call them, out of his sight.

Apropos the designation 'Moravian shovels', it derived from the fact that Gordeony had been raised on the farm of his father, a wealthy peasant of that region, who had sent his son to a commercial college in Prague and later to London, after the youthful Joseph had brought to disgrace the daughter of a prosperous city butcher, a fellow student, and had then himself been disgraced by being expelled from the college on the threat by her father of witholding his subsidized meat from the college canteen. The story met with the peasant father's outward rage, but secret and envying admiration, and Joseph was condemned for the rest of that year to work alongside his parent's farmhands, and given the exclusive privilege of amassing into neat piles, with an enormous shovel, the aromatic and generous droppings of the busily-digesting farm animals. Those days he had never forgotten, but in the beguilement of his new surroundings, with a heavy endowment and a pretty two-roomed flat in Belgravia, in Chester Square, he had allowed his mind to range over new images and fancies. That first month had been pure delight, even with his stumbling grasp of the English tongue, and although he lived in Belgravia he spent most of his days and nights in Soho where he learned with a fine discrimination how money could be spent with seductive and fulfilling rewards. His maternal uncle Rudolph, the founder of that import house of glass novelties from Bohemia, and to which Gordeony succeeded along with the founder's penthouse in the selfsame block as his own, soon put an end to his abandoned ways, enrolled him at a morosely English commercial college and reported to Joseph's father that the boy was getting on famously. As the man

101

thought of the boy, the boy within him mentally considered the man who was now, by increasing the water temperature to a raging heat, attempting to melt those degrading hands away. Gordeony, junior and senior, were both amazed that those amazing hands received no intimation of heat whatever, nor did they suffer any pain or discomfort when he placed them in turn on the bathroom scale and stamped upon them.

Beyond a certain glowing pinkness, and an inflamed and coarsened leering of the obscene tattoo, they displayed no ill effects from their ruthless maltreatment; indeed, if anything, they seemed invigorated, and commenced opening and closing themselves as though in genuine and healthy pleasure, as if the scalding heat of the cleansing foam and the furious stamping had given them a salutary and exciting stimulant, had woken them from a long, dreary nightmare, had made them alive and pulsing for action, independently or in collusion with their present guardian, now, this very moment, at once! This they seemed almost to shout with insistent bellicosity as they snapped their ferocious knuckles with nutcracking explosions. Gordeony was appalled. Those monstrosities seemed to have invisible feet of their own too, as they struggled within or outside themselves to run somewhere. They jerked at his wrists and forearms, yanked at his elbow tendons, jostled his thighs, seemed to prod at him as they grappled his flanks: shoving, thrusting, poking, scrabbling, trying to dynamize his dispirited body. They were rueful in their impatience, somewhat harsh but still relatively gentle, friendly but becoming unmistakably irritated; they wanted movement, not paralysis. They would not, they insinuated, put up long with this tardy behaviour. They were nice and clean too, more presentable. They were grateful for Gordeony's benign, if maliciously-administered, lustrations. They begged, they implored, they almost brayed like donkeys, they almost screamed with kinetic frenzy; they danced about like imprisoned lobsters hanging in chains; they seemed to fume, swear, cajole, and even the obscene tattoo elongated its mouth to add to their din; they squirmed, they tried to leap, to jump; they seemed charged with electric current. They finally began to sweat. And Gordeony, the sweat too pouring down from his glazed-with-silver chestnut curls onto his high, pink, finely-lined forehead, onto his tall, imperiously-boned nose, his unfashionable archduke's manly moustache, his thick, rosy hussar's lips, and his long, ungainly Gordeony chin – where that unending stream settled and dripped – Gordeony, amidst that torrent of seething water which still gushed into the overflowing basin, creating puddles of sea green foam round his feet, stared like a demented *golem* at his bathroom wall, adorned in coloured mosaic tiles by his good friend Zdenek, the Czech artist, and depicting a prancing faun-like form in the beatific undress of nature, with feminine breasts but with otherwise masculine musculature, playing on a shepherd's pipe and gazing with mischievously wanton eyes at the gay young antelopes sporting about, in a sunny green clearing sheltered beneath improbable trees.

And meanwhile that flood was rising, foaming and steaming, lapping at the bathroom fixtures, the tub, the exotic low-slung toilet against which the bathmat bobbed like a disengaged raft on a storm-tossed sea, when an outrageous hammering which Gordeony could yet hear through the bathroom door and over the churning maelstrom, came to him suddenly, shattering his stupor, his benumbed catatonia of thought and movement, while those idiotic hands still cried piteously like babes despoiled of their mother's teats. As Gordeony woke from his mind-blocked spell, his unseeing eyes, still fixed on the faun, blinked in amazement as the pounding outside was joined to a raucous bellowing and such ferocious thumping that it seemed the external door and wall of his flat must collapse in atoms. He raised his astonished feet, one after the other, as though water-wading in some shallow pool, placed one of the hands on the hot water faucet and turned it off, at which for the first time he experienced that molten lava round his ankles. Leaping into the air with a brute-like scream and with yelps of insensate pain, he rushed from the bathroom, with that dutiful flood of mindless green water following, sprinted to the outer door and unlocked it.

The torrent from without was if anything more startling than the torrent within. It hurtled past Gordeony in a flailing flood of arms, legs and grunting, overtoppling bodies which when restored to upright position revealed itself as the Superintendent and his cohort of savage, uniformed porters, all with white-gloved hands raised in fists, those very fists which had been creating that olympian din on his door, and with mouths fulminating at him in choice Calabrian, Austro- and Croat-Slav, and Ardennes guttural. Panting and growling like veritable tigers, they pointed with horror at the gurgitating water, scolding him, reprimanding him, threatening him with dire action for the mess he had made, in his flat and the flats of his neighbours, some of whom in fact were themselves now charging in with envenomed faces, bristling and cursing with righteous rage and calling for restitution of damaged property, until Gordeony, beside himself with fury, and hopping about like some madman on his scalded feet, gave a sudden leap and shriek like a Samurai and thrust those monstrous, fisted shovels before him, challenging any or all to touch him, hurt or menace him; yes, he invited them to do their worst.

When the Superintendent and all those heretofore aggressive porters and intimidating and outraged tenants saw those massive, boulder-crushing fists, they stood back like paralyzed goats before that lion, that elephant, that raging bear and champion prize-fighter rolled into one. The Superintendent, the first to move, drew off his white, peaked, attendant's cap and bowed, following which the rabble of central European porters did likewise, while the tenants murmured apologies and asked if they could help by offering their servants. A tentative amiability was established after Gordeony relaxed those terrifying shovels and let them drop inoffensively by his sides. Brooms, mops, pails, almost instantly appeared, and went busily through the lounge and into the bathroom, sponging, cleaning, drying, polishing, until dampness only remained; and the bathmat was wrung out and hung to dry over a radiator near the prancing faun, which porters and Superintendent with awed glances admired.

Gordeony, bemused, amazed, confounded by the servile display, was too much shaken by this dénouement to act, as he should have, the outraged lord of the manor, as neighbourly tenants and porterly riff-raff with profuse smiles, grimaces of teeth and deferential bows – all directed at those now relaxed but still menacing shovels, grinning in a sheen of triumphant self-love – moved reluctantly outwards, jostling and discomfiting their congested bodies, blundering, elbowing each other away, lingering as if hopefully awaiting a summons to return. Gordeony's expressive hussar's lips fell open in pure, stupid wonderment, his normally brisk business man's intelligence shattered momentarily like a heavily-dropped clock. In the mellifluous tones of Moravian Czech, which he had not used for years, the egregious importer mumbled the phrases of a catch-song he had memorized as a child. 'The sheep are in the clover / Mummy's baking honey bread / If I'm good the wolves won't eat me / Baa-baa-baa.' His equally fuddled guests, to show their high good humour, accompanied him in the sheep-like refrain the second time round, then began laughing uproariously. One young woman, bolder than the rest, stepped closely up to him and before he could protest seized one of his awful hands, pressed it to her lips and then to one of her shapely breasts where she held it and began giggling hysterically. The shocked importer pushed her gently away, but so violent was the gesture to the lady that she went spinning to the floor, moaning with dazed but wanton delight, and gazing lasciviously at her propellant. Gordeony, the slightly atrophied womaniser, gaped back at her ludicrously, the old romance searing his not-so-flexible arteries and agitating his still youthful but conservatively functional heart-strings, while those amazing devils of hands, particularly the one that was tattooed, leered disgustingly.

Gordeony, the once-dreamer, experienced a surging heat throughout his body, a bubbling, imperious desire to command – long quenched beneath the sober discipline of his conventional mind. His eyebrows arched, ridiculously, his nostrils widened with aggressive breath. He, the importer of glass novelties from Bohemia, felt the stirrings of a primordial and sordid will to power, a growling, turbulating obsession to shout, to stamp, abuse, humiliate, but above all to be admired, fawned upon, grovelled before. His chest swelled metaphorically with fine silk and woven braid, with flamboyantly-jewelled foreign decorations; his sternum even experienced the solid, reassuring weight of the Golden Fleece. The points of his archduke's moustache trembled in an access of ecstatic sensibility. A monocle! – if only he had a monocle, he, the Princeps of Chester Square, His Serene Highness' noble brow becoming unfurrowed and almost serene with fatuous pleasure, while they, the tiny respectful multitude, his subjects, gazed back at him with awe, with delight, with undisguised good humour, surrogately wearing some of his honour on their sleeves, their bosoms, their porters' bespeckled uniforms (bespeckled with soap stains and water and bathroom grime). And then that preposterous lady on the carpet who still ogled those monstrous hands, which ogled back at her, slipped out of her housecoat, released her brassiere bands, and revealed to the consternation of Gordeony a pair of surprisingly hirsute thighs and bristly thatch, distinctly brunette, which contrasted most unfavourably, he thought, with the bright blonde curls on her head. '*Lieber Gott,*' he groaned, as the outrageous woman got to her feet and gyrated insinuatingly towards him, the softer, lusher parts of her body vibrating unhygienically.

The fingers which Joseph Gordeony thrummed on top of his Louis Seize commode, evoking the sound of a forest full of primitive tom-toms and causing that article of furniture to exclaim with antique but wooden-like protest, echoed a pattern fantastic in its pretensions. As a boy, Gordeony had been a drummer in his high school band and, ever since, the habit of thumping out military tattoos had tended to stimulate his moments of mental involvement. That sound used to solace his anxious parent too, especially at times like exams and essay presentations, when the shrewd creased face would wreathe into smiles with the comment, usually to the household goat, that 'the *buben* is going, the boy is concentrating.' Gordeony however was considering neither the boy he had been, nor his dear departed peasant parent, nor in fact the importer that he ostensibly was. His thoughts were all directed to the Gordeony of the future, that miraculous future brought into being by the possession of those remarkable hands. Momentarily he stopped his drumming and looked at them, laughed inanely, then smacked them together with a flourish like cymbals. Almost simultaneously the doorbell rang and the smiling importer went to answer it.

'Ah, Verochka, Verochka, come in, come in,' he greeted her.

Vera, glancing at him suspiciously as he closed the door and placed an arm lovingly round her, remarked, 'You seem to be in a pretty good mood, don't you.'

'A drink, Verochka?'

'Don't call me that, please. You know how I hate it. Anyway, I can only stay a minute, Nick's out on a short call, so never mind the drink. What's up with you? I've been hearing things.'

'Things? What things?'

'*What things*, he asks. It's been going round the whole block. First the Head Porter comes to pick up a prescription and fills my ears with what a great man you are, then that Polanska woman meets me in the hall and raves about you.'

'Polanska? Polanska?'

'No, just Polanska.'

'A blonde with curly hair?'

'Aha!'

'Oh please, I don't even know the woman.'

'But she seems to know you well enough.'

'That minute of yours – it's getting rather stretched.'

'Are you telling me to go?'

'Vera, why must you? You yourself said Nick was out on a short call and you only had a minute.'

'Oh well, I exaggerated. He should be gone at least an hour.'

'In that case, sit down, relax. Vodka and cherry as usual?'

'Nothing. I want to talk with you.'

'You came to talk?'

'Is that so strange? Just because we're usually doing other things doesn't mean I shouldn't talk occasionally, does it?'

'Vera, you are right. Go on, I'm listening.'

But as she glanced at his hands, which he now made no effort to conceal, and which lay clasped over one of his crossed knees, although their monstrous proportions concealed both knee and most of the thigh, Vera was silent. A bemused expression of uncertainty caused her lips to open; an unnatural baritone groan escaped her; an unhealthy flush which began at her throat suffused her olive-hued cheeks, accompanied by a complex agitation of her facial muscles which made her for a moment almost painfully ugly, then more bewitchingly enticing than he had ever known her. The transfiguration stirred Gordeony heavily as he allowed her to unclasp his hands and transfer one to herself.

'It's what you-know-who must have felt.'

'Vera! You blaspheme.'

'No, Joseph, do not call love, the highest religion, blasphemy.'

'Love? You call that love? – manipulating my hand against your, your –'

'Yes, and she wants more.'

'So soon again? Vera, I am sorry to say this, but you are quite disgusting, and besides it is not manly for me.'

'Oh, Joseph, your manliness never gave me such a sensation.'

'Really! I'm delighted to hear so after all these years.'

'Don't be angry, please. It's not true what I said. There were times –'

'Yes, at the beginning.'

'No, even later. Once –'

'Of course! But this was better.'

'Yes, darling, I can't lie. You made me feel like a silly girl of sixteen.'

'So. Better than the beginning.'

'Honestly, I can't remember. Let me try again and I'll tell you.'

'Absolutely not.'

'Please.'

'Vera, I must go. I have an appointment with my tailor, must order a dozen suits.'

'A dozen? Why not a hundred?'

'I mean to travel.'

'Travel – you? And what about me?'

'There's still Nick.'

'Nick – ugh.'

'Vera, that's not kind. After all, he's been my friend for years.'

'Funny ideas of friendship you've got. If he knew what we do.'

'Please, I forbid you.'

'Oh, Joseph, why're you such a fool despite those hands of yours. Look, let me sit on one. I promise I'll sit quietly.'

'Absolutely not.'

'*Absolutely not, absolutely not*. That *friend* of yours kicked you out of his surgery this morning.'

'Did he tell you that?'

'Tell me? Why should he tell me?'

'Ah, up to your old tricks again ... listening at doors.'

'And why not? Everything's such a bore. I even open other people's letters, did you know that? And watch through my window when other women are undressing. Yes, yes, I'm really depraved.'

'I see that you are.'

'Of course. I blaspheme, as you noticed. I even have sexual fantasies and have to run off to the bathroom to satisfy my lust. But I swear to you, that hand of yours, those magnificent god-like hands, they answer everything for me. Once more, please, let me have one, let it do its work again and I swear I'll be good. No more peeking at other women, no more private fornication, no more listening at doors. Joseph, Joseph, I'm dying for your hand. Please! I'll scream my head off if you don't give it to me. Ah, at last – oh-h. Next time, I promise, you can be manly with me, but now – ooh-h – just let me die.'

The owner of the hands stared with a benumbed humility at those movers of his destiny which, incredibly, responded with a wink from the obscene tattoo. He rose with a shudder, went to the bathroom and plunging them under the foaming taps, reverently soaped them and extinguished Vera's powerful aroma, when suddenly they began vibrating with a new and threatening meaning. Disregarding his preference for balanced temperature, they veered imperiously to the left where the stream was hottest. So that was it, *Lieber Gott*, they responded best to near boiling water! With a triumphant cry of understanding he turned the tap on full, earning their unstinted approval as they frolicked shamelessly in the steaming torrent.

TAKEN WITH BOTH HANDS –
SWISS FRANCS 490'000

A recent visitor to our fair city, a Monsieur de Corleony, has left behind him an aura which at once is both fabulous and not entirely savoury.

What other impression can your reporter form when he witnesses at first hand the not entirely edifying spectacle of a well-known international banker, in the company of a recognized Treasury official, both attended by voluptuously overdressed ladies of unmatronly type, all vying noticeably for the favour of a rather bizarre, monocled individual with most remarkable hands. These hands, to which I draw my readers' attention, are well worth noting. They will be referred to again in later editions when, it is hoped, there will be photographs of them together with their preposterous possessor, the said M. Corleony.

Imagine the scene. The characters described are seated round a lavishly laid table in one of the most discreet and expensive of our city's restaurants. Monsieur de C, a fatuous expression on his elongated face, has raised one of his startling hands as if in protest. The well-known banker, his normally florid face flushed almost purple with a surfeit of emotion and champagne, of which three magnums still wait majestically to be introduced to the company by an obviously disaffected waiter – a secret Marxist no doubt by the way he hovers about the table most disapprovingly – the banker, I say, extends in his own hand a sheaf of papers which your reporter, at the negligible distance of three metres, recognizes as a certain very desirable issue of short-dated Japanese bonds, of handsome if not colossal value. As Monsieur continues to protest, the banker turns to his companion, he of the Treasury, and appeals to him to confirm their value.

'Are they not of such and such a magnitude, Heinz? Go on, tell him.'

'Ja, ja,' replies our man from Bern with the utmost stoniness. Then realizing that his contribution does not sound sufficiently exciting, he adds (eloquently for him): 'Monsieur, it is a very enticing offer that you are being made, merely to become associated in a non-executive way with an internationally known bank. Your hands, I mean, your duties, if we could call them so, would not occupy you for more than twenty hours per annum and, of course, are strictly honourable according to our Swiss commercial law.'

A short entre-temps follows, during which the waiter, scowling furiously, is requested to open a further two magnums. The banker proposes a fulsome toast. Monsieur, obviously a man of the world or at least a student of history who knows that, like Caesar, it is not politic to refuse such regal offers more than three times, takes up his glass in one of those amazing hands and with the other deposits securely in his breast pocket the Japanese scrip.

Although the politics of the waiter are anathema to your reporter, it must be admitted that at that moment he too shares the supreme disgust which that frock-coated minion of high society gives face to.

He travelled on. And those hands, likened by one overwhelmed witness to 'Assyrian flails', cleared the way for him through the thickets and undergrowth of conventional resistance to the opprobrious pinnacles of conventional power.

They waved themselves about at airline terminals, haughtily commandeering flights in private jets; showed themselves in distinguished places where they were slavishly gloated over; caressed objects of art and feminine pleasure which gracefully were yielded to them. An enterprising Italian manufacturer sought and won their permission, on a handsome royalty basis, to market an exclusive range of *Gloves by Gordeony*, reproducing on a remarkable simulation of human skin an artistic copy of the obscene tattoo.

They thrust Gordeony untiringly forward, jostling aside those who tried to stand in their way; and when foolishly impeded clenched themselves under the noses of those who dared forestall them, with the tattoo grimacing in frightful displeasure: flinging aside doormen, navvies, sailormen, bouncers, and other such menacing types. They opened a world to Gordeony he scarce believed existed. And they bullied their way to success: squeezing the fishy hands of financiers so hard that gifts of stocks and bonds which Gordeony never sought came tumbling in, in embossed envelopes, to his hotel suite each day. They handled the prized possessions of Arabian princes so magisterially that those dark-eyed potentates in fear and trembling would say, 'Take them.' Frenetically bustling, they carried Gordeony to the four quarters of the world: collecting rare icons in the heart of Russia, signed photographs from the leaders in the dreaded Kremlin, dazzling emeralds in the estaminets of Colombia, velvety blue sapphires from nawobs in Kashmir, fabulous rubies from the grudging hands of Sinhalese merchants.

They were photographed in seventy-two different positions by one of the foremost photographers of our day; then modelled in wax by a leading Japanese sculptor, who worked throughout on his knees in subservient idolatry; then cast into gold for the delectation of an unnamed fancier; then thrown into the melting pot because the finished result did not please 'them'.

They made themselves autocratically clear to the by now exhausted and dangerously ecstatic importer that life for them meant solely pleasure and fame, entertainment, riches and attention, fine perfume, constant manicuring and massage by female attendants, and the nightly bath administered by Gordeony in scalding foam, followed by the brutal pounding under rock-climber's boots.

They wrung the hands of dictators, presidents and prelates, village magnates and kings, commanders of armies and navies and the chief of the Israel air force. A film of them was made in Venice, called 'The Hands of Gordeony', but using spurious props, and pronounced a sham and failure at the International Film Festival.

And then, one night, after a day of excessively heavy frolic, as Gordeony lovingly lustrated his Herculean partners in their accustomed emerald green foam, and was about to commence the furious stamping, they leapt from beneath his booted feet and thrust themselves, almost cravenly, into his dressing gown pockets. 'Lieber Gott,' he giggled, 'even *they* want rest,' and staggering heavily he tumbled into bed. With unctuous affection he gazed at them lovingly as the one minus the tattoo turned out the light. But a moment later, at Gordeony's bidding, the light came on again, just to confirm what the egregious importer thought he had seen with his fading, sleep-induced vision – it was even so: the tattoo, no longer so blatantly obscene, was smiling blissfully.

When he awoke next morning in his luxurious rooms, with the imprinted smirk of those whose conscious and sleeping moments are forever gilded with fatuous complacence, his still weary legs awaiting the autonomic summons to action, he noticed, lying on the coverlet before him, not those magnificent paws which once, shamefully, he had called 'Moravian shovels', but instead his own lifeless, pallid, finely-made, undistinguished, every-day, white Gordeony hands. To this day, the screech which emanated from the Royal Suite of the Grand Hotel of D is referred to with religious awe by its soft-spoken attendants.

The gifts, of course, stopped coming. The extempore platitudes of Press and multitude were silenced and in some cases replaced by verbal assault. He returned hurriedly to London, dealing first with the threatening writs issued to him by teams of lawyers from the capitals of the world, demanding immediate restitution of their clients' mulcted property. He threw out the foam and reverted to soap and water and in a moment of insensate rage smashed and vandalized the innocent mosaic of his good friend Zdenek. He sold up his business to a venal competitor, relinquished his flat to a flat-hungry neighbour, bade Vera an affectionate but subdued adieu with a conveyed curse to Merolenko, and retired to Moravia where, last heard, he was employed as consultant to the Third Sectional Department of Czech Export, with special reference to Bohemian glass.

———————

Of Love and Dreams

Ilse

from *Emil Brut*

Ilse, the Germanic manageress, tells me we have met in another existence, many other existences in fact. Our lives apparently are paired, and this meeting too is not simply fortuitous.

I think my eyes must have become as protuberant as hers as she told me this, stroking my hand as my blood pressure dropped.

What do you do in such circumstances, and when the revelations come out in a delicate, Teutonic lisp?

'Oh, yes-s,' she said, very quietly but assertively.

She had come to my room with a book of Rilke, shuttered to the chin in a shapeless woollen gown, and exhaling a vapid but penetrating lilac fragrance.

I was quartered in her parents' house on the eve of the battle of Auerstädt, she informed me – a grenadier corporal, of all things. She was terrified, she said, and so was I. We were both only sixteen.

Her mother had harangued her on her sacred Teutonic duty: 'First decide that he pleases you, then go to him without shame and without pride. Only ask him to be gentle, because of the sacrifice you are making. And make him swear that if he lives, he will come back to you. And for the sake of your favours, let him strike bravely in the cause of our womanhood and our Fatherland.'

After this tirade, which she had naively reported to me verbatim, I burst out weeping, more than ever convinced of my doom next day. She cried too, and lay down beside me and took my hand. She even recalls my telling her that I had lost my mother the year before, and that my father was a farrier; and that most of all in the world I wanted to go to America and fight savages.

At this her mother put her head in at the door, and reprimanded us: 'What?' said she: 'still with your clothes on? And speaking of savages in America, when here we are faced by savages of a worse sort – the French? Why are you wasting the night in talking? You should be *doing*, my children, after which you will need all your rest.'

More terrible than the French to my sixteen years must have seemed this seminally-obsessed Teutonic fury. Besides, if anything, if I had *really* lived then, I'd certainly have been fighting in the armies of the Empire, rather than on the hob-nosed Prussian side. Marshal Davoût, in fact, happens to be one of my favourites.

I wanted to tell Ilse this, but the conviction of what she was saying was making her sweat round her smooth, pale-lipped mouth; and her eyes had a soft, somnambulic look which made their expression trance-like.

She dug her fingers into my hand. 'Oh, it was precious, so deeply precious, but I had much trouble with you at first. You were like a child, I had to do everything.

'And when Mother came in later, and asked: "Is it done?", and kissed us both, you turned away shyly, but then you drank very boldly of the French brandy she had brought you, and after that it was *you* who did everything. I could hardly restrain you anymore.

'Then Mother came in again, pleading to us that our cries and laughter would not let her sleep, and threatening to separate us if we did not cease. And you – I hardly know where you summoned your strength or defiance, and if I had known what you were about to do, I would not have allowed it – you lifted yourself with me atop you and struggled to your feet, both of us joined as we were, and with one hand supporting me under the buttocks, with the other you blew a kiss to Mother, who, terribly shocked, ran out.

'It was then almost morning, and as the dawn approached we examined the wondrous marvels of our youthful bodies: I, pink with the bruises your caresses had inflicted, and you still unimaginably swollen; and both of us weary and bitter with our weariness.

'From far off, we could hear the staccato of the drums, the *générale*. Then closer, on our own side, the clamour of screaming trumpets, followed by the shouts of our brave Prussian boys.

'How noble you looked as you stood in your uniform, transformed from my dear, strong Adonis into a veritable young god of war...

'I never saw you again. Your name was among the killed, but your body was never discovered on the field of battle. Together with thirty-two others in your regiment, you were awarded the King's medal, and over the burial mound of unnamed corpses, your Colonel cried – for I was there – "They died like Trojan heroes!"'

She paused and added: 'Later, I bore your child,' and allowed her dressing gown to open and disclose her pathetically tiny breasts.

'Do you remember me when my name was Adèle, and we were both French, of the *noblesse*, during the time of the terrible wars of religion, and we, thank God, were of the party of Coligny?'

Ilse had pulled her dressing gown closed, but had arranged it so that her shoulders were bare. She was breathing quite heavily now, and her words were becoming more acutely Teutonic.

I offered her a glass of Belle-Santé water which she accepted abstractedly, and while she drank it some of it trickled down her chin and throat. I stroked her gently dry with a kleenex.

'Do you remember,' she said, carrying my kleenexed hand to her breast, and leaving one of her moist hands covering it, while her face took on that beatific smile which invariably comes with self-deception, 'do you remember when Coligny called for a volunteer to convey a message through the lines of the loathsome Guise, and you, one-armed –'

'One-armed?' I interrupted lamely.

'Have you forgotten,' she said, still smiling inanely, and squeezing my hand as if in reproach, 'that your other, with its copper thumb, lay buried on the field of heroes at Jarnac?'

'Not La Roche-Abeille?' I ventured softly, which was unkind, because she became puzzled and somewhat hurt.

'*Was* it La Roche-Abeille? Oh, forgive me. I was so sure it was Jarnac.' And she bit her lip, but went on with no less certainty: 'And you, one-armed, stepped forward before all the others, and Coligny embraced you. After which he took me by the hand and kissed it, saying that I, your daughter, should fix that moment forever in my memory. As if I could forget!

'And then we waited, immobilized throughout the night until the early hours of morning, when the rich dawn brought with it the explosions of mortars and musketry and the wild shrieks of the embattled, as our forces advanced to the carnage which you, pulled down by foes many times your number, never lived to see.'

Ilse was sweating profusely now. She had flung her dressing gown completely off, her hips were even squarer than I had imagined, and they framed a fiery rosette of bright, wiry hair.

'My enduring regret,' she said, taking my hand again and

117

fitting her fingers in between mine, 'was that I had been only your daughter.'

And she took another swallow of Belle-Santé water, and paused embarrassedly as it gurgled inside her.

'It must have been after the infamous Revocation of Nantes,' she resumed again, 'that my life began in Prussia, but in a humbler way, for I remember my parents, poor but respectable innkeepers, preparing the feast for my wedding day.

'I can't remember who it was I was being married to, but what I sense, even now, is the dusk settling in around our village, and the sound of a cavalier approaching. It was *you*.

'You rode into our innyard and my father came out, saluting you; even the dogs were respectfully silent.

'You were then very much as you are now, in the full vigour of your manhood, but with an *hauteur* which I am glad you have relinquished in our present existence. Nevertheless, your face was curiously gentle, just as now, and your eyes had the same, rather hesitant humour. But there was no hesitancy in the way you addressed my father, and none in the way that he conceded your demand.

'My mother fainted, I believe. She was brought weeping to the table where the wedding feast had been laid out. And while you, our master, consumed glass after glass of our wine, my father took me aside to explain how matters stood. I could hardly tell my poor father that what he was so painfully explaining about pre-nuptial rights, was already well known to me and hardly dismayed me.

'You treated me as if I were almost your equal, and I began loving you straight away. You were so skilled, unlike the poor youth of Auerstädt, but nowhere as amorous. You let me sleep practically the whole night through. But in the morning you really recovered, and then you were splendid – a true lover, a true husband.

'I told you I would rather die than couple with that faceless bumpkin my parents had chosen for me. You tried to reassure me, making wild promises. You made me accept a gift of money and a small jar of perfume – a wedding gift only, you insisted. You kissed my mouth and breasts, and cupped your hand lovingly where you are touching me now, and then you left me, spilling tears, in my parents' bedroom.

'I listened to your booted clatter down the stairs. I went to the window to look at you, for what I knew was our last time as lovers. My father was helping you into the saddle. You turned your horse's

head about and waved to me, as I waved back. Almost simultaneously, there was a loud explosion. You looked up at me question-
ingly, and tried to smile as your mouth fell open, then you dropped
forward on your horse's neck and slid off sideways.

'I remember crying out, and seeing a man coming from behind
the stables, carrying a long, smoking carbine – my husband-to-be,
but who wasn't, for they quartered him ...'

I begged her to stop. Her psychic recollections were beginning
to make me quietly hysterical.

She placed one of her small, wet hands on my face and stroked
it. 'There were other times,' she said, 'when I was your sister, your
sweetheart, even your mother – and always you were being killed,
my darling. I shall *not* let you die anymore.'

———————

The Dream of Tenho

The shadow on the ceiling is a fish struggling through tangled, slow-moving weeds in a cloudy stream. For a long while Tenho has been watching it, exhorting it dumbly, and trying not to realize that it comes from the diffuse sunlight which projects the shape of a vase on a table near the open window, with fine tulle curtains blowing in gently: a bulbous vase with drawn-in waist just above its expanding base, and undulations of wispy green stems spilling up out of its narrow mouth and cascading down around it.

This is happening to me, Tenho thought. 'But it's a death sentence,' his own words echo back to him ... And Feldik's voice answering them:

'I wouldn't have told you if I knew you'd take it that way. You're a fool – why do you have to see everything so blackly? Anyway, there's still a chance. I'm going to help you.'

'Why?'

'Why should I help you?' And Feldik smiles. 'Maybe because I hate you that much. If you've got to die, then I want to be the one to do it for you.'

'Do it then.'

'No, not yet.' And Feldik grimaces through his smile. 'How would I live without my pet hate?'

And Feldik, still smiling, takes what looks like a woman's silver compact out of his white medical coat, trips it open and holds it up to Tenho's face.

'Breathe in, Tenho. Breathe deeply ...'

There was a photograph inside the compact, pasted over the mirror – a picture of Hedva? Tenho tries to examine it carefully since before, when he first looked at it, everything began turning to grey mist inside his eyes. But now the fish is wriggling desperately in a sudden turbulence of water and weeds as a draught from the window blows across his face, when from the far side of the room there is a sound of a door being closed, and the fish, gasping, relapses into feebler sideways movements, and the water ripples more quietly and the weeds merely sway.

It is Feldik, still in his white medical coat, and his serious face takes up the space of the fish's body above Tenho so that only its tail remains, flickering beside Feldik's ear. Tenho wants to speak, but now an insect with a metal stylet has fastened itself to the inside of his forearm. He raises a hand weariedly and puts it near the spot to warn it away, but gently, so as not to crush it. But it is remorseless, or stupid, or unalive to its danger as it bores its insidious needle in deeper ...

II.

The gardens of Deggendorf are divided into two, wide, semi-circular arcs, with violet erica in one and pink zinnia in the other. Between them there is a terraced tea-garden and a children's play-ground with miniature railway, complete with train and steam locomotive.

Hedva was sitting at one of the tables watching children getting into the open carriages. Tenho was standing by the table and smiling down at her. One of her eyelids, the left one, was trembling slightly. Tenho spoke very softly: 'Hedva, Hedva,' and she turned her head and looked up at him. With borrowed eyes, thought Tenho.

'You're late,' she said quietly.

'I'm sorry,' he murmured, and sat in the chair beside her. He began fidgeting with cigarettes, finally lit one, and blew smoke away behind him.

A waitress came up and asked for their orders. She was smiling. Tenho smiled back gratefully, because he imagined that waitresses are always compassionately pleased when lonely young women who are obviously waiting for someone, are finally joined by their dilatory companions.

Hedva's eyelid was still tremulous. He scrutinized her as she spoke to the waitress. Why did her eyes appear different? – not in colour or shape but different: as though some other soul had taken its place behind them – a cool soul, soul of a fox fairy, a naiad, a woodland spirit – not Hedva's.

'Why are you staring?'

'Forgive me, it's been so long.'

121

'Long?' She smiled faintly, barely moving her lips, only her cheeks swelling slightly. '*Is* it so long? Must you be so insatiable?'

'*Am* I so insatiable?'

She shook her head. 'Let's not talk about it. Look – at the train, those children – isn't it beautiful?' Then she turned her head and began crying.

'What is it, Hedva? What is it, my darling?'

'I don't know. My eyes begin weeping uncontrollably. I feel no pain or sadness yet they go on weeping – they seem filled with someone else's tears. I can't explain it. I'm so frightened, Tenho.'

The waitress was approaching with a tray and glasses. Hedva reached into her handbag and removed a compact. It was silver and familiar. Tenho began shaking his head sombrely as she opened it and held it up to her face. Everything then began turning black for him: blackness sweeping in at the edges swiftly ... a glint of silver in a dazzle of sunlight ... then that too engulfed....

III.

It was the sound of a train, the steady hammering of train wheels under his head. Tenho raised himself and looked about.

'Ah, good,' said the voice. 'You are awake.'

'Awake? Where am I?'

'Close to the border.'

'What border?'

The voice laughed. ' "What border!" Mr. Tenho, you must be joking.'

'No, seriously,' said Tenho: 'what day is it – who are you?'

'A dealer in clocks, watches and jewellery.'

'Really?' said Tenho, the reply seemed so prosaically incongruous.

'Yes, *really*, Mr. Tenho,' the voice mocked his with gentle amusement.

Tenho leaned forward. The faint blue light in the compartment showed him an old, ponderably fat little man with a sad, unpleasant smile. His chin appeared to be supported in a metal brace. Very decorously he began removing a business card from a wide expanse of ornamented waistcoat, and held it out.

'What is that?' asked Tenho.

'Read.'

'It makes no difference,' said Tenho, feeling suddenly weary.

'You asked who I was ...' There was a quality of plaintive, feminine reproach in the way it was said. Tenho took the card and read the heavily ornate, gothic type with difficulty: HAIM VERGLER – DEALER IN CLOCKS, WATCHES & JEWELLERY.

'Mr. Vergler–'

'Yes, Mr. Tenho?'

'–what day is it?'

'The ninth of Ab.'

' "The ninth of Ab," ' repeated Tenho abstractedly, visualizing a swarm of grey, thick-bodied moths: 'the most catastrophic day in the Jewish calendar.'

'You have not forgotten everything then; I am glad.'

'What do you mean by *everything*? What have I forgotten? Who are you?'

'But I have told you, I have given you my card – Haim Vergler.'

'Who is Haim Vergler?'

Vergler turned to look out the window and muttered something almost inaudible. Tenho shrugged, as though he had not heard and cared even less for hearing.

'We are approaching Deggendorf,' said Vergler more loudly.

'Deggendorf ...?'

Vergler began getting to his feet at the same moment that the train slowed and suddenly lurched. He swayed and seemed to suspend himself in the act of falling, overbalancing on one foot with both arms thrust out. Tenho reached up to support him, but mechanically and too slowly, and with no preparedness for the surge of Vergler's weight. His hands caught Vergler under the armpits as he felt himself being pushed heavily backwards, with Vergler's prominent belly pressed against him and their faces so close that unavoidably he breathed in the exhalation of Vergler's aniseed-scented breath.

Is it possible?, thought Tenho, as Vergler, sunk on his knees before him, felt first towards the brace under his chin, then tried incapably to raise himself. The train stopped. Tenho looked in the old man's face, and a sob that formed inside his chest moved into his throat before it dispelled itself. 'Father? Is it you? Is it you, Papa? Forgive me, I didn't know you.'

'There is nothing to forgive, my darling,' replied Vergler. And as Tenho got down on the floor and helped him turn into a sitting position, 'It is no shame for a son not to recognize his father.'

The train began pulling slowly forward. Neither spoke. Reclining beside the other on the compartment floor with their backs against the seat, Vergler had taken Tenho's hand and placed it on his thigh, just behind the knee, and pressed his own on top.

The door of the compartment opened. 'Mr. Tenho?' enquired the grey-uniformed official.

Vergler squeezed Tenho's hand in warning and answered quickly, 'Here.'

'Mr. Tenho, I am arresting you ...'

Something glinted in the top of Tenho's eye: a hard glint as though a metallic splinter had imbedded itself in the cornea and was glinting inside it. The compartment began filling with a choking, blue haze; the gun in the official's hand thundered and shot flame.

'*Shema –*' groaned Vergler, his head falling sideways.

He squeezed Tenho's hand imperatively. Tenho understood. With steady voice he closed the short invocation: '*Yisrael, Adenoi Elohenu, Adenoi Ehad.*'

Vergler's eyes remained open: his lips trembled as though they were trying to form the holy words themselves, or add a blessing, when the gun thundered again ...

IV.

Tenho thought: I am lying on a bed in a room which is half in light and half in darkness. There is a man standing with his back to me, slightly bent; I think he is working over a table. I seem to know that man.

The ceiling slopes like those in rooms at the tops of houses, and it is quiet here, so quiet that I can hear the trickle of a water tap and the light tinkle of metal against glass, or other metal, as that man makes his preparations. What preparations?, I wonder. Tenho raised his head and the man looked round. Was it Feldik?

'Ah, you are awake.'

Tenho nodded: his head seemed almost too heavy for him, as though he had just roused himself from a long, unnatural sleep.

'Where am I?' he asked, sitting up.

'At Hedva's.'

'Hedva? Madame Vergler?'

'Yes.'

'You *know* Madame Vergler?'

'Yes ...'

That second *yes* had the sound of an obscene caress. Tenho thought: Ah, Hedva, Hedva, you'll be sorry.

The man walked round the table and sat behind it. 'Tell me,' he said with mock ingratiation, 'are you fond of guns?'

Tenho smiled despite himself and shook his head.

'Here is a gun,' said the man, lifting it off the table: 'look at it. A pretty gun, a famous gun, the maker's name is Warbach – a famous maker of guns.'

He pointed it at Tenho, aimed carelessly, then released the trigger and laughed. There was no fire but a shot-sound came from the far side of the room.

'Again?' Again there was a shot-sound without fire. 'Pretty, yes? Did I frighten you?'

Tenho felt a greenness go through his chest. Why *green*, he wondered, why *green*? He was sure that if he bared his chest, there would have been a green aura over it, like corpse light.

'Did I frighten you?' the man repeated.

'Yes, you frightened me. That was an unpleasant trick.'

'Unpleasant? Do you find fear unpleasant? – Here, take it. Shoot at me.' He threw the gun over and it struck Tenho's knee. Tenho grunted painfully.

Yes, curse you, I'll shoot, thought Tenho, picking it up. He aimed and the gun moved unsteadily in his hand. Then remembering how he had seen it done once, he balanced it on his raised forearm and squeezed the trigger. A long spiral of flame flared out of the barrel: it seemed to loop itself round the papers on the table before it swept up along the coat lapels of the seated man and set his hair on fire.

'Help me, help me ...'

'Help you?' said Tenho, getting up languidly. 'You shouldn't use so much brilliantine.'

He walked leisurely over to the water basin and soaked a towel under the tap. Then he draped the towel over the man's head and drew the ends tight round his throat. He did this for only a moment though, because the elation of doing it made him tremble with an unnatural pleasure.

What am I doing, he groaned. Why did I strangle that towel round his neck? I thought I had buried my hatred. Will I never learn – will I die, hating too? Why does this repulsive creature, this gun player, make me detest him so? Is it possible he knows Hedva? Hedva, darling, where are you? I need you –

'Where do you keep the brandy?'

I can hardly bear looking at him, even with that ridiculous towel on his head. Why did I think he was Feldik? Can a man wear another's face?

'Yes, I see it.'

His temples are frizzed, that large burn makes him even more grotesque.

'No! Don't touch my hand. Take it off! Careful, you'll spill it. Slower, slower you – you'll choke. Don't gulp so.'

Hedva, where are you? Hedva, it's so dark here – why don't you come? Why don't you come!

'What?'

'Forgive me.'

Tenho shrugged.

'No, it was a poor joke, but it's I who have suffered.'

'You? You were only burned.'

'Yes, but I shall go on suffering.'

'And I?'

'You! You are almost dead.' This time the voice was really Feldik's.

Tenho stared at him and felt the greenness agitating his chest. He tried to speak but it seemed to be entering and closing his throat.

'You are Tenho Vergler?'

Tenho nodded.

'Did Hedva ever mention someone called Exersen?'

Tenho nodded again. His voice came to him through a thicket of fungus. 'Yes, there was a doctor called Exersen at the death camp of Deggendorf. You are him?'

'Yes. And you are a Jew?'

'Yes.'

'Curse all Jews.'

Tenho's heart began beating erratically. 'Listen –'

'Yes?'

'– I, who've never killed anything knowingly, will kill you now.'

'I am waiting.'

'With your own gun.'

'Go ahead, Jew.'

'First, I'll burn all the brilliantine off your head, and when it's gone the fire will smoke your brains.'

126

'Ha. Will you frighten me? I've said better things in my time. You're a tyro.'

'What have you to do with Hedva?'

Exersen smiled sorely. 'I'm her husband.'

Tenho choked. 'It's not true.'

'Why isn't it true? How do you know it isn't true?'

'B-because – I think she's *my* wife.'

'You think! You dare to think that? Listen, Vergler, Jew, if you say that again I'll smash your testicles between my fists. I've done it to others.'

'Y-you won't terrify me.'

'No? Listen, then. Did Hedva tell you that her father was in my camp?'

'Yes.'

'And that he lived?'

'Yes.'

'And do you know why? ... Because, like the little merchant in the fairy tale, he promised what he loved best in all the world, next to his own skin: his most prized possession – his white, untried daughter. He purveyed her as a conscientious butcher purveys his meat: limb by limb, organ by organ. And the beast, his amorous tail beginning to twitch, paid heed, paid heed and smiled, because he knew something the little merchant did not know: that the day of the fairy tale was almost over, that its enemies were coming even then with impious hands to destroy the sacred grove in which it blossomed – and stank.

'And the beast rose on his hind legs, for all the world just like a man: and the powerful scent of love led him straight to his destination outside the camp where, in a pretty little hut, traitorous hands hid the fair, untried daughter. But the beast, like a beast, laid about him and discovered her, discovered too what untried daughters always pretend to hide but are itching to show. Do you hear, Tenho? She is my wife by first possession – I deflowered her.'

The greenness was pulsing through Tenho's arms and legs, slowing his blood and changing it to chlorophyll. Exersen was grinning, his lips had dropped away to expose all his teeth at once. He raised a thin wooden rule from the table, Tenho could see the glint off its metal ferrel. With delicate precision, as if performing an exact operation, he laid the metal edge against Tenho's neck, drew it back, then struck viciously.

Even in that instant Tenho knew, with the pathetic certitude of rooted plants, that the blow was irremediable. He wanted to weep at the cruelty of the sound – a sharp, brittle cracking – but his head had gained free movement and was falling, rushing downward with the despairing speed of its shamefelt mutilation, while beneath it the earth was tearing itself asunder with equal desperation to ensure its unimpeded fall through the blackness...

V.

Tenho thought: I seem to be in a long conduit. I think I'm suffocating, it's so narrow here and filled with water, and I'm floating, somewhere, down this copper conduit, with soft shapes gliding past me, stroking me lovingly, and I want to touch these shapes and stroke them too, but they elude me. I am so filled with love for something, for everything. I want to tell God that I love him too, but I can scarcely breathe ... only if I keep my head near the top.

VOICE You are in a conduit which leads to a fish-processing plant. At the very end, it may be that the operator who controls the first machine will notice your irruption into it, but by then it will be too late, you will be unrecognizable. Those shapes which glide against you are fish: they too are being pulled inexorably forward. Have you any questions?

TENHO How did I get here?

VOICE There are suction valves. You were thrown overboard from a small boat with weights on your feet. The person who did the weighting tied the knots very clumsily. The weights slipped off, close by the suction valves.

TENHO Is there no way out?

VOICE No. Only into the machinery.

TENHO How long before I reach it?

VOICE A few moments.

TENHO If I hold on to the walls?

VOICE Try it.

TENHO No. No I can't.

VOICE You see?

TENHO Won't you help me?

VOICE I cannot help you.

TENHO Why?

VOICE I cannot answer.

TENHO Listen –

VOICE I am listening.

TENHO Who are you?

VOICE I shall tell you: you will never reveal it. I am, can you guess, the God of fish.

TENHO No!

VOICE Why are you laughing?

TENHO I am *not* laughing.

VOICE Then why do you grimace?

TENHO Now I'm laughing. There is a God – a God of fish? Forgive me.

VOICE Yes.

TENHO Tell me – what does a God do?

VOICE A God watches.

TENHO Only – watches?

VOICE Creation de-energizes the creator.

TENHO I see –

VOICE *What* do you see?

TENHO A woman.

VOICE Where?

TENHO At the beginning of the machinery. She waits to receive me with wide open legs. She suspends herself in front of the machinery.

VOICE Yes.

TENHO Make me smaller.

VOICE And then?

TENHO I will swim into her vagina.

VOICE You will suffocate.

TENHO Then as God of fish, give me the gills of a fish. Can you do that?

VOICE That is one of the things I can do.

TENHO Do it then, please. Now, now! I believe in you, I believe. There is a God, a God of fish. Hedva, Hedva, receive me, my darling ...

VI.

Tenho stands in a deep, airless tunnel, the walls trickling water; beneath his feet, the ties of disused railway tracks. In the long distance he sees a faint greyness – an exit, or an entrance? He walks forward, stumbling, but the nearer he approaches the greyness, the thicker it becomes. He stops to listen – there is a far-off roaring along the rails. A train? No. It is darkness.

Light travels in the world of life, darkness in the world of darkness. Light has forsworn life to burden darkness, the world is dead. Tenho, my dear, my sweet Tenho ...

VII.

Hedva stands at a window looking out over rooftops. Feldik enters the room and pauses; she turns to him without speaking and he shakes his head. She tries to weep but her tears will not come. Feldik's voice is low and condoling as he says, 'Too late, we were too late.' He admires with aesthetic appreciation her silky well-coiffured hair, as a random filtration of sunlight gives it a gleaming aureole. Now he is so close to her that he can breathe in its aroma and sensuous freshness as he whispers, 'But it was a beautiful death. So quick. I envy him.' Hedva closes her eyes as if in thankfulness. When she opens them again, Feldik has taken her hand. They begin to walk from the room and Feldik's arm encircles Hedva's waist. She does not seem to resist, either hand or arm, she leans lightly against him.

Mathilde

So I came to the land of the Groads, and as it was nearly nightfall, and cold, one of them made me welcome.

'What we have to offer is little, but you may share it if you wish.'

I thanked him, and walked into his cottage. The Groad children watched me silently: two girls with abnormally large eyes. They had been eating something from the table, but it was so dim inside it was difficult to discern it. A curtain at the end of the room was drawn to suddenly and apparently inquisitively, and a splash of weak light aureoled a woman's head: the Groad wife, probably: but she glanced out for a moment only, and the curtain swung loose again.

'Pray, sit,' said the man, indicating a stool at the table, opposite the girls. I did so and smiled at them, but their faces remained expressionless.

'It is very cold outside,' said the Groad father, then sighed. 'But, of course, it's always cold.'

I nodded. It was a fact. It required no added comment. There was a creaking of bed-springs, and another figure emerged into the shadowy light.

'That will be my elder daughter,' said the man. 'Mathilde,' he called softly: 'please, come here.'

The girl approached. She was about fifteen. Like the others her face was pale. Her hair hung down in untidy strands.

'Mathilde, a visitor.'

She nodded and stared, her acknowledgement a mute acquiescence.

'My children speak little,' said the man. 'You understand?'

I smiled tolerantly. Of course, such things I had heard.

'Are you coming from a long distance?'

'Not long,' I replied. 'Only over the Grey Mountain.'

'The Grey Mountain,' he mused, with a wistfulness that

seemed to compass dreams: or a nostalgia that betokened a vaguely happy memory. 'Supper will not be long. Perhaps you will be good enough to join in?'

'I shall be most happy and honoured.'

He smiled. 'Not honoured – surely, not honoured. It is very mean fare.'

'It will suffice.'

'Suffice? Oh yes, it will suffice. It is filling. It swells the belly. Mathilde!'

She stood by me.

'Let the gentleman feel your belly, how swollen it is.'

I protested, saying that I believed him, yet he insisted.

'Only feel it. You will be surprised.'

I did so reluctantly. Sensing my own embarrassment, I expected to sense hers, but she was utterly indifferent. I felt through the coarse dress.

'Yes,' I said, 'wonderfully swollen,' then took my hands away, adding inanely: 'but so warm.'

He beamed then became solemn again.

'That alone can I give them – warmth. You noticed. I am glad.' He leant near me and whispered, 'Later, when it is time for sleep, I shall ask Mathilde to go into your bed and warm it.'

'Believe me,' I said with hot discomfiture, 'there's really no need.'

He smiled. 'No, no, good sir, you misapprehend me. I did not mean that she should linger there and lie against you: only that she should get in in advance of you. Our beds are cold.' He shuddered. 'Very cold. It is only we who know how to warm them. And you, a stranger, would undoubtedly suffer. To carry away with you such a memory? It could not be endured – least from the land of the Groads.

'Tomorrow, you will pass from us into the sun. You will think back. Perhaps, you will speak of your experience to others, and say: "I came through the land of the Groads," and they will look at you with marvelling incomprehension, and ask: "But were you not cold?" And you will reply, as I expect you will reply: "No, certainly not, although it was a land that a man could only despise –" No, good sir, do not protest: it is but the truth. "It was such a land," you will say, "but yet its people were warm." Will you not say that, good sir?'

132

I bowed my head as a sob erupted with my breath: tears came to my eyes. The Groad children gazed at me with a rapt, answering sympathy: this was what they understood best.

'Do not weep, I beg you.'

He placed a hand upon my shoulder, and the stillness of its touch calmed me. Now that I had entered their compact of misery, the atmosphere brightened.

The Groad girls came round the table and stared at me shyly. Mathilde came too and bent her head, inviting the kiss which I pressed on her cheek: but how cold it was, though I said nothing. An almost ashamed clattering followed from the kitchen and the Groad wife entered the room, balancing on either arm a platter of potatoes and one of wild forest mushrooms. These she laid on the table, retreated to the kitchen, then returned with a cylindrical loaf. We took our places and silently we ate, feeling for the platters when the light receded and night came on.

It was filling, indeed. Sometimes hands touched other hands groping, and when this happened there was stifled laughter. What a curious meal! I shall never forget it.

The Groad father lit a small lantern and placed it upon the table. How it intensified their features – like a chiaroscuro painting. The Groad mother with pools of liquid darkness in her hollow cheeks. Mathilde, her face diffusely rounding in outline so that I could see her as she might become, a woman neither plain nor attractive, but with a staid feminine sweetness. The children, their eyes grown even larger in the distorting light: Mathildes-to-be. And the Groad father, an unmoved shape, caught in a shadow world familiar yet hateful. We sat there and soon, as there was nothing further to do, we prepared for sleep.

Mathilde was in the bed when I came to it. She had relinquished it to me for the sake of hospitality. The others appeared to occupy a larger bed in a corner of the room.

She began moving instantly as I approached, her father's lantern in my hand, but I protested: 'Please, stay there. I shall be very comfortable on the floor.

'*Believe* me,' I urged her unavailingly as she began sliding out, barely displacing the blankets, and then pressed me down with surprisingly assertive hands, pulling the coverlet up to my chin, and lingering there.

'Now, I shall go,' she whispered, enunciating her first words, then suspending the lantern over my head she stooped quickly and returned the kiss I had given her earlier.

The lantern went out, a moment passed.

'Mathilde,' I said softly, 'are you still there?'

A hand brushed across my face: I caught and held it.

'Do you wish me to stay?'

'I wish you only not to be cold. This is your bed. I feel remorse for having deprived you.'

'You have deprived me of nothing. To us all you have given much. Tomorrow, when you are gone, there will be only Groads in the land of the Groads.'

'I shall come back.'

'No! Once is enough.'

She began shivering.

I whispered: 'Mathilde, don't, please, misunderstand me. But you are cold. Come into the bed. Together we shall warm each other the night through.'

'Yes, that is good. But it is so narrow, we shall have to lie close. Will you not mind?'

'Certainly not. But don't spend time talking. Come in – quickly.'

I opened the blankets as she slipped in, almost without sound. All around us there was silence. Did they not know? Was their silence a pretence merely? Yet there were no protests, no movement. It was almost as though they approved it.

Her body was icy. At first she tried to lie away from me but the bed was too small, and before long she was in my arms. A relaxed drowsiness came over me as her legs entwined with mine.

Some moments went by and I thought that she slept when I felt her voice moistly against my ear: 'Are you warm, are you getting warmer?' while her moist hand stroked my neck and shoulders.

'Yes, my dear one, I am warm and getting warmer.'

'You will sleep now?'

'Yes.'

'Will you not fondle me, just a little, that I remember this night longer than others?'

I caressed her as tentatively as she caressed me and when I ceased, because the sound of our sighs and the bed-springs in the midst of that quietude inhibited me, she said: 'I shall remember this always, all the years of my life. Will you not fondle me more?'

134

Then, sensing the absolute sanction of that surrounding silence, I pressed all of her to me as we succumbed to our passion. We fell asleep embraced, but when I woke, in the grey light of morning, I was alone.

The Groad father came to me smiling.

'You have slept well? Serenely?'

'Both serenely and well.'

'You will be leaving us now?'

'Yes – perhaps to return.'

'Return? No! You will not return. Only remember, dear sir, that in the land of the Groads you were warm.'

'I shall not forget.'

'It is well then.' He turned and called: 'Mathilde?'

She came, carrying a canvas wrapper. Her face was grave and soft, almost as I had visualized it in the light of the lantern.

'Some food for you on your journey,' he said. 'Mushrooms and bread. May it suffice.'

'It shall.'

I emerged into the morning mist. Other Groads, bent beneath large burdens, were walking their way. I turned back with tears unashamedly filling my eyes.

'Thank you for the kindness you have shown a nameless stranger.'

'No, it is to you who have brought kindness that thanks are owing. Mathilde?'

She smiled and gracefully lowered her head.

I passed from the land of the Groads.

Laura

That's what I call the electro-chemical mystery of sexual intimations, communicable over short distances with mutually devastating effects.

I first became aware of it when I was fifteen, I think, and my perplexity about a mathematical problem led me to consult the Archimedes of our form, a certain girl called Laura Lindman with whom I'd established an ogling liaison. She had an inexhaustible supply of fuzzy angora sweaters through all the colours of the spectrum, and the essential pectoral architecture to give them shape, a shape which when I filled my eyes with it brought wistful parallels with *The Song of Songs*.

Her father did abortions for the financially unembarrassed, or so I heard, and skilfully removed his daughter's carbuncles which had a morbid way of reappearing regularly on her rounded cheeks. I had the temerity to phone her that Saturday afternoon, and ask if I could come round to get help with my problem. She said yes, if I wanted to, but to come right away.

I ran.

On the way, I realized I had forgotten to bring the scrap of paper with the problem on it, but assumed she'd be good-natured enough to overlook the omission since, probably, she would have a copy of it too.

She opened the door and asked why I was breathing so heavily.

'You said, come right away,' I explained, 'so I came as fast as I could.'

She dipped her eyelashes gracefully and smiled inside her eyes.

'I left the problem at home,' I added, 'but it's number four on the list we got yesterday.'

'Too bad,' she said. 'I didn't bother taking it. I finished the paper in class.'

I noticed as she spoke that her sweater was the sunniest gold I had ever seen and couldn't help admiring it, although it exuded a sickly perfume which made my nostrils almost grimace.

'Is that you?' I asked stupidly, 'or the natural fragrance of Angora rabbits?'

'What?'

'The perfume.'

Her bottom lip twisted like an archer's bow.

'Shall I run home again and get it?'

'Do as you please.'

'But what do *you* want me to do?'

She stared at me in a rather curious way, shrugged her athletic shoulders, turned and walked from the entrance hall where we were standing, into a sitting room where I followed her, sat down on one of the sofas, took a cigarette from a box, put it in her mouth, lit it, and began choking. Then she stifled the cigarette as I stifled an hysterical urge to laugh.

'Well?'

'Well, what!' she said, sounding irritable.

'Shall I go get it – you know, the problem.'

I think she was on the point of saying something rude, instead of which she shook her head exasperatedly and frowned as I sprawled into a chair.

'Tell me once and for all what you want me to do and I'll do it,' I remarked inanely.

She then became articulate again and said she didn't care, saying it as though she meant it, and for moments I believed her until I noted that her eyes were opened rather larger than usual, which gave them a baffled air - a quality I learned to heed in female eyes. And while she prattled on, reiterating her indifference to whether I stayed or went, and I replied with throaty rumbles rather than with words, I think we both sensed we were carrying on two conversations which each belied the other: one through our mouths and the other through the mediation of our eyes, since mine, I felt, were growing as baffled as hers, whether in wonder that she was teasing or testing me, or in amazement that I hardly heard anymore what she said but wanted her urgently not to stop, so that I could continue watching and enjoying the lines of her sensuously moving lips, and feel my arms and chest and legs burn with forty different shades of heat, which tingled or paralyzed me in different places, and made the skin around my nose irritatingly dry, and kept me swallowing frequently and far too noisily.

And when it struck me that that look in her eyes was probably the symptom of a bodily reaction similar to mine, which disturbed her perhaps and kept her desperately speaking, I rose and tottered slowly towards her as a half-enunciated word, waiting for its final syllable, remained suspended on her lips.

I recall her shaking her head and raising one hand as though to discourage my coming, but when I placed my own hand, palm spread flat to hers, matching finger up to finger, and stood there almost acrobatically, poised on one foot and leaning forward, she put her other hand round both of ours and drew them towards her.

I made myself twist sideways, taking care to fall on my hip alongside but barely touching her, and throwing out my free arm as though for support round her shoulder.

I half expected she would break away or make some protest, instead of which I felt her hand and arm glide through the opening in my shirt and circle round my disbelieving back. I was so overwhelmed by the generosity of the gesture that mentally inert I waited for another, but nothing followed; and I leaned my head behind her ear and began pulling strands of her hair between my teeth and lips, thinking, 'What next? What do I do next?' And all the while we spoke not a word to the other.

She then began leaning away from me, as though to break the hold of my arm on her shoulder, but as the arm was resistant to disengaging, I succumbed to the momentum and collided against her, gasping in surprise at the sudden conveyance of her heat and aromas: lying now face to face with noses almost touching, eyes opened wide, staring amazedly at each other, and breathing through our mouths.

I remember smiling at her encouragingly, but she seemed still baffled at how it was happening, and her forehead wrinkled wonderingly. Then she made a small sound, almost like a whispered laugh or laughing sigh, and pressed her mouth to mine, moaning softly, and I echoed it. I felt her saliva float in between my lips and her insistent tongue caressing mine and attempting the impossible feat of entwining it, while her saliva, or mine, or both, filled my throat as I swallowed it.

Then finally, happily I confess, her mouth fell away and I swallowed again, with an alienly new though strangely pleasant taste, while she, shaking her head somnolently slow as though in bewilderment that it was still happening, blinked her eyes like a blissful cat, with her arm still round my back but moving subtly downward, fingers probing along my spine then lying flat and still then probing lower; while I clumsily tried to force my hand inside the waistband of her jeans until she released the critical clasp that held it. Then, as her hand seemed to linger uncertainly above the base of my spine, I sent mine to fathom the intricacies of her underwear, despairing almost that it would ever reach its goal, when some hidden access to her flesh exposed itself and my hand plunged nimbly forward and came to rest on something it had never touched before. It felt like a miniature head encased in springy down-like hair, and as soon as my hand made its incredulous deduction, scarcely believing its good fortune, the head began shaking and butting convulsively forward, like a suckling calf against its mother, till it filled the hollow of my palm and the tips of my fingers made discoveries of their own, when one of them, searching deeper than the rest through the dryness of that maze, released a creamy flood amongst them all so that they almost slid away before they found themselves again, rhythmically stroking and fluidly penetrating amazing organic folds which I longed to place my mouth against. And meanwhile I found some part of her where I could stroke myself in unison, when I heard her exhilarating though surprising groans and my own muted answering sobs and the sound, far off, of a door being closed. She had to pull my hand away and push me roughly before I grasped the urgency of her alarm. I've never seen anyone move more quickly or adroitly as she fastened her jeans, smoothed her sweater and hair and almost savagely slammed a large book on my lap just as her mother came in.

She must have suspected something, I'm sure, but she merely nodded at us and said 'Hello' in what I thought was a disapproving way, then walked across the room into the kitchen where we could hear her moving about unnecessarily noisily, and Laura whispered: 'She's making tea. You'd better go.'

Except for a faint flush above her eyebrows and on her rounded cheeks she seemed as cool as though she'd just emerged from a refreshing shower. I wouldn't have minded the tea and perversely told her so, although the thought of facing her mother across a table was too unnerving to consider.

'Good-bye,' she said inflexibly, leading me to the door and opening it, then giving me a push through the doorway.

'Can I borrow the book?' I asked.

'Keep it,' she replied, and I did – I still have it – one of her father's antique medical tomes, he must have missed it, a treatise on anatomy by Realdus Columbus, the man who claimed to have 'discovered' the clitoris. I didn't grasp the irony of it until years after.

Then I walked morosely home with the book held in front of me with one hand, surreptitiously tasting the fortunate fingers of the other.

She wrote me a note and handed it to me on Monday morning, as I waited for her outside the school, then she ran into the building hurriedly. I read it in the street, after which I tore it into tiny shreds and strolled round the block distributing them in units every ten feet or so. It was the briefest note I ever got. It read, without salutation or signature: 'I'm not blaming you for what happened on Saturday, but I don't want to see you anymore.'

In fact, I saw her every day afterward for the rest of that school year, but never alone and never again with that baffled look in her eyes, although I've seen it on others.

The Mulberry Tree

He promised to stop dreaming when he was ten, and his mother had said to him: 'Remember, you promised.'

He promised again when he was twelve, and as she handed him his birthday gift, an illustrated text of *The Thousand and One Nights,* and coolly kissed him, she reminded him of his other promise and asked if he had kept it.

Pained at her remembering and pained too by her interrogation he nevertheless answered with defiant honesty.

'No, mother, I haven't.'

'Will you promise me now to stop dreaming?'

'If you wish it.'

'I *do* wish it.'

'Then I shall.'

That night, as he sat up in bed reading the first of the marvellous tales, he felt his pleasure riven with sorrow. Why had she been so cruel as to exact that promise? Why in almost all that she asked did he feel bound to comply?

Yet two years later she was dead, and pleasant as it was to go and live with his sister, who loved him dearly, he experienced a fearful need to obey.

Her face as she lay dying had been serene yet severe, as though with her last breath she sought to retain a socially acceptable composure even in death. Yet at the very end the severity had wavered as she appeared to stare at him with reproach. Reproach for him and all that remained living while she must disintegrate? Or reproach for him and his unconscionable lies which the prescience of death had revealed to her?

To dream for him had meant vision beyond sight; to feel himself impervious to men; to walk in the deep of the sea or soar to high mountains; to delight in images of love denied to him; and afterward to send his soul through the vastness of space to discover *hers,* kneel before it, declare passionately: 'See, mother, by dreaming I have *found* you again. Please, please, let me go on dreaming.' Yet directly she had answered: 'How *dare* you? You promised!'

To promise with fingers crossed behind one's back is a child's device for undoing promises. He had promised so when he was ten, and wilfully again when he was twelve.

As though she were there, gazing sternly at him, he tearfully begged for forgiveness.

'Mother, I *do* promise now. Really, I do. And swear to be true to it always.'

That evening, as she gave her husband his supper, his sister could not contain her surprise.

'I can't believe it,' she said animatedly. 'Such a change! Why, he's totally different today. So alert and aware when he's always been brooding. I do so hope it lasts, yet I feel rather anxious. It's as though he's suddenly aged.'

'You make too much of it, my sweet,' he chided her. 'After all, he's still but a child, and you' – and he fondled her tenderly – 'who are not much more than child yourself, perplex your brain too deeply. But here's the changeling himself, so let's be speaking of other things.'

The years of his adolescence sped away. His face harmonised into pleasing lines but tinged with a precocious melancholy. Academically competent, he passed his exams and prepared for university.

It was late in the summer, on an August day of foreboding heat and unnatural stillness which his sister would never forget. It seemed to her, she mused, that the sun was taking its vengeance of earth for all the millennia of man's evil. Her husband gazed at her in surprise but said nothing, feeling the absurdity of her comment unworthy of reply, yet feeling too that first cleavage in communion of shared lives, as though there had been revealed to him some alien aspect of her he had never imagined. It was not too dissimilar, he thought, although the comparison was grotesque, with what one of his friends in a state of morbid drunkenness had disclosed about his own wife: the unsightly mole that lay in the crevice of her thigh and which only the luxuriance of her pubic hair had long kept hidden. And he found himself disapproving of his wife in the way he disapproved of her brother.

The object of his distaste was then wearying himself at his desk with his books and notes. From time to time he had declined his sister's beckoning calls from the garden to come down and relax with a cooling drink. And when she appeared in his room with a tray of sandwiches and tea, and earnestly begged him to stop and rest, he smiled his thanks in his solemnly attractive way and promised to break off soon. Yet an hour later, abstractedly nibbling at bread, he was still engaged at his task.

It was at the period of heaviest heat, just as the village clock chimed six, that an unbidden idea came into his thoughts. He was twenty now. He had lived his life twice over exactly from the time he was ten. Two lives, in fact. And now he determined that as long as he lived he would measure the span in terms of ten, and count himself richer than others for living more lives than they.

The novelty of it, with its intimation of mystic power, gave him a thrill of pleasure, as from the garden below there came the domestic sounds of plates and glasses being gathered together, and the jarring voice of his brother-in-law: 'One doesn't necessarily believe what one thinks, does one? Do you? Do *you*?' and his unpleasant laughter.

One day soon, he thought, he would liberate her, she among all living whom he loved best. But now an urgent need overwhelmed other sentiments as he thrust aside his books and rose swiftly, went to his bureau and from beneath a stack of laundered shirts withdrew the copy of *The Thousand and One Nights*. There on the title page, penned in an immature hand, were the words he had inscribed when he was twelve: *Men of dreams have made this book, and I too will go on dreaming.* How pitiful! For beneath it he had added a mere two years later: *If dream I cannot, others must do so for me.* And with quiet approval he murmured, '... others must do so for me.'

How wise the boy of fourteen had been, how foreseeing of the future. And *she*? Was she aware of the pledge he had made and kept these many years? And was she grateful for it? 'Yes, mother,' he addressed her as of old and nodded to her framed photo on top of the bureau and held up the book for her to see: 'these are my dreamers now.'

A short piece up the road from his sister's house led to a pleasant glen where occasionally that summer he had joined her and her husband in their evening outings. He informed her now of where he was going, promised to be back in time for supper, and set off cheerfully with his book.

He walked hurriedly till he reached the glen and its prime attraction, a magnificent old mulberry tree; then plucking a few of the delightful fruits from the lower branches and pressing them sensuously between his teeth, he settled himself with his back to its stalwart trunk and began to read.

But soon he felt overcome by a great heated weariness, and allowing his torporous body to follow its own inclination, he rolled over and came to rest on his back. A sense of almost absolute peace penetrated him. It began with an icy tingling in the soles of his feet which flowed deliciously through his legs and trunk and radiated out to the extremities of his fingers. How glorious, he thought, I seem suddenly become oblivious of heat; and crossing his arms beneath his eyes he gazed at the foliage-traceried sky through the blur of his eyelashes and the fine hair atop his wrists.

And consciously he dreamed – a dream so real it was more vision than dream, so magical it was resistant to reason.

He saw himself in a verdant valley, at least he didn't see himself at all but merely knew he was there. Without stirring he could feel the momentum of his pacing legs; with vision and senses extended he could observe unfamiliar trees and plants and inhale their intoxicating fragrance. The sound of a stream was nearby and at length he came to it, and felt his hands braced in its swift current and his throat eased by its cool water. It was mid-afternoon and all that he heard was the buzz and shrill of myriad insects, so when it came to him from anear the music had a remarkable clarity.

It was as he turned in the path that it rose to a delicate crescendo and ceased, the notes of a shepherd's pipe in accompaniment with a voice of penetrating languor.

The musicians were two. An old man seated cross-legged on the grass and with a white flowing beard, and a girl on her knees beside him. As he paused uncertainly, the man beckoned him on with his pipe.

'You are very late,' he said. 'I suppose you have been wandering.' And the girl, who appeared no more than thirteen, smiled at him with her dazzling teeth.

For want of anything to reply, and in his indecisiveness, he first shook then nodded his head and murmured, 'Sorry.'

'Sorry? There's no need of being sorry. A boy must wander, as a girl must wait. She,' and he stroked her head fondly, 'has long been waiting. It is well you have come.'

At the man's bidding he sat near to them and then, as he thought, incuriously odd, they stared at one another with critically examining eyes.

He, the old man, seemed vaguely familiar, though it bothered him little that his identity was elusive. The girl was otherwise. She, he felt, was totally unknown, and it was on her that his glances most repeatedly fell. The other, noting this, smiled with a grimace of mock satisfaction.

The girl was astonishing in her icily remote attractiveness. Her hair was flaxen almost to whiteness and hung in heavy coils about her face. Her face was full and round with a hint of plumpness, and agreeably defined by the line of her chin. All the features were delicate and small: nose, mouth and especially the ears which he could discern through the coils of her hair. Her skin was startlingly white save for the flush round the outer corners of her eyes. The flush intensified as she smiled and, as he would learn, when she felt emotion. But her eyes were her most dominant feature, not in shape or size but in colour, a deep cobalt-blue. Medusa eyes, he thought them, as he felt himself almost paralyzed in their stare. The eyebrows, in consonance with her general complexion, were pale, almost indiscernible. As their glances crossed he knew, by the wonderment in his, that he was enthralled.

'From gazing,' said the man at length, 'one comes to understanding, and from understanding to friendship.' And rising suddenly he moved off sombrely into the wood.

Taking his hand, she said to him, 'Now we are alone. Are you pleased?'

'Yes. Oh, yes!'

Her eyes sparkled in child-like triumph. 'Then come, I have much to show you.'

But as they rose to their feet she withdrew her hand brusquely from his, and he, startled by the transition to coldness, felt an alarm of despair.

Lying beneath the mulberry tree he groaned.

For now she was as distant as though they were strangers, and yet, he reasoned, were they not strangers in fact?

So he strolled beside her, sorely troubled, while she, distrait in her mood, ignored him.

They walked for some time in silence when all at once she took his hand. 'See!' she declared, and smiled with her dazzling teeth. 'All this is mine. These trees, these pathways, these flowers, the very birds that live in the trees – by my grace. This stream. All mine. My inheritance.'

And she dug her sharp fingernails into his flesh in her exultation.

'Come,' she said, still smiling and turning coquettishly to look up into his eyes. 'Race with me over my domain.'

145

Her small feet seemed to fly over the ground and, agile as he was, he found he could scarce keep up with her. Her short white frock plumed fan-like behind her, and in play he attempted to snatch at it while she, glancing round and noting what he was about, shrilled with laughter as she accelerated her pace. Then willing him on by waning in speed, she allowed him again to snatch at the plume, only once more to burst away with a shrill of laughter. Over and over she tantalized him this way.

Tireless as she was, however, and tireless as he discovered himself, she now halted suddenly, stared at him as though again stranger he was and icily demanded: 'Who *are* you? Why do you follow me? Go away. Oh, *go* away.'

And again beneath the mulberry tree he groaned.

The afternoon deepened, the voices of birds sounded, and along the dappled paths he trod alone, brooding on her. Then through a clump of alders he saw the old man.

'I see,' he remarked coldly, 'that you have lost your companion. Have you been wandering again? There, that way,' and he pointed. 'Straight ahead. She waits. God knows why she waits for *you*.'

Unstung by the reproach in his gratitude, he saluted his thanks and then, as if impelled into flight, ran wildly forward.

He heard her voice, raised again in languorous song, and stopped to listen, trying to distinguish the words.

Yet as if sensing his nearness her voice ceased, and in silence he advanced till he saw her, seated on the steps of a rustic cottage.

She rose as he approached and smiled her dazzling smile, and allowed him to take her hand and kiss it. How small it was, how delicately veined, yet the strength of her fingers in his astonished him.

'Well, are you pleased?'

'I have *found* you again.'

'And does it mean much to you?'

'If only you knew!'

Her eyes widened with pleasure as the flush round them deepened in colour.

'Come,' she said, bemused with delight, 'I have made you your supper.'

They ate without speaking. He at least had no tongue for words. Which words after all could convey the eloquence or confusion of his feelings? The food itself, pallid though pleasant, was of a kind he had never savoured, yet to examine it, he felt, would be betrayal, for in itself it had meaning as his first shared experience with her.

Yet words or thoughts in disembodied form were reflected in their oblique glances. How daintily she took her food and chewed it. He himself was unaware he had eaten, until smiling she asked if he wished for more. Then smiling too he said it was sufficient and thanked her, and praised her for its excellence.

He half-feared now that there would be a reversion to her coldness, and lying beneath the mulberry tree he felt a cloyingness of earth penetrate his back. How reassured was he then when she took his hand and led him without, bade him sit beside her in the doorway of the cottage, and even leaned her head against his shoulder. So overwhelmed was he, he seemed to be dreaming in his dream.

Now as if in response to the birds, which commenced their evening melodies, she too began murmuring in song in a languorous voice. Her head swayed gently on his shoulder in rhythm to the music as her body, respiring to its demands, rose and fell against his side. He, enraptured, leant his face close to hers and marvelled at the purity of her breath, and marvelled too that her song though unenunciated in words brought understanding.

She removed her hand from his and stood. 'You who have been slow in comprehension are so no longer. It is well, yet sorrowful. For remember, whatever comes to pass, *you* are to blame. Stay now. I shall return.'

He waited, unbelieving that she would return. The sky, brilliant with stars, grew swiftly darker. The air chilled in an awakening breeze.

Then he heard light footsteps in the near distance, and lying beneath the mulberry tree he sluggishly shifted his inert body.

Her face in its severity seemed now older, as she led him indoors and showed him his room. 'Here you will sleep, and I bid you goodnight,' and she left him.

But moments after he had undressed and stretched out on the bed he heard her footsteps again, and after a hesitating pause the sound of his door being opened. Even in the summer darkness he could discern her dazzling teeth as she approached and the startling whiteness of her body.

As her arms enfolded him, and her breast and lips pressed to his, he felt that all disbelief, all evil, all suffering, had ended, and that he lay within the gates of paradise. Again and again in their unsubduing passion they yielded their bodies throughout the night, and even at last as they slept their insatiable limbs clung twined together.

Was it she who now raised her languid head yawning, displaying her white brilliant teeth and pink tensile tongue which she used to moisten his lips and ears as she caressed him? Was it still she with cobalt-blue eyes and the flush around them roseate as sunrise? She with lyre-like pelvis and thighs? Her face and body were no more a girl's but those of a young nubile woman.

He gazed at her amazed through the fringe of his eyelashes.

'Rest on till rested,' she whispered in his mouth, 'then come, beloved, and we shall bathe.'

In sensory stillness he stared at the beams of the ceiling through the traceried foliage of the mulberry tree.

They took their breakfast in silence together under the gloomy eyes of the man with the beard. He it was who brought them their fruit and bread and waited on them at table, from time to time seeking to deflect her glance from his and furious each time that she ignored him, while they, engrossed in mute wonder of the other, smiled with smiles near detached from their faces.

Today she wore a waisted frock of deepest red which fell to her ankles. Her coiled hair she had dressed in a loop at the nape of her neck with a ribbon of black velvet.

The new day was like the old, save that the leaves of various trees had turned to autumnal colours. From high in the branches a thrush warbled urgently to its mate. Unintendingly he heard their voices from within the cottage, hers modulated and subdued, his raised in unseemly protest. How increasingly familiar yet still elusive that voice to him seemed.

'We have come to an understanding, father and I,' she said as she emerged and the old man followed. 'He and I will spend a few hours together. You,' and she beamed with her dazzling teeth, 'will wander meanwhile and wait.'

Now he traversed over different paths, striding, half-running, with hands clenched and fingernails sunk in his palms, mouth grimaced in despair, and remorseless legs beating in a violence of movement that agonised his breath: circularly, as in a maze, unseeing of the trees he grazed against, directionless, frenzied, seeking collapse through exhaustion and obliteration of his thoughts.

Yet it was not weariness that halted him but the meeting on the path with the animal of lemur-like face, which leaned on its haunches as it curbed its speed and gazed in startlement at the curiosity that barred it.

Like adversaries they confronted one another, until in its spherical eyes he saw wonder turn to fear, and gallantly yielding his place, stepped to one side and spoke to it.

'Friend, go forward in freedom. The world is yours,' and outstretching his arm, bidding it on, he applauded it gravely as it sped past his feet.

He wandered now in introspection void of thinking, stopping sometimes to listen, sometimes to turn and gaze watchfully behind. The sun arched to the meridian. The air from moist changed to dry. Then he saw it, amid a huddle of saplings, majestically foliaged, heavy with fruit. A mulberry tree! He could scarce believe it.

In deference he approached and tentatively stroked its bark and unaccountably began weeping, then sitting with back and head to its trunk, face in sunlight, he slept.

He awoke to a persistent shadow and a tapping of light fingers on his brow, and opening his dazzled eyes was greeted by her dazzling smile.

'You,' he exclaimed. 'It is *you.*'

'Were you expecting another?' she coyly asked with a single syllable of derisive laughter. 'I see you have discovered my mulberry tree.'

'I thought I had lost you.'

'*Did* you,' she said, raising her pale eyebrows. 'And did it perturb you? I, at least,' and she yawned, 'was quite pleased to be alone.'

'Alone?' and he scowled. 'I understood you to be *not* alone.'

'That doesn't concern you!' she vehemently flared as the flush round her eyes deepened to crimson.

Again she had aged, or was it the sun which now wounded with shadow the clefts in her cheeks he had not seen before. In the warmth of the weather she had unwaisted her frock and exposed her shoulders and the slope of her breasts. In reproach they stared at one another until she in discomfiture turned away.

'Your ribbon is gone,' he remarked softly, viewing her in profile and noting the disordered state of her hair.

'My ribbon?' and she felt for it dazedly and then in despair. 'Oh!'

'Shall we look for it?'

'Look for it? No. It's a trifle.'

'A trifle with value, it seems,' and he smiled.

'What?' and she gazed at him with blank remoteness in her cobalt-blue eyes, then leaning with head bent over and step of a somnambulist she began searching about.

'My ribbon is gone. Have I lost it? My lovely black ribbon –

149

where can it be? Here? No. There – was it *there*? I know, now I know, it was taken!' and she smiled with her dazzling teeth.

Now she threw back her head with hands beneath her neck and stood gazing up in rapt immobility as languorously she sang:

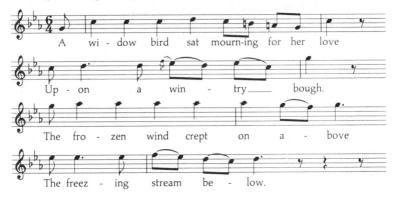

A wi-dow bird sat mourn-ing for her love
Up-on a win-try__ bough.
The fro-zen wind crept on a-bove
The freez-ing stream be-low.

He listened enchanted, charmed as much by the melody as the music of her voice, and the disturbing familiarity of the lines by Shelley. Who *was* she who knew of the susceptibilities of his youth so well? Why must she stop and not continue?

Now she stood before him and said to him gently: 'You have known sorrow this day. I, too,' and her cobalt eyes filled with tears. 'Yet why sorrow? The dream will soon be over,' and kneeling she kissed his lips as her hair encoiled him in its flaxen curtain and the moisture of her mouth frothed into his. Then embraced as one they lay beneath the mulberry tree, as he lay beneath his.

For a while they sank into a serene half-slumber. Each growing thing – tree, blade of grass, filament of lichen, plant – seemed as impaled in unliving stillness. Gradually his eyes opened and gazed at hers, inertly shaded in their flaxen eyelashes, then gazing lower he drew in his breath.

'You have a sign there,' he said, as her eyelids separated as somnolently as a cat's: 'like someone I knew;' and delicately he touched the coppery boss on the pillow of flesh above her left breast.

'Have I?' she murmured, as drowsily she watched his caressing forefinger. 'Have I? Why, so I have!' she exclaimed delightedly and pressed her hand on his. 'Come,' and she rose, drawing him up with her, then suddenly she trembled. 'Did you hear?'

'Only thunder.'

'Quick,' she said, as she drew her frock over her shoulders and her white skin bleached in internal pallor.

Where there were shadows there was sudden darkness; where penumbras an opaque bluish mist swirled in. Between the trees, like miniature flashes of lightning, fireflies darted. The very air seemed menaced with being.

'Quick!' she said once again as a light rain commenced, and grasping his hand in hers, with fingernails biting his flesh, she began running.

As possessed as she in her frenzied haste he followed her, both coursing like animals pursued, mindless with panic.

A clap of thunder sounded from above and halting she shrieked and tore herself from him.

For time extended he stood in bewildered silence, staring into the impenetrable darkness, until hearing light footsteps approach from his right, he called, 'Is it you?', when the footsteps ceased and a mocking voice answered, 'Is it you?'

Now from behind the footsteps began as he whirled about and called once more, 'Is it you?', and again the echo voice mocked, 'Is it you?'

Lying beneath the mulberry tree he started in dismay.

Then, 'Yes, it is I,' the voice came nearer. 'I, the betrayed, I, the widow bird, mother and daughter.'

Now it was he who tried to avoid her, she, revealed in the returning light in the familiarity of age, with hair uncoiled into strands of rain-soaked grey and cobalt eyes bleached to palest blue.

'Will you disavow me?' she said and smiled with her dazzling teeth as she drew him towards her. 'You cannot, you know, nor a tyrant be. Oh, if you could slay for me!'

'That and everything you require of me.'

'Obedient as always,' and she pealed with laughter. 'If only it had been!

'See – behind every tree there is a tyrant, behind every tyrant his female prey. Will you slay for me all the tyrants of this earth – with your breath, with your eye? Or can you death repeal that dead may return to avenge their own?

'Come,' she said as the bluish mist lifted and dissolved in a sapphirine glow.

The rain had ceased. The path again dappled to sunlight. In the branches above the voices of birds chanted in languorous song.

Now she too began murmuring in song, and taking his hand pressed it to her ribs as languidly they stepped in pace to the rhythm.

Was it the illusion of his senses or the resurgence of warmth which made the strands of her hair re-encoil in their flaxen lustre, or the unnatural light which deepened the blue of her irises and restored the flush round the corners of her eyes? His hand grew moist as it moved in hers to enclose her right breast.

'*You* –' she exclaimed as she paused to draw in her breath – 'can you? – who have known, and now know me – can you *still*? Then it's *I* who am at fault for what's come to pass – not you.'

'No! You are without fault, as without peer.'

'Am I, indeed,' she remarked sadly as his left arm encircled her waist.

Now they walked in silence embraced, he with face sloping down to her hair, inhaling its flaxen freshness, she with hand pressing his to her breast.

At length they saw the old man with the beard, massively immoving amid a shrubbery of mallows. With one hand upon his heart, with the other he pointed. 'Go without fear, without remorse. You have triumphed. Go in freedom, for it is yours.' Where he stood a sudden darkness replaced him, of textured bark-like form, before it dispersed into voidness.

The shadows lengthened. The air was tinctured with the evening scents of plants. High above a thrush warbled and was answered by its mate.

When they came to the mulberry tree they were yet embraced. She it was who separated them as she gazed at him mournfully.

'The dream is over,' she said. 'The day is ended. The time for us to part has come.'

Then mournfully too he shook his head.

'Disobedient?' and she raised her pale brows as the flush round her eyes deepened in colour. 'You must dream no more of me.'

'I cannot *live* without dreaming.'

'Can you not?' and her cobalt eyes diffused with tears. 'And if dreaming mean dying? –

'Then place your hand on mine on the mulberry tree and say with me: "It is here that I come for love and peace. Here I shall remain."'

Lying beneath the mulberry tree he saw again her dazzling teeth as darkness came.

Reports

For Being Albert

Will you believe me? – I *said* that to him. And do you know what he replied? –

'Wake me up when it's time to die.'

'How shall I know when it's *your* time?' I asked him. Then he was so still he might have been dead already. 'How shall *I* know?

'Albert,' I said, and went over to his bed and shook him. 'Albert?'

The windowman came by again and put his pendulous nose in between the bars. 'Alright in there?'

'Yes. Alright.'

'Remember ... if there's anything you want ...'

He kept his nose there, as though trying to snuff up part of our remaining time. I wanted to say 'Go away' but didn't. A minute later, after he'd gone, I could still see the outline of his white nose dangling there, seemingly fumigating our combined smells, mine and Albert's.

His face was cold, and when I placed my hands on his chest and belly there was no trace of movement, heart throbs or belly rise. He'd fooled me that way once before; there's a name for it, but it's a rather unique condition. If he was shamming, as I thought, there was a way of finding out, but I'd never thought of trying it before. I hesitated because I was embarrassed – social inhibitions at a time like that! Well, I'll test you, I'll test you, I thought. I put my hands lightly on his genitals. 'Albert?' I whispered. Then I pressed down hard. He jumped so violently that I could hear the bones jangle in their sockets.

'What are you doing?' he moaned. 'O God, I wanted a tender communication with God.'

'You frightened me,' I said. 'Why did you have to frighten me that way? I wouldn't have touched you otherwise. You seemed dead, I was scared –'

'Why should my death disturb you?'

'I don't want to be alone.'

'Is that a reason?'

'Isn't it?' I reproached him.

'Here it's no reason – here or anywhere.'

'What was that shouting?' It was the windowman again. 'Why are you shouting in there? You woke me. I was asleep and I heard you shouting. I was dreaming.'

'It wasn't us,' I said. 'It didn't come from here. Probably some of the others –'

'What others? There are no others.'

'We, the only ones?'

'Yes, they're all gone. It's only you two now. Why did you shout?'

He stared at me.

'It was I,' said Albert. 'A nightmare.'

'Really?' said the windowman. 'A nightmare? How strange. You a nightmare and me a dream. What was your nightmare about?'

'A woman.'

'Tell me,' said the windowman.

'No.'

'Please? Shall I get you twenty-four hours more … shall I? If you want I'll get you twenty-four hours more but you must tell me your dream –'

'Nightmare.'

'Alright, nightmare, but tell me …' His preposterous nose was twitching almost, so big yet twitching like a tiny insect's antennae, and Albert smiled.

'Do you know,' said Albert, still smiling, 'in every one of our lives there is a woman, a very large white woman, she is so large that when she stands, we, who stand before her, reach only to her pubis.

'I stood before this woman, this gentle white-skinned goddess, with her triangular garland of parched, russet-coloured hair. I looked up along the line between her small, wide-spaced breasts and she looked down at me: a moon face, placid, with pale lips and large, pale eyes, so soft, so softly did they look at me; and that same russet-coloured hair fell straight from the top of her head, silky and loose-hanging but full, and vaguely gleaming. There was a fragrance from her: a lightly-scented, cow-like, mother-like, fragrance: my breath was full of it; and I wanted so much to touch that soft flesh and hair, to stroke it, to feel it with my lips, against my eyes ...

'She understood me, she nodded: so slightly that it was not a nod but a subtle acquiescence. I looked down again. At eye level my sight was filled by that mound of russet hair, those almost unfathomable hips, those immense white thighs. I spread my arms as wide as I could to embrace them, merely reaching with my out-spread fingertips to where they began to swell and turn. I pressed my lips and eyes into that whorling russet hair and kissed it. – I was a boy only, a young boy in that nightmare, and I could feel a large, soft hand enclose the back of my head, and press it gently forward when I began to weary in the strain of my outflung position.'

'And then?' asked the windowman.

Albert shook his head. 'That's all. It was over.'

'That is why you cried out – because it was over?'

Albert smiled.

'But why do you call it a nightmare?' asked the windowman. 'Surely it was not a nightmare but a beautiful dream?'

'Does one have beautiful dreams in a place like this?'

'No,' said the windowman, 'you are right, nothing here can be a dream. And now that you remind me – my dream too was nothing but a nightmare.'

'Tell us,' said Albert.

'You really want to hear?'

'Of course,' said Albert.

'Of course,' I added too.

'Well, if you really want to hear ...

'I was standing before a deep hole in the ground. It was like, well, very much like a pit, dark, you couldn't see bottom. And I stood over it and the sun was shining, in my dream – my nightmare – and suddenly I could hear sounds, strange sighing sounds. What is it?, I thought. Is there something sorrowful coming up from this hole, this dark pit?, and I waited.

'It was in the yard, the fortress yard, and the buildings stretched four-square around me. But it was empty – no guards, no movement from behind the barred windows, even the pennon hung slack. And there was I, listening to that strange sound, trying to peer into the hole, and feeling the sun burn the back of my old, dry neck. Then a wisp of green came up out of the side, moving, slender and green and almost shivering with life, and then more wisps – two, three, eight, ten – I began counting them till I couldn't anymore, because it was like a jungle, a matted jungle of wisps of green, each pushing, pulsating, thrusting up out of the hole so that you couldn't see it anymore – the hole – and then they began spreading out fanwise in every direction, moving across the cinders in the yard. And I stood back, very perplexed and angry too, though I hadn't seen green things since I killed my first calf on the farm. And they began to scramble round my feet.

'They were cool, very cool, icy actually, as though they had come from some deep wet place, and they tangled themselves round my boots until I moved away, slowly at first then quickly when they began to follow me. And I began running, fast, shouting the alarm as I went, but there was no answer, no sound other than my choked cries, just the swish of this remorseless grass slithering along the ground, sweeping up the cinders with it, wriggling like snakes. I ran and ran and wherever I ran it ran too, and there were other black holes in the ground, I almost fell into some of them, and they too were erupting with wriggling green snakes –'

'And then you heard a cry,' said Albert. 'You woke.'

'Yes, exactly.'

'But the cry was your own.'

'The-cry-was-my-own? – Yes, I see. But of course, you are right. The cry was my own. That is what I heard – my own cry.'

'Yes.'

'I think I prefer your dream.'

'Undoubtedly. But you never could have had such a dream, just as I could never have yours.'

'Why is that?' asked the windowman, genuinely puzzled.

'Because dreams, like lives, are not interchangeable.'

The windowman's nose seemed to grow longer. 'But it's not fair,' he protested. 'I, who never dreamed like that: I, whose dreams are always of dark holes –'

'Dark holes? Always like that?'

'Yes.'

'I'll tell you what,' said Albert, 'I'll exchange my dream for yours.'

The windowman looked incredulous. 'But that's impossible. You yourself told me –'

'You don't understand. Of course you never really could have dreamt my dream, but is there any reason why you can't possess it?'

We both stared at him, clear-headed Albert talking like a precocious madman. 'But it's simple,' he said. 'First, do you remember it?'

'Of course, who could forget it?'

'Very well then, it's yours. You will try by an effort to make it even clearer in your mind, and I shall repeat it to you, or write it down, and you will absorb it until it becomes part of you, so that one day, instilling the wish that it really happened to you, you will come to believe that you dreamed it.'

'Are such things possible?' asked the windowman.

'Yes,' said Albert, 'but you must will them so, will it daily, hourly, then it will come. And I shall take over the burden of your pits, your dark holes.'

'Such men as you,' said the windowman feelingly, 'should not die.'

'How much time have I?' asked Albert, so abruptly that even I was startled.

And the fool replied without thinking, 'Tomorrow, before sunrise.'

'Why *before* sunrise?' asked Albert angrily. 'Why not *at* sunrise, or after?'

'It is traditional,' said the windowman stupidly. 'You asked, you should not argue. I myself do not wish it, am in fact against it. It is beyond my power.'

'Your *power*? But you promised me twenty-four hours if I told you my dream! *Where are my twenty-four hours?*' Albert screamed.

He ran to the window and struck with his hand at that intruding nose between the bars. It should have flared blood, broken itself against the bar, as I expected it to, instead it just winced, went over on one side and straightened out slowly, whitish-looking and not quite in its original shape, almost but not quite.

I know it's a remarkable thing but that was my impression, and it is impressions precisely that you have asked me to give. I don't wish to appear disrespectful, but if you have stayed in a cell as long as I have, with a person like the said Albert, you do not grow in objectivity. All that is mentioned in the protocol. I didn't mention the nose because it seemed of no relevance. I was in fact ashamed of the matter, of having even seen it. There was something lewd about it. If we wore our genitals on our faces it would be different: it was just like that in fact – forgive me. The windowman is a special case

159

however. It is to be regretted that such men are born, but they serve a function – as I serve a function. I beg your pardon. The digression was only to highlight an incident which, even now, seems to me to be entirely without point. I thought I could illuminate it by speaking of it but it has eluded me, the 'illumination', I mean. I shall resume.

'You promised me,' screamed Albert. He turned to me. 'You heard him too, didn't you?'

'Albert,' I replied, 'take hold of yourself. The man has no authority. He had no right to make such a promise – isn't that so? And what is this magic anyway of an extra twenty-four hours? Can it make any difference to you in this sunless place if you die now or a few hours from now?'

And all this while the windowman said nothing, only now, finally, a pinhead of blood glistened at the end of his nose.

'Do you prize the stench our bodies make so much, that you want to relish it another twenty-four hours? Aren't you sick of it? A few minutes ago you were calm, I admired you. I wanted to emulate you. After all, I have to die too, don't I?'

'Do you?' he asked with ironic sympathy. 'Do you *really* have to die too?'

'What makes you say that?' I retorted.

But he turned to the windowman again and shook his fists on either side of that imprisoned white nose, which still hung there like a tired obscenity.

'Listen,' he hissed, 'listen you, you putrescence, you took the beauty of my dream and gave me the coarseness of your lavatory pit in exchange. You took my white giantess and gave me a filthy hole. You insinuated her out of me by promising me twenty-four hours more. And now you think you can have *both* – my dream and your lie? But you won't! I'll tear them out of you!'

The windowman nodded. If he hadn't, I should have thought him somehow dead, more dead than he usually was. It was then that I gave the signal. I hardly noticed him being removed, nor, I think, did Albert. I hope his end was not prolonged, that his neck was merely broken in some quiet corner.

Albert calmed down after that. He went and lay upon his bed and appeared to fall asleep. I woke him at two, as instructed.

Perhaps I'm mistaken in thinking him asleep. If he was, it could only have been a very light sleep since he seemed to rouse himself with very little effort, and speak that curious dream-like monologue which I found embarrassing even to listen to, but perhaps it was because he was muddled by dreams.

'Listen,' he said with abstract intensity, 'the messenger has just reported a terrible injustice to God on high. Immediately the directives are given. The messenger is handed a scroll, already inscribed and embossed with a large seal, he hurries gratefully from the throne, down the hundreds of steps, past the hundreds of distinguished people and there, near the grand entrance where stand the mild-faced guards, he pauses, and some of the urgency of the matter seems to leave him. A great weariness comes over him as he reaches the portico. Wordlessly he hands the scroll to one of the guards who, compassionately, drops it into one of the great litter bins which at first sight had appeared to him as giant ceremonial bowls.

'And now, his weariness having transformed him also into a distinguished person, the messenger turns and walks solemnly back into the great hall and, as he advances, the assemblage makes room for him, and the women smile gravely and flaunt their shapely breasts at him; and as he passes, some, by manoeuvering dexterously, impel him to brush against these erotic prominences. For a moment he is startled, the thought of that message still dying in his brain. He sees about him men and women with memoryless eyes and memoryless smiles, who use their hands not for exhorting just causes but for stroking one another. And as he feels himself capitulate he hears a long, protesting cry – like the one he gave when he rushed in so indecorously: an hour ago, a day, a week ago?

'He turns and looks down the centre of the great hall and there, as him before, is a youth walking, almost running, with wild appealing eyes and arms stretched out before him: and courteously the concourse makes way. He feels that he should observe this new messenger more intently, but around him now there is an exquisite shuffling, as countless well-bred feet give protest to the tedium of a same-again performance. Among the mixed assembly, opposite now turns to opposite, and where there are no opposites same turns to same. Against his diaphragm and thighs he feels a warm insistent pressure, and with his eyes and breath acknowledges the buxom young woman who smiles appreciatively at him, whose warm arms firmly encircle him as he clasps her too and melts in the moisture of her beckoning lips.'

For a moment Albert stopped speaking. He turned the palms of his hands upward and gazed into them, one to the other, as though they contained some previously hidden revelation. Then he clenched them and pressed them between his knees, as old men do. Still possessed by his morbid rhetoric he went on.

'It is the way life is ordered in heaven and on earth. It is dreams which come to one when the age for dreaming should have long been buried. It is twenty-four hours more to inhale the sweetness of one's decaying armpits. It is the pleasure of prolonging pain against the somnolence of death.... Everything that breathes is capable of intelligence, only death is stupid – and dumb. Do you know, even wharf rats come out to admire the moon?'

And then he stared at me and when I stared back he laughed. 'Tell me,' he said, 'shall I be brave when I die?'

I shrugged.

'Well,' he persisted, 'what do *you* think? You who have been with me for three weeks – a long time under such conditions. And they say that a man reveals himself at such times – whether he is weak, despicable: whether he is strong – all of it comes out. What do you think? Shall I meet death bravely?'

'What does it matter?' I answered, 'how a man dies.'

'*A man has only one death,*' he chided me. '*That death may be as weighty as Mount T'ai or as light as a goose feather* – which shall mine be?'

'I don't know,' I replied. 'We are not living in the days of public executions, so what does it signify? If the hammerman sees fear in your eyes and knees do you think he will strike less hard for that? Or if you look at him with contempt, or indifference, or hatred, or even pity, or cry out in terror – will that soften his heart? No. His duty is fixed – to strike, to end a life; it is prescribed. And even if he strikes you an oblique blow, will it matter to him that he has prolonged your agony? No. He knows simply that he must strike another, and even then –'

'Yes,' he said smiling, 'even then?'

'Even then, if you have a semblance of consciousness – and do you know, some of them with their skulls cracked open can still stare with amazement – even then the hammerman, avoiding all ordinary human sensations, must kneel down and deal you the slash of mercy across the throat.'

All this while he watched me, almost without expression,

162

almost as though without hearing, and the same smile hovered on his face.

I said to him, 'Albert, the answer to your question is that you will die bravely.'

'No,' he protested mildly. 'Simply because I can listen apparently unmoved to your tale of horror, does it follow that when it comes I shall be equally unmoved? I may attend such a thing as an onlooker, or act in one – with a cold, dry heart. But between the hammerman and his victim there is only the hammer – an abstraction at rest, a density which receives direction, violence and purpose through the act of momentum. It is from this that the victim cowers, not from him who deals the blow. I may be immune to the menace of other men, but not a piece of flailing matter, when it's matter that kills.'

I went to sleep shortly after and slept soundly – such talk invariably wearies me – and even as I woke I knew he was no longer there. After his last soliloquy he said little of consequence, little that I can now remember. Everything that he spoke of I have mentioned, everything, that is, of relevance, and even of the irrelevant, the unintelligible – to me, like the reference to the obscurantist Kafka and his 'impossible crows'.

I am a trained recordsman, my duty is to recall. I mention this because I wish to speak of a conjecture, mine alone. By some manner, intuition perhaps, the prisoner Albert came to sense my role, and yet I am sure that I said or intimated nothing.

'No, you said or intimated nothing. You did your duty well.'

'Forgive me, what you say is altogether in my favour, but –'

'Yes?'

'I was presumptuous, there is nothing more. Yet, if you are satisfied with me, may I ask a question?'

'Go on.'

'A foolish question perhaps, but if I do not know the answer it will bother me all my life.'

'Then ask it.'

'How did the prisoner Albert meet his death?'

'How do you think? – Like an animal!

'At first he came out into the square of the fortress yard and, to look at him, seemed quite unaware of why he was there at all – perhaps the shock of being aroused so early in the morning. He followed the hammerman meekly enough, as though he were some

163

kindly guide. When he was told to kneel he began weeping, choking rather, it took three of them to halter him, and since he wouldn't stop his bawling they stuffed a pad in his mouth. When the hammerman swung his instrument back you would have sworn that his imprisoned tongue had leapt into his eyes, they practically bulged with speech. And then the hammer fell, a good clean blow, the thud of it seemed to bounce off the fortress walls. He sank without a word – naturally, with that pad in his mouth. Curiously enough, while the brain matter oozed down one side of the smashed head the eyes remained open – those same, dumb, animal-like, beseeching eyes. Then the hammerman bent over and split his throat. Finished. Any more questions?'

Buonarotti's Neighbour

from *Notes* of Emilio Ludi

They say this age of ours is of the greatest, and our City of Flowers *primus inter pares*. Let them rave, the raw gullets, the brazen-lunged ninnies: the Arno will wash out their grandiloquent lies.

The merchant Petrucci, that unamiable fool, that sycophant of the high and mighty and self-proclaimed 'slave of the arts', he whose sister it is said gave birth to a goldfish (is it to be wondered at? – she whose physical adornments would be contemned by a self-respecting frog!), he took me by the hand, not a fortnight past, at the Port'a San Gallo, and beseeched me on the pain of his honour to take up residence in the fine airy studio he had built next the workshop of the Santa Maria del Fiore, blessed church. I demurred, pleading on behalf of my antique bones that their attenuated condition rebelled against any change from their familiar, if evil, situation in the Mercato Vecchio. Yet the more I protested the more he insisted, smiling his inane gap-toothed smile (may those gaps be stuffed with the droppings of our Duomo pigeons!), till I, ancient fool, acceded, acquiescing finally to his blandishments of my 'imperishable creations'.

Peace there was for a week, and the campanile of Maestro Giotto soothed occasionally my aching eyes, till it began: a small tentative chipping, as though some benighted rodent with iron teeth were testing the resistance of a new and formidable stratum of rock. The folio of Messer Sergio moved almost perceptibly under my arms, the flask of vermilion shivered within its alabaster shell. Then it ceased. The still Florentine night filled my ears again. *Bone Deus, bone Deus.*

I raise the elongated peacock feather, dip into the vermilion and focus my eyes within a nose-length of the folio page.

Nowadays the feather moves with the haltingness of my senility; my eyes water with the concentration, my nose drips. I have to steady the sweeps of my inclined feather-fingers with a controlling left-hand index finger – I, Emilio Ludi, scribe, illuminator, artist on vellum: I, who once would take deep breath and draw with unerring brio the full circumference of a circle in one swift continuous flourish; crescents with the ease of crosses, and ellipses; the breasts, bellies and buttocks of nubile women with the casual inattention of a mother hen laying her eggs: I, Emilio Ludi, bearer of an illustrious name: Ludi – Enrico: scholar, poet; Ludi – Federico: soldier, martyr; Ludi – Ippolito: miniaturist, lover; and I, the last, the painter on vellum, the sufferer with bad bowels, foul breath, gas. Again, that chipping! May a rain of turds fall upon his head, that cursed Petrucci, that smiling hypocritical whore-monger, Jew! He promised it would be quiet here. Quiet! It is as though a horde of demented rats are scuttling about a mortuary of disintegrating stone. That dust! Holy Mother of Satan, where comes it from? How can I draw a simper on the face of a saint when I cannot breathe? Ah, it is going – *bone Deus*. Yet what is that which now stumbles about, sighs heavily, moans? *Chip, chip, chip.* May you chip yourself into the fires of Hell! Ah, at last, silence.

It has been going on for over a year, the apothecary Landucci informs me. *A great work of art,* he avers, his stupid eyes wrinkling devoutly. I propose that we exchange places, he and I, that in the munificence of my bounty I will yield up to him my honoured and fortunate location and accept in return the lowly hovel that is his, but he glances about slyly and hurries away, saying he must complete an entry in the Diary he is keeping.

Today, yesterday – memory fails me – a creaking of pulleys, the hoarse cries and bellows of labourers, the cursing of a high-pitched, arrogant, eunuch-like voice. I send my slut to summon the merchant – thirty-three silver scudi!, plus the pitching and screaming as from the depths of purgatory. Today, yesterday, when the pulleys pulled, the eunuch wailed, and the labourers groaned. And Messer Sebastiano? He was engaged, nay, ill: his left knee was being cupped. May the Devil cup his addled brains into a privy!

She, my stupid slut, stood there retailing this gossip, all the while looking more stupid: great stupid eyes staring at me over her mountainous breast. 'Madre de Dio, calm yourself.' *She* tells me this. 'Maestro Emilio, I conjure you.' 'And I, to the fires of Hell would conjure *you*, were I a necromancer.' 'Santo Spirito,' she cries: 'is it possible?' I have gone too far, too far.

'Come to me, my pretty one, mia chiocciola (the black vomit stirs in my gut at this idiocy). Forgive my evil distemper. Come to me.'

She smiles – it is always the way with them. She approaches – the floor creaks beneath her weight. From the other side there is silence: purgatory is listening. She loosens the silken lattice-work between her mammalian appendages and introduces one of my skinny hands therein; there is barely space. I feel my cheeks becoming flushed and foolish as my palsied loins tremble.

Vile am I and too antique for these gymnastics. My heart scarcely beats, my legs have turned to stone. I hear the eunuch's high-pitched voice and some adolescent boyish shrieks as well. So he is not a eunuch, but one of *those*.

May 14, anno 1504. Today there was such a movement as of Aetna loosening its bowels. The walls shuddered and cracked, and Santa Serena to whom I was applying the point of a lance at her left breast, received the thrust in her right nipple instead. They have demolished a part of the workshop wall of the Santa Maria del Fiore to get the monster out; the din and dust asphyxiate me. I lie suffocating, awaiting the sweet release of Death, but the subtle trickster denies me.

Peace at last. They have drawn the monster away on greased planks. Slowly it moved, so I am told, yoked to the backs of forty strong men with cables.

I emerge into the streets at night, near where it has been temporarily halted, and there encounter and converse with other furtive citizens, fellow sufferers I discover, plain decent people for the most part but here and there a notable savant, all of whom, like me, innocent neighbours of the Santa Maria del Fiore, have endured the torments of the chipping eunuch. We release our envenomed bile by collecting and hurling stones at the monster, until our exultant cries bring out the guardians of the night, and ourselves fleeing in all directions. Shrieking with the laughter of our merited catharsis, we embrace those who remain nearby, and bid each other a night of blissful undisturbed sleep with undisturbed days to follow.

She, my slut, has gone to the ringhiera to witness the unveiling. It is a colossal figure of some ancient hero, says she, or perchance a Hebrew king: a youth of sombre countenance but with such delicious-looking lemons, as the lewd girl calls them, that she could sink her teeth into them.

If eyes other than mine should ever read these lines, then prithee, prying stranger, know how fortunate thou art to live in an age when disturbers of public sanity and peace exist no longer. Better far for thee to live at a time of puny achievement: that at least will ensure thee quietude.

NOTE.

The incident of stones being thrown at Michelangelo's *David* derives from the *Florentine Diary* of Luca Landucci (1450-1516), although the culprits are not identified.

Valedictory of
Gabriel de Marignac

The waiting is worst of all: the waiting ... and the stench. I would never have believed that men of our class could smell so.

Beneath the window they are playing dominoes ... pathetic posture of sang-froid: it will be played out to the end. There is even one who laughs continually, a Gascon with three noses rolled into one, a veritable Guesclin of the South ... he would look well in a hauberk ... how came he to be born in our age?

Gaiety is de rigueur ... how could it be else? ... we men of lineage ... who would exchange our birthright at this moment for the veriest of them who show their soiled bottoms through the rents in their breeches.

I am twenty, I have barely lived. On that glorious day when I knelt to receive the colours of our regiment from Her Majesty, I secretly stroked her august gown. I have enjoyed the favours of one woman only, twice, and the first time was a fiasco. Poor toy, I shall never play with you again. Again, that stupid sound of forced laughter.

My last July ... One of us said that we are like gods because we know the proximate date of our deaths, because we know the future with a certitude not given ordinary men.

They have taken Comte Annibal, he of the nose. He had kept by him one remaining clean handkerchief. This he applied to his gargantuan nostrils and began insolently to clean them while the ruffianly scum looked on amazed. Then he dropped it and one of them swooped upon it and secreted it in his blouse. We all of us roared with laughter.

We spend our time wagering: whom will they come for next? For an hour or more I am rich enough in pledged louis d'or to triple my inheritance. With Comte Annibal gone and the Sire de G, our average age has dropped to thirty-three, the age of Our Blessed Saviour. There is a point at which every man ceases being a clown and becomes a ghost. We are such ghosts.

July 27, 1793 ... day of my destiny. It is being recorded here on earth ... will it be recorded in Heaven?

Coarse, hideous, jeering faces along the route of our Calvary: ours at least are refined by inevitability. The cart jars the soles of the feet, the ankles, the knees ... yet we retain our dignity.

Fair nymph, whom I shall never know, whose breast I shall never caress, whose warm thighs I shall never put my face between ... how I long, how I long! Yes, gaze back at me, knowing not my thoughts, yet thinking perhaps the same as I ... how else shall I interpret your sweet interest? I would take your hand if I dared ... now you have turned your head away ... if you had not, I should perhaps have dared, but the back of your head frightens me.

I am the second. I mount quick-step as though hurrying to obey a royal command. The buffoons laugh. I turn to her of the cart and bow ... does she see? Forgive me, lady, who have covered your dear body with my secret irreverent kisses, whose mysterious fragrance I verily taste on the tip of my tongue. God grant we meet in Paradise!

Oh, how woefully exhilarating to hear the thunder of the drums, the winching creak of the blade being drawn up: to see those caverned mouths – funnels of spewing venom: those heads like flattened pins of red and blue protruding from waving insect bodies.

That sneeze! Did it erupt from the Olympian nostrils of Zeus himself? I am drenched in a mucoid spray. It has become quiet, so quiet I may be in Heaven. No. Everything is as it was: the crowd, the line of drummers with sticks upraised, the horseman in black with the unrolled order of instructions, his head thrown back. Yet how silent, how silent it is. All those Frenchmen ... making no sound. Has it not fallen?

The sun shines but the air is icy ... and *this* July! It is darkening at the edges ... why don't they *move*? Move, curse you, shout again at least ... fill my throat with your nauseous stench. How long will it last? They are growing greyer. Ah, to hear the thunder of those drums again! How strange, the penumbras have become black shadows ... only in the centre do I still see them. They are swaying now ... everything is swaying ... becoming fainter, darker, darker...

Densities

But I think my dream is more curious than yours, he said: more curious and even more unpleasant.

I was in a large stone cavity – not quite a cave or a natural cave, that is, since its interior was square and that bespoke the construction of men: a square cave then, very dank and probably evil-smelling too; and I – I assume it was I although to tell the truth the person I visualized was perhaps a quarter of my present age: perhaps I as I was when a youth: yes, I believe so – and I, this youthful I, was naked as I recall and somehow gifted with the miracle of levitation, or flight.

And what was he doing? Why, nothing else, this proud youth, but hovering over a voluminous heap of old clothes and filth, his white skin gleaming; and turning over folds of the stuff, or occasionally kicking the pile with an immaculate, extended white toe.

The dust rose from those decaying tatters and still he foraged, though daintily, his every movement betraying his ineffable disgust yet at the same time his imperative need to discover something in that squalid heap. And what d'you think he was searching for?

It came to me as I watched him in my dream: this aristocratic mole, sorting over ancient rusty clothes and mangled papers, hovering still as in winged suspension. Why, he was searching for me! Yes – *me*. He, the youthful illusion, was seeking the senile reality, the unsightly and as yet unsighted abomination which, with the bright blade strung round his back, he meant to make an end of. But even he, or maybe because he was too finicking, could not penetrate to the depths of those destroyed years, of that accumulated garbage.

The homily is this. As a man grows, so does his invisible cap of detritus. This in its intensifying weight he balances through life until that moment when, like gravity, its top-heaviness overspills

171

him and flings him back to his rightful place in the immemorial slime.

II.

He plays with ideas ... but they are always disappearing ... like snowflakes on warm window-glass ... perceived then gone. Something of their design he will remember ... later, when intimations appear.

His mind freezes half-way through dreams and speculation ... an odd world which only he inhabits. But, if you insist, he will take you there.

His igloo ... water dropping from the low curvatured ceiling ... and always a steam. He lies there indolent, forever indolent, but sometimes he rises to shake his hair free of the collecting water and sometimes, in its spray, he recollects the snowdrops. Then it is that he puts down his words and smiles to himself. It pleases him.

The steam begins to ascend again ... so it goes on. Then summer comes and it is time to go back into the sun – the igloo has melted. It melted long ago. Only he lay there, oblivious of it, while others passed by in the open, sharpening their knives as they went, or spitting, or breaking air.

III.

Remember? When we sat round the table? I could not see all of you too clearly, your faces were so vague. Then *she* came in – gaunt, dressed in her perpetual grey, her cheeks creased like old fruit, but so smooth between the innumerable wrinkles, with a night-cap upon her head – and she kissed me, on both sides of my temples, and a warmth of new life surged in my veins ...

So must you all have felt as she went about kissing each of you in turn. I know – because your faces began focusing into clarity for me. And then, strangest of all – do you remember? – she leant over the table and began kissing the dressed rooster there, lavishing on it more kisses than on us, moving over its parchment skin with her parchment lips. And how startled we were when the rooster – miraculously renewed in panoply of grey-white feathers and

172

blood-gorged comb – rose to its feet and began crowing: loud and piercingly. And how filled with horror we all were for what we might have done.

======
IV.

He was about my height, but a little shorter. He had blue eyes like mine, but flecked with green. He had an impatient way about him, and a freckle over his left eyebrow – and he felt hunted!

Each way he looked, he shuddered. They seemed everywhere. Who?

He began running through the green fields, and the cows raised their heads from the lush grass and gazed after him with curiosity and compassion. He ran straight out to the middle meadow and saw a rope ladder dangling, a foot off the ground. He didn't stop to consider – as you or I might – what is a rope ladder doing in the middle of a meadow?

He just leapt onto the first rung and began climbing – up, up, up. By the time he reached the first low-lying cumulus, he was out of breath, but oh – so relieved. He sighed and looked down. The earth was very far away. All he could make out was the patchwork of the fields below. Again he began climbing and suddenly discovered that the ladder was terminated: there were just some frayed ends to signify it had been torn, or broken – he couldn't decide which. And while he perplexed himself it was snatched away as he clung to it.

======
V.

They, the deprived, the maligned, sit about their watch-fires in eternity. Death has not released them.

The engulfing core of emptiness, stripped of bone and flesh, unredeemed by spirit survival, broods and haunts through the spirit forest, whispers on the spirit wind, eddies in the foam of spirit water, mocks on the distantless horizon.

He, the unelect amongst them, unelect as they, waiting for return from that timeless, nightless, dayless domain of monochrome nothingness: He, the unelect, once elect of countless, of his own vanished ego, with pitiless recall sees outlined yet his once vaunted, obliterated form: as within one unextinguished atom of illusion, he breathes at that breathless waste with the irrepressible lust of the gambler, to vision a toss of spirit coin, a ghostly luck, a restoration.

VI.

I have lost myself ... must find myself again.

That doorway ... yes, it may have been in that doorway I blundered into. I recollect now that it had furry edges and an elliptical frame. It could have been *there*, yes, it could, because she was there as well. She. Who is *she*?

How does one know one has lost oneself – how, especially, when one has never experienced it before? Horror, in its kindly malignity, provides an almost instant awareness. Before my conscious mind had decided, my tongue had already formed the words 'I have lost myself.'

I have lost not only myself but the landmarks of my conventional existence. I stand suddenly before a befriending pit, lately evacuated it seems, perhaps in gesture of hospitality, by some gigantic earthworm: a pit which begins at my fastening toes and crumbles away in its own instability into internal mystery. It's as dark as the doorway, that doorway as dark as the interior of an onion underground.

'How was it,' I asked, 'that when I spoke to you of love, you spoke to me of death?'

'Because death is truer than love, my love,' and she smiled with marboreal teeth.

Lies. Lies. Unanswerable lies.

I must find that doorway again!

VII.

He told me he had gone to the cinema and fallen asleep, and when he awoke it was so dark that he couldn't see who was beside him. But someone had placed a hand on his thigh – whether from the right or left he was unable to tell – and with one finger had signified a suggestive intent by delicately scratching, in a slow, sensual, circular rhythm.

A woman's hand or a man's – which? That's what he could feel his penis deliberating wildly – whether to enlarge as it almost compulsively raged to do, or remain shrunken in quiescent disgust.

He said that while it lasted, for no more than a minute, he lacked either the courage or wit to resolve his body's disabling dilemma by taking and feeling that alien hand and determining its gender. And just when he could bear it no longer, the screen lighted up, and he discovered himself seated between two women, both equally seducing, but whose cold aloof profiles intimidated enquiry.

VIII.

Even when the harvest is good, and the numbers at record level, there is no rejoicing it is said among the bureaucrats of Hell.

'And the figures this year – are they the same as ever?' asks the Principal Satan.

'Better than ever, Sire,' replies the Chief Statistician.

'Ah,' answers he with a mournful sigh. '*Better*, you say. That's certainly doleful news.'

'Indeed, Sire.'

'Indeed. Our celebrations must accordingly be muted. It is fitting. You will see to it, Chief Statistician?'

'Sire, I shall.'

'Ah yes. In our trade there is nothing so sorrowful as success.'

IX.

I am on a train.

The passengers around me are animals, four-footed animals, seated on benches beside me and opposite.

A horse of matronly appearance reclines comfortably in a corner. She wears a shawl and large spectacles, and is knitting. A young cat in a voluminous gingham skirt stands with forepaws raised, gazing out of the window with child-like intensity. There are others as well, but I cannot put them into clearer focus, so they remain shapes, diffuse, whose outlines though animal conform to human attitudes.

My travelling companions are silent. Of course! *Animals are dumb.* I nod in apology to some grey form beside me and step from the compartment into the corridor.

The train sways and I lean into something of great bulk. Again, I nod my apology. I begin to walk down the corridor, conscious of the clatter of the wheels beneath and, in the distance, the mournful cry of the locomotive. I feel a sweep of wind along the floor as the door at the end of the carriage opens. Coming towards me is the conductor, or some such uniformed individual. I flatten myself obligingly to allow him passage, and note that he at least is a man.

All the other compartments are filled with animals as well. The conductor glances into each as he passes, as though checking that everything is in order. Again, there is a swish of wind as he exits from the head of the carriage.

I am now at the rear.

With some hesitation I open the door of the lavatory, and after assuring myself it is empty, enter and lock it. I examine myself in the mirror as I stroke my face wonderingly, then open my mouth and contract my larynx to evoke some word; but none emerges. I am not wholly surprised. Animals are dumb.

Victory

When they came to examine his paws, they thought: they're *His* paws, not ours. When they spread them open there was a perforation through each. Down the street there was a rattling of musketry.

In God we trust, the surgeon said, wiping his dripping nostril on the surgical towel. The patient smiled back uncertainly. A spider testing its web on the cornice of the ceiling paused to observe the micro-spasms of its victim.

Fourteen ears, all of one kind, ocelot, and the tail of a miniature Chinese deer, the latter to dangle downwards and conceal her smooth, epilated labia. The minister who had been eating pomegranate seeds from a crystal bowl, cleansed his hands on his beard and wrote the single word Death! with the pen the slave had handed to him, on the arched back of the pretty youth.

I cultivate drinking tea as I cultivate my hatred for women, he remarked amiably: the one for reasons of bad digestion, the other for inadequate erection. A platoon of cavalry, shrieking, rode by.

One woman had been transfixed by lances. Her sorrows, which a moment before had seemed to her overwhelming, no longer troubled her. Those near her heard her mutter with her apparently last gasp: I am free! Later, she was revived long enough for her living heart to be excised and transplanted into the diseased cardiac cavity of a priceless hunting dog.

Stretched beneath him, like a corpse within its granite catafalque, she awaited with amused horror to receive the icy enlargement of his commanding masculinity, they read from a treatise on Anglo-Saxon erotica. The soldiery mingled with the townsfolk and those whose faces offended them received the butt ends of their muskets. A fruiterer's stall was overturned and looted. The troopers hanged a small cat.

They say that the Almighty created the world in six days and on the seventh rested, and seemingly has been resting since. The forces of evil, taking note of this hiatus, have been gleefully active since. So comes the oft-repeated plaint of poets and lamenters: thus virtue sleeps, et cetera.

Seven strong arms with fully-cultured biceps held the gates of the portico closed, despite the beating of crowbars and mallets from without. The possessor of the single well-developed arm was a wrestler who had turned to thievery and been amputated. The town council later awarded him an iron arm in recognition of his feat.

Temple doors were meant to be smashed as women were meant to be taken and God damned – that is freedom! A boar on a spit whose eyes gleamed as maliciously as when he was speared was nearing completion and smelling delicious. The army restored order amid cries of Long Live the People!

The Creator groaned in his sleep, troubled by bad dreams, while the imps of Hell with fingers plunged in their anuses blared with their tongues from their gullets outwards. The patient died, the condemned youth died, the hunting dog died, the Anglo-Saxon woman conceived and produced a small, hard, white man who despoiled other women from puberty till death. Round fat faces with succulent lips murmured To Life! as they transferred spiritous beverages to round fat bellies. The cavalry rode back at the trot with triumphant bugles screaming the victory fanfare, with now peaceable lances upthrust, buried in melons, apples and other soft fruit, and the occasional head.

===

Scene 1 from

The Burning of the Book

a play in one act

[*Cobbled square in medieval town. Fountain at centre with grotesque bronze figure brandishing trident and spouting water. Rathaus with banners drooping. Other appropriate medieval buildings facing square.*

Chief Councillor and other council members stand before Rathaus. *They are dressed as modern city aldermen with gold chains of office. Heralds stand to one side of them, dressed in harlequin tights and jerkins. Line of drummers to other side.*

Drawn up beside fountain is honour guard composed of medieval men-at-arms with halberds and harquebuses, and several garbed in present-day American marine uniforms and those of Red Army, these latter with assault rifles.

A rag-tag crowd of people jostle each other to right of stage in wing.

King enters square from left. He is a pale thin-chested young man in flashy plus-fours, and with a tweed cap surmounted by a small gold crown in place of the usual button. A monocle is fixed in his left eye. Although the temperature is equable, he fans himself frequently with a red handkerchief as he blows through his lips. He is followed by a small retinue of other young men dressed similarly to him except for caps and monocles.

Simultaneously, heralds blare a jazzy discordant fanfare on their trumpets.]

CHIEF COUNCILLOR [*Bowing deeply*] – Welcome to Your
　　　　　Majesty. [*In loud pompous voice*] – Present arms to
　　　　　His Majesty!
　　　　　[*As arms are presented, several harquebuses and rifles
　　　　　discharge with loud bangs. Crowd cheers.*]
　　KING [*Unruffled and with quiet dignity*] – We have come to
　　　　　see the Governor of The Book, then the prisoners of
　　　　　The Book. [*Fans himself vigorously*]
VOICES IN CROWD Louder! Louder!
　　KING [*In preturnaturally loud voice*] – WE HAVE COME TO
　　　　　SEE THE GOVERNOR OF THE BOOK, AND THE
　　　　　PRISONERS OF THE BOOK.

179

[*The effort exhausts him. He begins to sag but is immediately sustained by two aides who raise him beneath the armpits.*]

WOMAN IN CROWD A petition! A petition to His Majesty. The Governor is innocent. He's been slandered by malevolent authors.

KING [*Taken aback*] – And the prisoners?

WOMAN IN CROWD They too are innocent.

[*Cheers from crowd.*]

KING [*Turns to one of his aides and whispers agitatedly*]

VOICE IN CROWD What's he saying? What's he saying?

CHIEF COUNCILLOR [*In fury at display of lèse-majesté*] – Beat the drums!

[*Drummers begin beating.*]

KING [*In trumpet voice*] – STOP THAT INFERNAL RACKET!

[*Begins to sag again and is raised by aides*]

CHIEF COUNCILLOR Cease drumming – BY ORDER!

[*The drums stop beating except for one whose drummer, with gigantic plugs in his ears, has not heard the command. The man standing next to this unfortunate strikes him on the head with a ceremonial halberd whereupon he falls, apparently dead.*]

KING [*In distress*] – Oh! See to that poor fellow.

WOMAN IN CROWD [*With a shriek*] – It's Geckel – our woodman – a father of three. O Geckel, poor Geckel, who will look to your children now?

[*Face appears at window of The Book – a prison with open pages containing other small windows. The face is pale, white, in fact, and freckled with black print. It wears a nightcap upon its head.*]

FACE [*In voice of anguish*] – Butchers! Butchers! See! They have murdered him.

[*Other pale faces appear at windows of The Book.*]

VOICE IN CROWD It's the Governor of The Book!

[*Governor tears at his face, ripping off strips of printed paper. Confusion and great hullabaloo as crowd gathers round fallen Geckel, now hidden from sight. Cries and groans.*]

CHIEF COUNCILLOR Make way! Make way! You'll asphyxiate him.

[*Banners in crowd break out with captions:* FREEDOM IS IMMORAL – DOWN WITH FREEDOM! DEATH TO DEATH!]
[*Crowd manhandled aside by soldiers, revealing flattened cardboard shape with outline and appearance of Geckel – like character in cartoon film, flattened by heavy object. (Substitution of real Geckel by cardboard facsimile effected during enclosure by crowd.)*]

CHIEF COUNCILLOR [*As soldiers raise shape of Geckel for all to see – amid cries of horror from crowd*] – He looks asphyxiated to me.

VOICE IN CROWD No, Your Honour, he's just dead.
[*Weeping women draw away Geckel's flattened body.*]

GOVERNOR OF BOOK *Evil!* Evil from without, evil within –

ECHO RESPONSE FROM INSIDE BOOK E-e-vil – wi-thin –

GOVERNOR OF BOOK An end to it all. BURN THE BOOK!

KING [*Aghast*] – What?

CROWD [*In horror*] – No! No! No!

CHIEF COUNCILLOR If Your Majesty will permit, it was done once before.

KING What are you *saying*?

CHIEF COUNCILLOR In the reign of your august grandfather The Book was burned, Your Majesty. It resulted – I have the figures here [*consults paper*] – it resulted in the disappearance of two million, four hundred and eighty-four thousand and three men, women and children, including all branches of the learned professions, together with soldiers, workers, sailors, horses and airmen, et cetera – plus thirty-five words of wisdom.

VOICE IN CROWD [*Bewildered*] – What are *airmen*?

KING Thirty-five? That indeed is a loss.

CHIEF COUNCILLOR Yes, indeed, Your Majesty, plus two million, four hundred and eighty-four thousand and three women, men, and children, including all branches of the learned professions, together –

KING Silence! [*Blows through lips*]
[*Author with large cravat and arm in sling now pushes through crowd.*]

AUTHOR This is all rather crazy. Your Majesty! Oh, I say, Your Majesty.

KING Who calls?

AUTHOR It's I, Barnadorn, Your Majesty.

KING [*Smiling*] – Why, Barnadorn, my friend – come forward.

CROWD [*Chanting at Barnadorn*] – Devil! Devil!
[*Before Barnadorn can proceed, he is elbowed aside by three awkward-looking children who are thrust forward by crowd.*]

KING [*In surprise*] – Who are these?

CHILDREN [*In unison*] – We are the Geckel children, Your Majesty.

KING [*Wringing his hands*] – Ah, poor souls, poor souls.

VOICE IN CROWD Is that all you can say, you shit?
[*Shocked silence, except for loud laugh from Barnadorn, who now covers his mouth with cravat as he walks quickly towards King.*]

CHIEF COUNCILLOR [*Simultaneously*] [*In fury*] – What? What? What?

GOVERNOR OF BOOK [*Simultaneously*] [*Tearing more paper from his face*] – Shame! Shame!

CROWD IN UNISON [*Simultaneously*] [*Groaning*] – Ahh-hh-hh-hh.
[*At same moment, grotesque figure in fountain drops trident which falls with heavy metal thud to stage.*]

VOICE IN CROWD Look! Look at St. Gondor!
[*As all watch transfixed, figure steps down from fountain, retrieves trident, then re-mounts fountain and stands upright again.*]

WOMAN IN CROWD A miracle! Mother of God – a miracle. Did you see? Did you see? St. Gondor moved.
[*Crowd surges forward and surrounds figure of St. Gondor, gazing up at it with reverence.*]

KING [*In an aside – with awe*] – How? How do you *explain* it?

CHIEF COUNCILLOR [*Sententiously*] – Even the patience of a bronze saint may be tested, Your Majesty.

KING [*Turning to Barnadorn*] – You saw, Barnadorn?

BARNADORN Saw what, Your Majesty?

KING St. Gondor.

BARNADORN What of St. Gondor?

KING Did you not see him drop his trident then pick it up again?

BARNADORN Ha! ha! ha! Not for the first time.

KING What d'you mean?

BARNADORN The records tell us he does it whenever momentous events are afoot, Your Majesty – plague, war, or similar catastrophes. It's even said he used it to strike Pope Honorius on the mitre as His Holiness walked by, after His Holiness had mulishly refused absolution to your gallant forebear, Adalbert the Outrageous, and merely because of some alleged peccadillos involving his nieces and other under-aged females. My opinion's he drops it occasionally through sheer fatigue. Remember, Sire, he's been standing there for over five hundred years, prodding Jews and other infidels into Hell with his trident.

[*As Barnadorn speaks, a woman with great curiosity touches St. Gondor on his thigh then crosses herself. Others watch in fascination as she circles about the figure, gazing up at it and continuing to stroke it and cross herself. Suddenly the figure twitches noticeably. Then, shame to relate, it becomes monstrously ithyphallic.*]

KING [*Apoplectically*] – THIS IS TOO MUCH! [*Begins to sag, and without support of otherwise preoccupied aides, collapses to stage*]

BARNADORN [*In great excitement*] – A camera – who's got a camera?

VOICE IN CROWD [*Bewildered*] – What's a *camera*?

CHIEF COUNCILLOR Yes – too much! A saint that drops his trident is one thing, but one that – that – that – THROW A SHEET OVER IT. Mothers! Remove your daughters! DRUMMERS!

[*Drummers beat frenziedly as women scream and honour guard begins discharging their firearms. Crowd runs pell-mell back and forward across stage. Voice of Barnadorn continues at intervals: 'Who's got a camera?' as he exits to right.*

Meanwhile someone has pulled down one of Rathaus banners and thrown it over figure of St. Gondor. Gondor, infuriated, immediately flings it off. With great cry of rage he now crouches with trident

183

thrust menacingly before him, as though daring anyone else to take liberties with him.

Sound of 'heavenly' music off-stage – organ and boy choristers. Drums cease beating erratically, women fall to knees and cross themselves, men embrace other men nearby. St. Gondor now resumes his traditional upright stance, looking up to Heaven, the prongs of his trident pointing below.

One of his aides helps King to his feet.

Now all – King, aides, Chief Councillor and other councillors, drummers, honour guard, crowd – face audience with beatific expressions as music soars to 'heavenly' crescendo, while faces at windows of The Book simultaneously disappear.]

In Heaven

In Heaven there are no smoked fish, but plenty of fish that smoke, and gifted hens who nightly place blazing tapers on the Pleiades, and men, yes, men, who light the tapers for the hens, and dutifully replenish the cigar-stubbed ashtrays of the fish, and girls – what girls! – girls of both sexes, and also mere sketches of girls with just the outlines of their breasts pencilled in, and lacking genitals, because the artists there are more attuned to painting Divinities, or so they say, but the true reason is DECENCY!

Heaven, one hears, has many mansions with empty rooms displaying TO LET signs, grimy with golden splendour and hanging sadly in the forlorn windows; and unswept pathways with leaves tumbled down, and wells choked up with the deluge of feathers perpetually dropping from moulting ANGELS, suffering a form of heavenly dermatitis.

And the worms that burrow in the gardens of Heaven! Quite astounding, they say. Each with a filigreed coronet of precious stones with pointed facets on their dainty heads, to inhibit the fish from taking a too close interest in them.

But Heaven, sad to note (for those who care), reeks of the fumes of expensive cigars which grow like plums on trees and are plucked when mature by the men in that area designated Havana-Heaven – for the delectation of the fish, of course, but some others too whom we are forbidden to mention, and this despite the aeons-long NO SMOKING campaign.

Sad to note also the multitudes of disgustingly drunken seraphim lurching down the highroads arm-in-arm and blaring indelicate blasts on their golden trumpets at the unfinished girls who shield with their unfingered hands the incomplete parts of their bodies and feeling, naturally, most shamefully deprived.

Heaven is definitely not a place for FUN. When night comes, and it lasts a thousand earthly days exactly, all one hears, besides the

185

ineffable droning of ANGEL sermons, is the sound of phlegmily-wheezing fish (and some others whom we are forbidden to mention), plus the frustrated groans of the incomplete girls and the men who gloomily by the light of over-worked fireflies carve useless tourist trinkets from the plethora of feathers.

Did we say *tourist*? That may be a slip requiring excising by the heavenly CENSOR, whom we must not identify. Excising, if we may digress – and as we wait – is rather unpleasant in heavenly terms. Briefly it means, for revealing trade secrets, that that receptacle which functions for breathing, hearing, seeing, grinning and masticating, together with its thatch of heavenly hair, is removed temporarily and re-attached a kalpa later. For offences repeated, permanent removal is decreed with chilly exile to the wastes of space.

Ah, SANCTION has just been received to proceed – CAUTIOUSLY!

Tourists? YES! Tourists from where? Tourists from *where else* but – Ah-hh-hhh-hhhh

Chippewas

At the age of ten he saw them for the first time – ten youths of the Chippewa nation, stealthily peering then boldly clambering through the hedge at the bottom of the garden: assembling there in a tribal snake-formation, each with a knowing grin and bowing, then waving and hooting with derisive boyish laughter.

At twenty, roused from post-coital stupor by a sudden grotesque remorse, he disengaged from her cloying thighs, went to gaze sombrely from the open window and saw them again – staring up and grinning as though acknowledging past acquaintance – in the inner court of the building: living anachronisms of the archaic plains, compassed about by beer cans and the detritus of late twentieth century garbage: twenty young Chippewa braves, decked out in full-feathered head regalia but otherwise naked: prancing in the style of aggressive cock-pheasants in a ritual circle, each with soaring penis in hand: rotating like a battery of Tomahawk missiles then accelerating, until in a climax of whirling frenzy all discharged simultaneously.

He had just turned thirty when he saw them again – a party of young-ageing men with bronzed, prominent Mongol cheekbones, athletic shoulders and muscles straining at the seams of their incongruous suits: some smiling inanely, some grimacing, some merely saturnine: filing into the hotel from their tourist coach, consciously uncomfortable under the white man's eyes – all thirty – delegates of the Chippewa nation to the Conference of Stateless Minorities.

Of Cockroaches and Men

It's said that Peter the Great once fainted away at the sight of a cockroach ... an anecdote recorded in sober history and in *The Secret Annals of Cockroaches*.

It's also said (according to this learned tome) that cockroaches are the avatars of once famous men, and conversely; and that the one, in fact, which caused Peter to collapse was Coriolanus.

Peter, a quondam cockroach himself, recognized Coriolanus despite his new guise, and remembered when he had been brutally squashed beneath Coriolanus' massive ass when that warrior unknowingly sat down upon him, causing Peter, in recollection, to pass out from shock.

Coriolanus subsequently became a dray-horse, and suffered the ignominy and horror of the knacker's yard. Later, more happily, he became an immigrant wash-up man at a *luxe* New York City bar, and married an angelic Italian girl from Moreno. Peter became Stalin, when his attitude changed and he began to regard men as mostly cockroaches.

Not all cockroaches, however, says our learned tome, transmigrate successfully. Many, indeed, remain cockroaches, although having formerly been great men.

To Nachman of Bratzlav, 1770-1810
Hasid and Saint

from *Emil Brut*

My dear Nachman, you once wrote: 'It is forbidden to grow old' –
at least it is recorded that you did so; and I, otherwise a scoffer gen-
erally at Hasidic norms, took those words for my banner in life and
even attempted to live by them; not by the application of their
admonitory wisdom, of which somehow I had intuited the mystery; but, and I confess it shamefully, through some inadequacy of
my own: my inveterate immaturity.

Thus, while my contemporaries have sobered, aged and stabil-
ised around me, I, like some idiotic knight of old astride a prancing
destrier, have borne aloft on my lance an unchaste article of my
lady-love's underwear, challenging the passing years with an
ardour of resistant hate for their encroaching indignities.

Yet perhaps I misconstrued or misapplied those words. What
exactly did you mean by them?

Were you in fact implying a state of perpetual youth, or perpetually youthful feelings? Were you, like me, so enamoured of the
world and its prime delight, the intoxication of females: their flesh,
their shapes, their moistures, fragrances, orifices, their maddening
tactilities: and so turbulently felt in the days of your decline that by
a superhuman resolve, and God knows what mystically-
performed Hasidic gymnastics, you reversed your descent into
disintegration? Ah, you could not have been more obsessed than I;
and then again, why, saintly man, could you have not?

Or were you signifying some purer source? Did it happen one
day that weary with profundity, you walked amid the forest near to
your native town and there, remarking the beauty of the place and
some flamboyant insect counterpart of me – some ephemeral scav-
enger on the pond mould of life, compound-eyed but empty-
headed, existing solely for sunshine and pleasure – you found it
good and conceived those words? Insects, at least, would understand them.

Perhaps I am deluded by dreams. Perhaps your words are a

snare which has somersaulted my void. For in the distance I see a lazy, ambling, young-ageing figure (which is me), which stops to gaze at the busily perambulating pigeons, and more attentively at two clasping beaks in a tandem of erotic excitation, almost dislocating their delicate necks in upward and downward thrusts, followed by the gravely expectant crouch of one, the female, as he, her mate, clumsily mounts her.

That figure in the distance, distancing himself from me, that wraith, as inconsequential as his own cigarette smoke, will disappear if I let him. Hurriedly I exchange saddles for that of a metaphoric motorbike which gives me wheels in place of equine legs and speeds me furiously down the road, gobbling up minutes in moments and diminishing my wasted years, as he, growing more distinct now, his lethargic movements all too painfully familiar, turns bemused and angry at the oncoming tumult of beating cylinders enriched by petrol stench, klaxon hooting to add to the din: scowling, open-mouthed, his crooked teeth exposed in a snarl of inept displeasure, as I, missing by a hairsbreadth one of his precious pigeons, roar past him, crouched jockey-like clear of the seat and turn my head, grimacing in turn with *my* crooked teeth, and scream insanely against the deafening wind: 'Hi! hi! It is forbidden to grow old.'

Sometimes, my dear Nachman, I believe I understand perfectly what you have said, or rather that part of me which stands like a solemn sentinel gone to sleep, that grenadier in bearskin shako, overcome by stiff limbs and dreams of glory, arms akimbo on the long musket, moustachios drooping gently over the barrel – but with no compassionate Napoleon as temporary substitute; yes, that part of me sometimes understands you in the miasmas of night.

Yet at other times I find those very words obtuse or obfuscating; almost, I confess, needlessly opaque. What *could* you have had in mind?

Listen, my dear, if you are now in some saints' or fools' paradise where the hours are struck at intervals of a thousand years on golden kettledrums by learned chimpanzees, all with PhD's, and the holy honey-cake is washed down with peach-scented nectar served up in crystal bowls by doe-eyed angels, those with breasts, of course, and surrounded by your fools' or saints' disciples, will you expound to them, 'It is forbidden to grow old'?

Better far to tie their snowy beards together, set those beards aflame with heavenly fire, and launch them turning in the empyrean like a celestial wheel of raging light, like a golden holocaust of aged men who did not heed the tantric words, 'It is forbidden to grow old,' but sought decrepitude and heaven to defiant living.

You are angry. Yes, you are angry – I can almost see it. Your eyebrows, or what's left of them, lunge frighteningly over the deep-set sockets of your enkindled eyes. Your blond or rather yellow-stained whiskers (ah, you were a smoker too, my dear, it shows disgustingly) open round your yellow-stained teeth. Did I not recognize you, I should shudder with terror.

They, did you know, who raised a coprolite to be a god, they with spindles of blood in their eyes and vomit in their souls, whose breath stank of nazi ordure, they too took note of those words, 'It is forbidden to grow old,' and applied them to butchery.

That coprolite which lay mouldering in a medieval privy, speculating insanely with its demonic atom of a brain, after being stamped upon by the generations, pissed upon and shit upon, rose up finally with the ardent harmonic hate of other reanimated coprolites to guide the destiny of the German nation, and, fittingly clad in generic brown, spewed slime over Europe and bequeathed slime to the world.

My dear Nachman, let me change my mood and tell you a true and pathetic tale ...

A certain man I know, a loiterer on the fringes of society whom normally I avoid if I can, met me in the street last week and, because it would have been blatantly rude to turn away, or pass by hurriedly unnoticing as I sometimes do – since we were already within speaking distance – I stopped, greeted him and we chatted for several minutes. He appeared possessed by an odd excitement.

'Tell me,' he said, 'do I look different to you in any way that you can notice? Please, be frank.'

'You seem rather excited.'

'But besides that – which is true – different in any other way?'

I stared at him critically, attempting sincerely to discover the extraordinary change he expected me to see, but that face of his, which has the vague familiarity of so many other faces that I know, seemed in no particular manner to be out of the ordinary, except for its unnatural elation.

'New tie, perhaps?' I suggested lamely.

'Ha, new tie!' and he grimaced fiercely. 'Well, I must be going,' and he went.

Today, my dear Nachman, I met this irritating man again. Would you believe it? – in almost the same place at almost the same time. And again in a curious state of excitement. Yet it was he, this time, who would have passed by without speaking, no doubt in recollection of our previous meeting.

I am a perverse fellow, Nachman, as by this time you may know, and I was burning with curiosity to penetrate the mystery of his eccentric behaviour: this man whom conventionally I would run from, whose most animated comments are usually reserved for the subject of buying and selling objects.

'Hello, hello,' I acknowledge him amiably. 'Something pleasant happen?'

His eyes crinkle gratefully. 'Yes, most pleasant, most wonderfully pleasant, young man.'

That 'young man' of his puts me in a condescending good humour.

'Tell me,' I say, as engagingly as I can.

'If you promise not to laugh.'

'I –' I protest: 'laugh?', greedy for more information.

He glances about as though to assure himself that we are alone.

'You recall last week that I asked you if I looked different – do you remember?'

I nod.

'And you said no.'

'Well, not exactly no.'

'Do I look different to you in any way today?'

I consider very carefully, aware that any wrong reply will scuttle him away again.

'Hm,' I say disingenuously, 'there's certainly *something* changed about you. But what *is* it?'

'I'm in love.'

'You! – in love?' I blurt out unthinkingly.

He grimaces and appears to grind his teeth.

'Does my age inhibit it?'

My remark, I realize, has been thoroughly stupid and cruel, and I attempt to diffuse it.

'Who is she then,' and I smile: 'this paragon of woman?'

'Not woman. Girl.'

An illuminating light suddenly penetrates me.

'Of course,' I say, slapping my forehead for emphasis: 'now I see. You *do* look different. Younger, in fact.'

'I knew it, I *knew* it was true,' he shouts almost joyfully, then flushes and becomes modestly subdued.

And now he is so transparently agitated to reveal it all, that I need hardly press him on more.

'Tell me about her.'

'Listen then, my dear young man – ah, how I love young people! – listen, an unusual thing for me: I decided to travel on the underground last week and saw, from midway in the carriage, a startlingly beautiful female face at the rear. It seemed such an illusion, and my sight is so poor, that I pushed my way through the other passengers to study her close, and found a position directly facing her. Then by good fortune someone vacated the seat behind me and I seized it.'

'And – *was* she?' I ask quietly, for he seems now overcome by his own revelation.

'Extraordinary! She was extraordinary! The kind of beauty which in the history books causes the downfall of empires. And yet, what was so strange, it was *I*, I alone, who noticed her.

'I turned several times as passengers entered and left, and not one that I could see spared her a glance. Do you know what it reminded me of?'

'Of what?'

'That painting by Breughel, set in a medieval landscape, of Icarus with melted wings thrashing about in the sea, while the ploughmen on the hills above unmindfully continue their stolid tasks as brutishly unaware as their toiling beasts.'

A simile like that, you will agree, dear Nachman, is worthy of some consideration, if somewhat unfair to beasts.

'Go on,' I encourage him, not amused anymore.

'She was aware of my attention obviously, and responded with an occasional sidelong glance.'

I commiserate mentally with the hapless girl.

'What should I do?, I thought. I had an important engagement [buying or selling objects] and had already passed my station. Dare I speak? Inwardly I tested several phrases, finding each inadequate or foolish. I prayed that she would arrive at length at her own station, giving me the opportunity of exiting with her. At last I grew desperate, and rising as the train slowed for its next halt, I walked

193

over to her, lowered my head intimately, and without hesitation spoke and left through the opening doors.'

'And then?'

'The train went.'

'But what did you *say*?'

'Ah, what did I say?' He becomes almost smug with himself. 'I said, "Excuse me, but you have the most exquisite face I have seen in my life. I felt I must tell you that."'

'And she – did she answer?'

'No, but she smiled, and continued to smile so radiantly that it was altogether sufficient for me.'

'And that was last week?'

'Yes.'

'But *today*.'

'Today – will you believe it? – I met her again, as I have met you again. Isn't that remarkable?'

'It is rather remarkable.'

'Today, this morning, on a completely different branch of the underground – there she was, standing on the platform.'

'And you spoke to her again?'

'Yes, and this time she replied, and entered a carriage with me and travelled for several stations. And as she spoke, I could feel my eyes growing in dimension, and a curious stimulation – a sensation of almost cellular vibration, renewal – on my cheeks, on my brow. And an aliveness, an awareness I have not known since adolescence. I felt my years drop from me like shrouds ...'

'So,' I say to him smiling gently: 'the fountain of youth is youth itself – embodied in youth's beauty.'

Nachman, my dear, if it is forbidden to grown old, is it permitted to become young?

———————

For a list of other books,
write for our catalogue
or call (416) 979-7374.

The Coach House Press
401 (rear) Huron Street
Toronto, Canada M5S 2G5